The Mysterious Jamestown Suitcase

Linda Salisbury

Drawings by Christopher Grotke

Tabby House

Cover design: Lewis Agrell
Author photo: Ann Henderson
Illustrator photo: Paul Collins, courtesy of MuseArts

Library of Congress Cataloging-in-Publication Data

Salisbury, Linda G. (Linda Grotke)

The mysterious Jamestown suitcase / Linda Salisbury ; drawings by Christopher Grotke.

p. cm. -- (Bailey Fish adventure series)

Includes book club questions and related web sites.

Summary: Before the Keswick Inn opens for business, two guests and a foster child arrive, and they all stir Bailey's curiosity as she and her friends try to find out what is in author Elmo Phigg's strange suitcase and how to encourage young Sparrow to speak.

ISBN-13: 978-1881539-43-8 (alk paper)

ISBN-10: 1881539-43-1 (alk. paper)

[1. Friendship--Fiction. 2. Authorship--Fiction. 3. Elective mutism--Fiction. 4. People with disabilities--Fiction. 5. Foster home care--Fiction. 6. Virginia--Fiction. 7. Mystery and detective stories.] I. Grotke, Christopher, 1964- ill. II. Title.

PZ7.S1524Mys 2007

[Fic]--dc22   2006045093

baileyfish@gmail.com
www.BaileyFishAdventures.com
www.BaileyFishAdventureBooks.blogspot/com

Classroom quantities available.

Tabby House

P.O. Box 544, Mineral, VA 23117

(540) 894-8868

Contents

1

Unexpected Visitors

"I'm home," called Bailey Fish as she dropped her faded lavender knapsack inside the front door. She kicked off her scuffed sneakers without untying them.

"Have a good day at school?" answered her grandmother, Sugar, from the kitchen.

"Pretty good," said Bailey, reaching down to pet her kittens, Shadow and Sallie. Sallie batted Shadow with her paw. "You are getting so big," said Bailey. She smiled and scratched their ears. "But I only got a B plus on my science quiz," she said loudly.

"That's not bad at all," said Sugar. "By the way, there's a note from your mother on the hall table. Molly said she likes the sandy beaches in Costa Rica."

Bailey pushed her medium-brown hair behind her ears. She could smell cookies baking as she read the printed copy of her mother's e-mail. Her mom didn't mention coming home anytime soon. Bailey sighed, folded the note, and put it in her jeans pocket. She headed for the kitchen. She knew her grandmother would let her have three cookies with a glass of cocoa milk as a special snack just because it was Friday.

Suddenly, a popping sound like a firecracker made the kittens dive under the hall table. Bailey peered out the screen door. A silver van with a rocking chair and boxes strapped to the rooftop had stopped in the road at the end of Sugar's driveway. Steam swirled from under the hood. Bailey saw a very large man, wearing a red Hawaiian-print shirt, get out. He waved his tweed golf cap at the steam.

"Sugar, people need help," Bailey shouted. She opened the door and hurried down the front steps in her stocking feet.

"I'm coming," yelled her grandmother.

"Oh dear, oh dear," they heard the man say as he looked in dismay at the cloud of steam.

A small, birdlike woman, wearing an identical floral-print shirt, hopped out of the passenger side. The woman wailed, "Whatever will we do?"

Sugar reached up to tap the enormous man on the shoulder and said, "Do you want to use my cell phone? But first, let's open the hood and see what the problem is."

"Thanks, but I'm not very mechanical," said the giant man. He put his cap back on his head.

Sugar popped the hood. "It looks like the radiator. Might not be too much of a problem to fix. Where are you headed for the night?"

"We're hoping to stay here," said the woman. Her hands fluttered towards her dyed orange hair.

"Here?" said Sugar, clearly surprised. "We don't have any motels out here in the country, and I'm afraid this is just *our* house."

"We didn't mean 'here' here, ma'am. We've heard talk at the diner in Mineral that a bed-and-breakfast is opening," said the man, adjusting his cap.

"Oh, Keswick Inn," said Sugar, "but I don't think the Keswicks are officially ready for guests yet. They have just moved in themselves and are still working on the house. I'll call them, though. And you are?"

The man said, "How rude of us. We haven't introduced ourselves. I'm Elmo Phigg—that's spelled P-H-I-G-G and pronounced fig and this is my darling wife, Feather."

Bailey covered a smile with her hand. "I'm Bailey, and this is my grandmother, Sugar," she said. She studied Mr. Phigg's short, white fringy beard and mustache. "Everybody calls her Sugar, by the way."

"We shall, too," he said grandly.

"We're evacuees," said Mrs. Phigg, buttoning a pink cardigan sweater in the cool afternoon air.

"From what?" asked Bailey. Her hazel eyes filled with curiosity.

"From the storms," boomed Mr. Phigg.

Bailey wanted to ask about the storms, but just then Sugar got off the phone. She said, "The Keswicks seem to be out at the moment. Why don't you come up on the porch and join us for peppermint tea and peanut butter cookies. Bailey and I were about to have an after-school snack. We'll call the Keswicks and then Herman's auto repair shop to see if mechanics are available to check your radiator."

"That would be lovely," said Mrs. Phigg. "Lovely, indeed."

2

Jamestown Author

"How kind of you," said Mr. Phigg. He sipped his mug of tea. "We hope we can stay in the area for a while. My darling Feather lived in this part of Virginia when she was a young girl. She used to ride the train from Mineral to Louisa. Took the No. 47 train to see the movies—Westerns. You know, cowboys, horses, and bank robbers—the bang-bang-shoot-'em-ups." He aimed a pretend rifle at a tree.

"Only cost seven cents for the ride," said Mrs. Phigg. "Other days we'd go shopping in Richmond on the C&O's No. 30 and come back on the No. 41. Those were the days!"

"Go ahead—tell them the names of the stops on the Louisa line, my dear," said Mr. Phigg.

"Oh, Elmo, let me see," said Mrs. Phigg. "I do it best when we make a train." She motioned for Bailey and Sugar to stand up and put their hands on each other's waists behind her.

"Chugga chugga woo woo," said Mrs. Phigg. She started slowly across the porch. "Shadwell, Keswick, Cobham, Lindsay, Gordonsville, Trevilians, Green Springs, Louisa, Mineral," she recited, speaking and moving faster and faster. "Pendleton, Fredericks Hall, Buckner, Bumpass, Dundas, Beaverdam, Verdun, and Doswell. I think I forgot one," she said. "Oh, Hewletts." She pretended to pull on a brake cord to stop the train. "Woo woo. Whoa!"

Mrs. Phigg collapsed in a chair. "Whew! Travel is so exhausting." Her laugh sounded like bells in a wind chime.

"Where are you from?" asked Bailey, slightly out of breath.

"Where the hurricanes hit," said Mr. Phigg. "We lost our home and many of our things, but we have each other. That's what counts."

"We were planning to visit this area anyway," said Mrs. Phigg. "Elmo's an author. He's researching a book for children about Jamestown. His assistant will be joining us."

"A real author?" asked Bailey "I've never met a real author. How many books have you written? Are they all for kids?"

"He's very modest," said Mrs. Phigg proudly. "Elmo has written ten books, and one received a literary prize."

Mr. Phigg's mustache twitched as he tilted his head and smiled.

"Sugar and I like to read a lot," said Bailey.

"Wonderful. When we get unpacked, I should be able to find sample copies of my books for you," said Mr. Phigg. He stroked the edge of his beard. "Feather is very modest, too," he added. "She dances and writes poetry."

As if on cue, Mrs. Phigg put down her mug of tea, bowed to Sugar and Bailey, and did three pirouettes, her hands moving like butterflies. As Bailey and Sugar clapped, Bailey wondered how Mrs. Phigg's spindly legs could support her.

"Do you like to write, young lady?" Mr. Phigg asked Bailey.

"Yes, but I haven't lately. I had a notebook at my house in Florida, but when I moved here, it got lost."

"Ahh, we'll have to change that," said Mr. Phigg. "Every writer needs a special notebook. I have an extra one in my van that would be perfect for you."

"Thanks," said Bailey, offering more cookies to their guests.

The phone rang inside the house. Sugar excused herself to answer it.

"Are you an evacuee, too?" asked Mrs. Phigg.

"Not really," said Bailey, "although a hurricane hit the town in Florida where I used to live. My mother is traveling—she's a writer doing an article about Costa Rica for a magazine and maybe a book about the bug man. That's why I'm living with Sugar for now."

"Ahh, a writer," boomed Mr. Phigg. "The bug man? Who is he?" He reached for another cookie, carefully selecting the largest that was not too brown around the edges.

"Dr. Andrew Snorge-Swinson. Have you heard of him?" Bailey said his name as if she needed to blow her nose. "He's an entomologist. A famous one, I guess."

"Ahh," said Mr. Phigg, thoughtfully. "Snorge-Swinson."

Bailey couldn't tell if he had heard of the bug man.

The screen door creaked as Sugar returned. She ran her hand through her short, dyed-brown hair. "That was Will Keswick. He said no need to call the garage. He'll come over to look at the van. The family homestead that they are turning into a B&B isn't finished yet, but since you are evacuees—if you don't mind living there while work is going on, well . . ."

"Oh, lovely," said Mrs. Phigg. "I was so hoping this would work out."

3

Mysterious Suitcase

Will Keswick poured some water from Sugar's sprinkling can into the van's radiator. The Phiggs were to follow him down the road and around the bend to the old house that the Keswicks were fixing up. Earlier in the spring the Keswicks had thought it would be at least a year before they could move in and take in guests.

They were making excellent progress, however, with the help of a handyman and his workers. Bailey and other neighborhood kids were hired to do odd jobs after school and on weekends. So the Keswicks moved in while the work continued.

Bailey and Sugar drove behind the Phiggs in case the visitors needed help unloading the van. Bailey wondered how the rocker and boxes managed to stay on top without sliding off. They didn't look securely tied.

As they rode, Bailey wondered how the Phiggs would want to be addressed. Mr. Elmo? Mr. Phigg? When Bailey met Will Keswick and his wife, Bekka, they told her to call them Mr. Will and Miss Bekka. "It's a Southern thing," Mr. Will said, "and the way children in our family always addressed our friends."

"Welcome," Miss Bekka said warmly to the Phiggs. She held out her hands.

"I feel like I've been in this place before," said Mrs. Phigg. She took off her sunglasses and surveyed the house and yard.

"It belonged to Edgar Emmett," said Mr. Will, taking off his cap. "He was a cousin of my grandmother, Miss Dolly."

"Oh, my!" said Mrs. Phigg. "What a small world. I knew your mother, Martha, and played with her in this very yard when I was a girl. What grand times we had! In fact, there is the oak tree where we made fairy houses out of sticks, stones, and flowers. We ate crunchy Winesap apples from your orchard."

"What a small world, indeed," said Mr. Will. "My mother would love to see you again, I'm sure." He looked around for the boys, who were standing off to one side. "These are our sons, Fred and Noah. They are my good helpers here at Keswick Inn."

The boys said hi, then Noah decided to tease the Phiggs the way he had goofed on Bailey when the boys first met her.

"Fred and I are twins," he said with a straight face.

Mrs. Phigg studied them carefully. Fred had dark skin and hair, while Noah was fair. His hair was the same color as his father's—like a yellow cat—and it stuck out like it was spiked. His eyes were greenish, not dark brown like Fred's. Mrs. Phigg said, "Oh, my, but you don't look at all alike."

Fred smiled. "We're both adopted."

Mrs. Phigg looked puzzled.

"Dad's actually my uncle," said Noah, as he poked Fred playfully in the arm.

"Aren't families wonderful," said Mr. Phigg. "I was raised by my grandmother."

"Really? I've been with my grandmother since winter," Bailey said, smiling at Sugar.

"Grandmothers can be positively grand," said Mr. Phigg. He cleared his throat and looked at the front door.

Mr. Will took the hint. "I bet our guests would like to get settled. Fred, show Mrs. Phigg to the guest room on the first floor. It's clean but still needs wallpapering. We have a lot left to do to finish the inn."

"I'm sure it will be fine," said Mr. Phigg. He slowly opened the back of the van. Bailey was sure all the suitcases would fall out. Everything

seemed to have been jammed inside in a hurry when the Phiggs fled the coming storm.

As quickly as Mr. Phigg placed boxes and bags on the ground, Bailey, Fred, and Sugar gathered them up and lugged them inside—all except for a small green battered suitcase tied tightly with straps. "I'll carry that myself. It is very special," said the large man as he snatched it up. "Very, very special."

"What's so special?" asked Fred.

"Ahh, it contains a Jamestown mystery. Do you like mysteries?" asked Mr. Phigg.

"We do," said Fred. He pushed his Harry Potter-style eyeglasses higher on his nose.

"The contents of this suitcase are so precious that they have been in a series of locked storage sheds for years. Now, where did you say our room will be?"

Fred rolled his eyes at Bailey, then dragged an oversized suitcase with wheels with one arm

and carried a shopping bag in the other. He led the way up the front steps while the big man cradled the Jamestown suitcase.

The room immediately became crowded as the boxes—many marked "books" in big black letters—were piled high along the wall by the window.

The Phiggs did not seem concerned when the boys' little white dog, Clover, jumped in the middle of their bed and put her shaggy head down on a pillow. Sugar helped Mrs. Phigg hang up what few clothes she had on one side of the closet. She folded Mr. Phigg's shirts and placed them on a shelf, and put the rest of the clothes in a tall maple dresser below a matching oval mirror. Mrs. Phigg unwrapped three framed photographs and carefully arranged them on the dresser so that she could see them from the bed. One was a wedding picture of the Phiggs. One was of a calico cat, and one was a high school graduation picture of a boy who resembled them.

Bailey looked around, but the old suitcase was no longer in sight.

Bekka Keswick carried in four blue towels and extra fluffy pillows. "I have a large pot roast cooking. I hope you'll join us for supper," she said to Sugar.

"Please?" Bailey whispered to her grandmother.

"I guess my pork chops and sauerkraut will keep," said Sugar. Her round face crinkled into her famous big smile.

"Wonderful," boomed Mr. Phigg. "Feather and I would be honored to get to know our new neighbors better."

4

E-mail for Bailey

Later, after Bailey finished her homework, she checked her e-mail. Her best Florida friend, Amber, had written:

From: jbs25@yermail.net
To: "Bailey"<baileyfish@gmail.com>
Sent: 5:45 p.m.
Subject: Like it

Cool picture you sent of you, Emily, and the boys. Noah and Fred sure don't look alike. Have you heard anything from Norma Jean and your dad? What about Justin and Chuck the crow?

She signed it SCR, for Sisters Club Rocks. Next she read one from her half sister, Norma Jean.

From: pjfish2005@yermail.net>
To: "Bailey"<baileyfish@gmail.com>
Sent: 7:40 p.m.
Subject: Hi

Sis: My best friend Nola is going to sleep over soon and Mom said we can make tacos. How's Justin? And Em? SCR Norma Jean

Bailey replied:

From: "Bailey"<baileyfish@gmail.com>
To: <pjfish2005@yermail.net>
Sent: 7:40 p.m.
Subject: Hi

People named Phigg are going to stay at Keswick Inn. He's an author and has a secret green suitcase that he won't let anyone touch. It's mysterious. Justin says hi. Chuck the crow sat on my arm the last time we were at the Rudds'. Justin is making a special perch with branches sticking out. Bailey

And there was one from her mother, Molly. It had been a few weeks since her last e-mail.

From: mollyf2@travl.net
To: "Bailey"<baileyfish@gmail.com>
Sent: 10:14 p.m.
Subject: Back

My darling Bailey: I'm so glad we were able to see you when we were on our way to New York. The city was so busy compared with the Costa Rican countryside. Before we returned to Tilahari, Andrew and I went to the gold museum in San Jose. I have never seen such beautiful gold. It was made by pre-Columbian Indians. The Conquistadors stole much of the gold, but fortunately this remained. Give Sugar a smooch from me, and keep three for yourself. Kisses, Mom

Bailey knew she needed to feed the kittens, but she decided to reply first.

From: "Bailey"<baileyfish@gmail.com>
To: mollyf2@travl.net
Sent: 8 p.m.
Subject: hiya

Dear Mom: The Keswicks have guests. They are evacuees from storms. Have you heard of Mr. Elmo Phigg and his wife, Mrs. Feather Phigg? He's an author. I might want to be an author some day. Sugar says even though we call the Keswicks Mr. Will and Miss Bekka, we should call their guests Mr. and Mrs. Phigg. Sugar says it's more polite to use last names when you don't know people well. Love ya, Bailey

Bailey heard the grandfather clock strike eight times. She quickly logged off and turned out the light in Sugar's study.

5

Writer's Notebook

"There's my favorite young writer-to-be," boomed Elmo Phigg. Bailey and Sugar opened the front door and walked into Keswick Inn. They were on their way to Fredericksburg to buy groceries and wanted to see if Miss Bekka needed anything from town.

Mr. Phigg was holding a small red clothbound book.

"Young lady, here is the writer's notebook I promised you," he said. His blue eyes twinkled.

 Bailey thanked him as she opened it. The ivory pages had lines like a school notebook, but they had a different feel—creamy—and the edges were rough rather than straight. There was a long thin pocket on the front cover for a pen or pencil.

"It's beautiful," Bailey said softly. "Thanks."

She felt the edges again.

"Those are called deckle edges. Fancy, don't you think?"

Bailey nodded.

"Now promise me that you'll fill your book with stories, thoughts, and dreams," said Mr. Phigg. "I try to write a little something every day. Some days ideas or characters pop up like toast and other days I have to tease them out of hiding. They are always with me. Your characters will be with you if you invite them."

What a strange idea. Bailey wondered how she could invite characters to be with her. "What's your new book about?" she asked.

"Jamestown—the story of that unfortunate English settlement of 1607. Did you know that Captain John Smith was trying to find gold and silver? Did you know he was attempting to reach the Pacific Ocean when he explored what we now call Chesapeake Bay?" Before Bailey could answer he continued. "I am writing my book for people your age."

"I know about Indians—Powhatan and Pocahontas," said Bailey. "Sugar and I read about them after I found an arrowhead in the Keswicks' yard."

"Ahh, so you are a researcher, too? That's good. It's so important to do your homework and get your information right," he said. "That's why my assistant, Dr. Robinson, is so wonderful. She helps me with the fact-checking."

"What does she check?" asked Bailey. She had never heard of a fact-checker.

Mr. Phigg said, "Good question. She makes sure names are spelled correctly, and that I'm using the right word. She looks up dates. She also tells me if the truth is being told."

"The truth?" asked Bailey.

"Yes. Take the Pocahontas story. Many books and movies have it all wrong."

"I know," said Bailey. "Sugar told me that Pocahontas was only my age—not a grown-up lady."

"That's right, and she was kidnapped and imprisoned by the white settlers for months and months," said Mr. Phigg.

Bailey said, "That's terrible. She must have been afraid."

"Very likely. There is so much to learn from history," said Mr. Phigg. "I want the information in my books to be right. That's why I value the help of Dr. Robinson."

"Is she an evacuee, too?" asked Bailey.

"Yes, but you'll have to ask her about her experiences when you meet her," he said. "Now, if you'll excuse me, I need to wake my dear

Feather. She didn't sleep well last night. She misses her little Poochie." He stood up and started toward guest room number one off the main hall.

"Poochie?" asked Bailey.

"Yes, Feather's little calico cat. She used to sleep on her side of the bed. Well, she wasn't exactly our cat, but she lived with us for years after she showed up at our door. But we couldn't take her to the emergency shelter where we stayed during the storm so we had to leave her behind. We don't know what happened to her," said Elmo Phigg, wiping his eyes with a large white handkerchief.

"I hope Poochie is all right," said Bailey. "Maybe Miss Bekka will let you get a kitten or dog."

"That's a kind thought, young lady. I must get to work now." He blew his nose. As he closed the door to his room behind him, Sugar and Miss Bekka appeared from the kitchen.

"I appreciate your offer," said Miss Bekka, handing Sugar a list. "Now that we have guests, I need to stock the pantry."

Bailey showed them the writer's notebook.

"What a wonderful present," said Sugar. "I kept a diary when I was your age. It had a tiny lock and key, which I promptly lost. I did very well with the daily entries during the school year. But when summer came and I was reading books and just plain lazy, I didn't write anything down except NMH."

"What did that mean?" asked Bailey.

"It stood for Nothing Much Happened," said Sugar, her face crinkling. "The truth was that so much happened on those wonderful summer days that I didn't want to take the time to write about them. Now I'm sorry I didn't."

"Here's a special green pen," said Miss Bekka. "I think it fits perfectly in the slot."

"Thanks," said Bailey. "I hope I can think of something good to write about."

6

Sparrow

Bailey was thinking about hurricanes as Sugar drove them to Fredericksburg to shop.

"Does evacuee mean that the Phiggs don't have a home anymore?" asked Bailey.

"That's what they said. We don't know much about them," said her grandmother. "It sounds like they lost almost everything. They'll tell us more when they are ready. Sometimes people who have had bad experiences need time before they can talk about them."

"It would be sad if they don't have a place to live," said Bailey. "Mrs. Phigg had to leave, Poochie, their cat, behind. You wouldn't make me leave Sallie and Shadow if we had to be evacuees?"

"Of course not. Remember those gray plastic cages we bought during a treasure hunt? They are to take your kittens with us," said Sugar.

"Good!" said Bailey. "The kittens wouldn't know what to do by themselves in a storm."

"By the way, Miss Bekka said they'll have another guest soon," said Sugar. "So I'll need your help shopping when we get to the mall."

"Who? Dr. Robinson?" asked Bailey.

"No, a girl called Sparrow."

"Sparrow?" asked Bailey. "And her parents?"

"Just Sparrow," said Sugar. "She's about seven years old and must use a wheelchair for quite some time."

"Why?" Bailey's eyebrows raised.

Sugar pushed her glasses up her nose, then rubbed her chin. "Sparrow has a problem with her hips. Her doctors said if she does not walk for a year or more, and gets the proper medical care, her hips should mend. Then she will be able to run and play again. Meanwhile, this will not be an easy time for her."

"Why can't she stay with her parents?" Bailey asked, twisting her hair.

"Sparrow has been in foster care—that means people other than her parents have been raising her—since she was a toddler. Unfortunately, her foster parents must move out of state and the rules don't allow them to take Sparrow with them. The Keswicks have been foster parents in the past and Miss Bekka can homeschool Sparrow and give her the special attention she needs. So the Keswicks have agreed to take her."

"I'll help," said Bailey. She was thinking that Emily's little sister, Nannie, and Justin's sister, Fern, could be Sparrow's new friends. They were about the same age.

"I knew I could count you," said Sugar.

"When will she get here?" asked Bailey.

"Sooner than expected," said Sugar. "That's why Miss Bekka asked us to get new clothes, books, and toys for her when we are in town today—and pretty sheets for her bed."

"Where will she sleep?" asked Bailey.

"In guest room number three on the first floor," said Sugar. "Mr. Will and Justin are going to make a ramp so that Sparrow can get up in the house in her wheelchair."

Bailey decided that she would write about Sparrow in her new notebook. She wondered if Sparrow was sad that she couldn't walk for a long time. *I would be,* Bailey thought.

7

Getting Ready for Sparrow

By the time they returned, the ramp was constructed. Mr. Will had also measured doorways to see if the wheelchair could get through.

"The social workers said that Sparrow will be here Tuesday at four," said Noah. "Now we'll have a sister, too." He grinned.

Fred said, "I'm going to bake brownies for her. Everybody likes brownies."

"It's a good thing you use a mix, dude," said Noah, gently punching Fred in the shoulder.

"Hey, if you don't like my brownies, you shouldn't eat them," said Fred, pushing back.

"Where are the Phiggs?" asked Bailey.

"They went for a walk to the little cemetery," said Fred. "Mr. Phigg said he gets inspiration for his books when he walks."

"He has a big walking stick with a duck head on the top," said Noah, "and a duck quacker attached under its head."

"A quacker?" asked Bailey, her eyes wide.

"He squeezes something and it quacks. Awesome," said Noah.

"You should have seen Clover when she heard it. She couldn't figure out where the duck was and started spinning in circles and barking," said Fred.

Sugar and Bailey made Sparrow's bed with yellow striped sheets and helped Miss Bekka hang matching curtains on the window. Bailey folded the clothes they bought—underwear, four T-shirts, two pairs of shorts, and two pairs of jeans—plus a hairbrush and a necklace—in Sparrow's dresser. She placed a fuzzy tan stuffed cat on Sparrow's pillow and neatly stacked the books on the bedside table.

"There," Sugar said. "This looks nice for a little girl."

"I know you and your friends will all want to meet her," said Miss Bekka as she came into the room, "but I'd like to give Sparrow a day or so to get adjusted. It will be enough to have just the Keswicks and the Phiggs around."

Bailey was disappointed. She had hoped to be waiting on the Keswicks' front porch when Sparrow arrived.

"That's fine. Call us when you are ready," Sugar said.

Quack. Quack. The Phiggs had returned from their walk. Clover barked and spun in circles.

"I think Clover is a dancer like me," said Mrs. Phigg. "How charming."

"How are her obedience lessons coming?" asked Bailey.

"Every time Justin comes over, he shows us how to make her behave," said Fred, wiping his glasses on his shirt. "So far Clover minds him, but not us."

"It takes time to train a dog," said Sugar, crinkling. "Especially the smart ones. They always have a better idea." She turned to Elmo Phigg. "If we can be of any help to you with your book, let me know. I have quite a large library and several books about Jamestown."

"That would be outstanding," he replied. "Most of the books and papers we were able to bring with us are still packed in boxes. Dr. Robinson will be joining us soon."

"She will?" asked Miss Bekka, sighing. "I'm not sure we'll have a third guest room ready by then. We've barely prepared two of them."

"We'll do our best," said Mr. Will, putting his arm around his wife.

"And we'll help, too," said Sugar.

"Marvey," said Feather Phigg, her hands fluttering towards Clover's moppy head.

8

On the Way

"I wish we didn't have to wait for a few days to meet Sparrow," said Emily. "It's not fair! Can't we sneak over or something? We could just look in the window when she gets here."

"I wish," said Bailey. She gazed out the school bus window. "Sugar promised that we wouldn't go over until they called."

"Have the Phiggs showed you what's in the green suitcase yet?" asked Emily.

"Nope. Noah thinks it's full of gold coins and Fred says it must have important papers inside."

"I think it's full of beautiful jewelry," said Emily. "That would be mysterious. You should ask them about it. I bet they'll show you. Besides, what else could be in there?"

"I don't know, but I'm not going to ask," said Bailey. "Sugar says they'll tell us more when they're ready."

"Then, I'll ask," said Emily, as she pushed dark curls out of her face. "You're too much of a scaredy-cat."

Bailey didn't like the way Emily called her that, even though her friend was smiling.

Justin nodded at the girls as he got off the bus.

"Nice ramp," Bailey called after him. Justin knew how to build things, not like the rest of the kids. He was patient, measured carefully, and took pride in doing the job properly. Mr. Will was showing Bailey how use tools. She now knew how to hold a hammer correctly so that she would pound the nail, not her thumb. She wanted to learn to make a bookshelf for her bedroom, like Justin made for Noah's room at Keswick Inn.

"Maybe when they aren't home, you could open it," said Emily. Her blue eyes danced.

"Open the suitcase? Nuh-uh," said Bailey. "It isn't mine." She gave her friend a look.

"Hang on. I was just joking," said Emily as they reached Bailey's bus stop. "Call me."

Bailey slipped the knapsack straps over her shoulders. It was so heavy with books that she felt like she was going to fall over backwards when she reached the bottom step. "See ya tomorrow," she said to Emily.

The house was empty. Sugar was at a meeting. She left two boxes of raisins next to a note for Bailey near the phone.

Dear Bailey—Get your homework done right away. Sparrow arrived sooner than expected and Miss Bekka said she needs our help. I'll be back by five.

Love, Sugar

Instead of heading for her room, Bailey spread her schoolwork out on the kitchen table, poured a glass of milk, and popped a handful of raisins in her mouth.

It will be so much fun to have another girl in the neighborhood, she thought. *I hope she likes to read.*

9

Bad Beginning

"Where's Sparrow?" Bailey asked Noah when she and Sugar arrived at Keswick Inn.

"In her room," said Fred. He didn't sound happy. He took off his glasses and wiped the smudged lenses on a corner of his shirt before putting them back on his turned-up nose.

"What's the matter?" Sugar asked Miss Bekka.

"I knew it wasn't going to be easy for Sparrow or us, but she's very upset. She refuses to talk to any of us."

"What would you like us to do?" asked Sugar.

"If you and Bailey would visit with her, maybe she'll talk to you."

"Of course," said Sugar.

Bailey looked around the living room. Even though the Keswicks hadn't finished decorating the inn yet, they had placed furniture in various rooms for themselves and their guests. The Phiggs were reading in tan armchairs near the fireplace. Mr. Phigg was taking notes on a large yellow pad. They seemed to be ignoring the problem of Sparrow's arrival.

Miss Bekka said, "I know it will take time for Sparrow to feel comfortable here, but I feel sad for her in the meantime." She buttoned her denim overshirt and tied her thick blond hair back with cloth-covered rubber band.

Sugar said, "C'mon, Bailey. Let's visit the newest guest at Keswick Inn." She knocked on the door to guest room three. There was no answer. Sugar turned the knob and opened it.

Bailey saw that the stuffed cat had been flung to the far corner. Books were scattered everywhere on the floor. Even a hanging picture of Bambi was crooked, like a terrible storm had whirled through the room.

There was a small wheelchair near the window. Its back was to the door.

"Hello, Sparrow," Sugar said gently. "We want to welcome you to the neighborhood. I'm Sugar, and this is my granddaughter, Bailey. She's new here, too."

Silence.

"I'm going to turn your chair around so we can visit," Sugar said. Bailey didn't know what to expect. Would Sparrow scream or throw things or start talking?

Silence.

Sugar carefully turned the chair around so that the little girl was facing them. Her mask-like face was frozen in anger. She looked briefly at Bailey and Sugar, then stared at her lap. Her long, dark-blond hair partly covered her face. She had a few freckles like Bailey. Her hair needed combing. The sleeves of her blue T-shirt hung halfway way down her thin arms, and she was wearing jeans.

"There're a lot of kids in the neighborhood," said Bailey. "They want to meet you. There's Nannie and Fern . . ."

Silence.

"I hear you've been a good runner," said Sugar. "I'm wondering if you're sad because you can't run or walk until your hips are healed." She waited.

Silence, but Sparrow blinked hard.

"And I bet you're feeling bad that you've had to change foster homes and school—all at the same time."

Bailey thought Sparrow looked like she would cry. The girl's tiny hands curled into fists.

"And maybe you're afraid to make friends here, because you're afraid that you might have to move again."

Silence.

"I'll be your friend," said Bailey. "We can read together, and maybe you can come to my house to see my kittens. They're really cute."

Sparrow said nothing. She stared at the ceiling.

"It's almost time for supper," said Sugar. "Let's go see what Miss Bekka has fixed."

Bailey opened the door, and Sugar pushed the wheelchair into the hallway. Bailey went back in the room and quickly put the books and toys where they had been before Sparrow arrived.

10

Silence

Sparrow picked at the spaghetti and took a few sips of milk. Bailey wondered if the girl wanted help cutting up the big meatballs on her plate. Sparrow hadn't asked for any, so Bailey didn't offer.

Everyone acted like they didn't notice that Sparrow still refused to speak. Noah and Fred told knock-knock jokes, including Fred's favorite. He said in Sparrow's direction, "Knock knock. Who's there? Norma Lee. Norma Lee who? Norma Lee I ring the bell."

Then Noah made a series of goofy faces that made Bailey laugh. Sparrow watched them, but didn't even smile.

Miss Bekka asked Sparrow if she wanted a little salt or pepper but didn't push the girl for an answer.

"These are the best meatballs I've ever had. Don't you think so, Sparrow?" said Mr. Phigg.

He dabbed orange sauce off his beard with his large paper napkin.

Still no response. Sugar and Miss Bekka talked to Sparrow as if she were listening and about to enter the conversation. Miss Bekka told her about their plans for Keswick Inn and the boys' homeschool. Sparrow also would be learning at home. She said she heard that Sparrow had earned good grades so far in school.

Sugar told her about how Bailey had moved in with her and the treasure hunts they went on to find bargains at yard sales and auctions.

Mrs. Phigg straightened the red comb in the bun of her orange hair and told the little girl that she would fix her hair like a princess.

Silence.

Bailey could see that Noah and Fred were tired of all the attention that Sparrow was getting. She saw Noah give Clover some of his peas, and then Fred nudged Noah to try to make him spill his milk. Bailey wanted to talk about something else, too.

"How's your book coming?" asked Bailey.

"The characters arrived today," Mr. Phigg said grandly. "They came tumbling like clowns out of a little car."

"That's always exciting for us," said Mrs. Phigg. "Then Elmo gets going with the story."

"What do you mean?" asked Fred.

"Look outside after supper, my friends," said Mr. Phigg. "My characters are camped on the lawn."

"Who are?" asked Bailey.

"The Powhatans and the English settlers."

Noah couldn't stand it anymore. He bolted to the window and peered out in the twilight. "Nobody's there," he said. "You're making that up."

"Noah, that's rude," said Miss Bekka sharply.

"I'm sorry," said Noah to Mr. Phigg. Bailey didn't think that Noah really meant it.

"They are *my* characters. I see them, and that's what counts," said Mr. Phigg, looking kindly at Noah. "I can see their campfires. I hear their voices and muskets. I hear the drums and smell the wild turkeys and corn roasting. Now, tell me what you think. Should I write my story from the point of view of one of the Powhatans, or one of the settlers?"

"Pocahontas," said Noah.

"John Smith," said Fred.

"Pocahontas's sister or her cousin," suggested Bailey. "Then it would be different from other books."

"I shall have to consult my characters," he said thoughtfully, "but thanks for your ideas."

Mr. Phigg sounded so convincing about the characters that Bailey wanted to see what was outside. Noah still looked like he didn't believe a word of it.

"Would you like a piece of chocolate cake, Sparrow?" asked Miss Bekka.

She ignored the girl's silence and placed a piece in front of her. To everyone's surprise, Sparrow didn't waste time sinking her fork into the fudge frosting.

"Would you like me to help you get her ready for bed?" Sugar later asked Miss Bekka. She placed the dirty dessert plates in the dishpan.

"I think I can manage. I was just a bit over-whelmed this afternoon, said Miss Bekka. She and Bailey stacked and dried the rinsed plates.

Bailey walked over to the wheelchair. "Bye, Sparrow. I'll bring books when I come back. Then we can read together."

There was no answer.

11

Night Sky

Sugar pointed out the Big Dipper in the sky as she and Bailey walked back home through the field behind Keswick Inn. Bailey traced its curved handle and bowl with her finger. She was learning the names of the stars and constellations from her grandmother. Bailey could see them better in the country where there were no city lights.

"The Big Dipper is part of Ursa Major, the Big Bear," said Sugar. "One of my favorites."

"Look," Bailey said, stopping. "There's Polaris, the North Star." She had found it on her own for the first time.

"The explorers, including Captain Smith, used the North Star to help them stay on course," said Sugar. "Reading the sky is an important part of navigation. By the way, both the Big Dipper and North Star are pictured on the Alaska State flag," Sugar added. "I have a little one in my library. The flag is especially interesting because it was designed by someone about your age."

Bailey cocked her head and studied the sky. "What do you call that almost-full moon? A gibson?"

Sugar chuckled. "Close, but no cookie. It's the gibbous moon. Gibbous means hump."

"Gibbous. I'll try to remember," said Bailey. She said it again. "Gibbous."

"Let's go," said Sugar, "or we won't be home before the morning star rises."

They entered the path in the woods that took them past the little cemetery. Bailey was glad both of them carried big flashlights to help them find their way. She wished she were as brave as Sugar. Her grandmother—a genuine wild woman—didn't seem to be afraid of the creaking, crackling sounds behind them, or of what might be lurking in the shadows on either side of the path.

Sugar hummed Popeye the Sailor's song, and soon Bailey joined in. She realized humming made her less afraid. *Wild things will know we're coming and get out of the way,* she thought.

Their humming stopped when they reached Sugar's yard. Bailey hated to go inside when there was still so much to see in the night. The bright moon cast long shadows from the tall trees. A rabbit scampered across the lawn when it heard Bailey say softly to her grandmother, "Look, Sallie and Shadow are waiting for us on the porch."

Before going upstairs, Bailey checked her e-mail. There were two messages. The first was from her father:

From: pjfish2005@yermail.net>
To: "Bailey"<baileyfish@gmail.com>
Sent: 7:42 p.m.
Subject: Hi daughter

We snorkeled yesterday in the reefs at Gab Gab and saw clownfish. Norma Jean and the boys enjoyed the warm, calm water. Did you ever snorkel in Florida? My plans to move are delayed. I'm waiting for the right job once my time is up with the Navy. How's school going? Have those kittens turned into cats yet? Are you practicing your clarinet? I'm writing a duet for us to play. I'll send the music soon. Dad

And the second was from Amber.

From: jbs25@yerrmail.net
To: "Bailey"<baileyfish@gmail.com>
Sent: 4:14 p.m.
Subject: Me

Hey, Bailey: I can't wait till school gets out. It is soooo hot here. I felt like a melting ice cream cone at the bus stop. There's a new boy named

Morrie in the neighborhood. He's cute. Mom is
going to see if he'll mow our lawn. I hope so.
SCR, Amber

Bailey logged off without answering either
e-mail. She made sure there was kibble in the
kittens' dish and refilled their water bowl before kissing Sugar good night.

"Thanks for helping with Sparrow," said her
grandmother."

"I didn't really do anything," said Bailey.

"You offered to be her friend, and best of
all, to come back, even if she wasn't respond-
ing. You didn't let her chase you off. That's what's
important. We must have patience," said Sugar.

Bailey gave Sugar another kiss. When she
reached her room she sat on her bed with the
special notebook and green ink pen. The kittens scrambled up to sit with her.

The blank pages were so nice she hadn't put
words on them yet, even though Mr. Phigg had
told her to write. Bailey printed the date, and
next to it drew the Big Dipper and North Star.
She wrote: "This book belongs to Bailey Fish. I
live with my grandmother, Sugar, and I'm going to be a teacher, spy, or a writer, if my characters show up like Mr. Phigg's do. Maybe I'll
name one Mr. Gibbous."

12

Sneaky Plans

"I can't believe how helpful the boys have been lately," said Miss Bekka when Sugar and Bailey stopped by with picture books for Sparrow.

"I usually have to beg them to help me with chores—the jobs they don't get paid for at Keswick Inn. All of a sudden they volunteered to clean the guest rooms. They offered to dust and vacuum," she said.

"A sign of growing up," said Sugar.

"Where's Sparrow?" asked Bailey.

"She's doing math problems in the kitchen. She should be done soon. There is nothing wrong with Sparrow's mind, even if she refuses to speak," said Miss Bekka. "She learns quickly."

Bailey heard a *pssst*. She saw a hand beckoning her to come into the living room. Noah whispered, "So, what do you think of my plan?"

"What plan?" asked Bailey very quietly.

"To find the suitcase."

"Huh?" she said.

"When we clean the guest rooms, we'll be able to look for it. Pretty clever, right?" he said.

"The suitcase isn't yours," said Bailey, twisting her hair. "You could get in big trouble, you know."

"Not unless you tell," said Noah. "Besides, we're not going to take anything—we just want to look. Phiggy shouldn't have teased us about it. He made us curious."

Bailey looked at Fred. His brown face showed worry. He took off his glasses and examined them for Clover's smudgy nose prints, which she put there quite often.

"Now, are you going to help us clean Phiggy's room?" asked Noah, his eyes challenging her.

Bailey thought about it. It wasn't right to be spying on people, especially nice people like the Phiggs.

"No," she finally said, but it didn't come out very strongly.

Noah said, "Well, will you at least be our lookout and tell us if someone is coming?"

Bailey guessed she could do that. It wasn't exactly the same as searching for the suitcase herself.

"Okay," she said, but she didn't sound like she wanted to do that, either.

"Won't it look weird if I'm just standing around in the hall while you clean a room?" asked Bailey, putting her hands on her hips.

"You can play ball with Clover," said Noah. "She likes to chase it down the hall."

"The Phiggs have gone for a walk, so the only people you have to watch for are Mom and Sugar," said Fred.

Sugar. Sugar would be very unhappy if she found out that Bailey was a lookout. Before Bailey could tell the twins that she wouldn't help them after all, Fred appeared with a ball. Clover danced to reach it in his hand, while Noah dragged the vacuum cleaner into the Phiggs' room.

The boys closed the door and started the cleaner. Bailey tossed the ball, which bounced off the wall right into Clover's mouth. The small white dog raced back to Bailey and dropped the

ball at her feet. Bailey sat down and threw the ball again. Clover sailed through the air to catch the ball before it reached the end of the hallway. The ball was gooey with dog spit when

Clover dropped it again by Bailey's knee. Bailey wiped it off on her pants.

"Good girl," said Bailey, reaching out to pet her. Clover backed up so Bailey couldn't touch her and barked. She only wanted to chase the ball again. The vacuum stopped. The boys must be dusting, or perhaps they had found the suitcase.

When Bailey heard Sugar and Miss Bekka coming down the stairs, she gave the signal, three knocks. The door opened and Fred said a little too loudly, "On to the next room, Noah, my bro."

"Nothing yet," Noah said quietly to Bailey. "We'll look more next week when we clean again."

13

First Laugh Tradition

"As I was reading more about Indians, I came across this," said Sugar. "Third paragraph."

Bailey got up out of her chair in Sugar's library and leaned over her shoulder to see where her grandmother was pointing. "Hey, that's really neat," said Bailey. "I didn't know there was a first laugh ceremony. I bet Noah and Fred haven't heard of it either."

Sugar said, "Apparently, there is a Navajo tradition that the first person who makes a baby laugh throws a party for the baby."

"I've got an idea," said Bailey. "Let's have a party for Sparrow to see who can make her laugh or speak."

Sugar's face crinkled. "What a wonderful idea. We'll talk with the Keswicks to see what they think."

"And Emily, Nannie and Howie, and Justin and Fern," said Bailey. "Everyone can help."

"And don't forget the Phiggs. They are around her a lot, too," said Sugar. "What kind of party should we have?"

"Maybe we could have one full of jokes. Clowns. Funny games," said Bailey. "We could all dress up in crazy outfits and do silly things."

"I like your plan, but that isn't exactly what the Navajos do. They have the party *after* the first laugh, not to make a baby laugh, but our situation is different. In the Navajo tradition, the baby is supposed to grow up like the person who makes him laugh, but your idea could work for us," said Sugar.

"I hope so. Sparrow always looks so sad."

Sugar continued reading. "Hmmm. Part of the Navajo tradition is to give sweets to all the guests at the party to make the baby generous, and rock salt to keep him or her from becoming stingy," said Sugar.

"We should do that at Sparrow's party," said Bailey. "They could be the favors."

"Are you ready for hot cocoa?" asked Sugar. "I think it tastes good on cool evenings."

"Yum, that would be great," said Bailey. She returned to her chair and her book, *The Lion, the Witch and the Wardrobe*. She loved this quiet reading time with Sugar. Bailey turned to chapter eleven. The story was getting scary.

Her grandmother pushed the creaky recliner footrest down and stood up. Bailey heard Sugar say, "Oh, drats!" just before the crash. Bailey looked up in time to see Sugar fall, hitting her head on the edge of the coffee table before landing awkwardly on floor. Sugar was bleeding badly from her forehead and her glasses were twisted.

"Sugar!" Bailey screamed. She rushed across the room and knelt beside her. "Oh, no!"

Sugar's eyes were closed and she didn't say anything for a minute. Then she blinked and said, "I twisted my leg, and my arm.... Call 9-1-1."

Bailey grabbed the phone and dialed. "My grandmother's hurt, please hurry," she told the dispatcher.

She got a clean towel from kitchen and put it on Sugar's forehead. Bailey patted her grandmother's cheek and held her hand. "You'll be okay, Sugar. I promise. I won't leave you." Tears streamed down her cheeks. Bailey was glad Sugar's eyes were closed again so her grandmother couldn't see her cry.

"Now, please call the Keswicks. You will need to stay with them if I must stay overnight," whispered Sugar.

"I want to go with you," said Bailey, holding back sobs. She patted her grandmother's cheek.

Before Bailey could dial the Keswicks, she heard a siren. The ambulance wailed up the driveway. She was surprised and relieved to see Mr. Will pull in right behind it.

"The rig passed me on the road, then I saw it turn up your driveway," he said to Bailey.

"She's in the library," said Bailey, pointing the way to the emergency crew.

Mr. Will put his arm around Bailey's shoulder as they watched the emergency technicians bandage Sugar's cut forehead and examine her leg and wrist. Then they carefully placed Sugar on a stretcher.

"We'll follow you," Mr. Will told Sugar. "I'll take care of Bailey. Don't you worry."

Sugar reached out her hand and touched Bailey's face. "I'll be all right, sweetheart. See if you can find my spare glasses in my bedroom. They're in the drawer in the table beside my bed. And please get my toothbrush and jammies, just in case I need to stay the night."

"I love you, Sugar," said Bailey as the EMTs wheeled her grandmother out the door and put her in the ambulance. Its sirens pierced the night as it speed away down the dark road. Bailey held back tears.

While Mr. Will phoned Miss Bekka to let her know what had happened, Bailey located the spare glasses. She wrapped Sugar's toothbrush and toothpaste in a clean washcloth, and found a pair of blue plaid pajamas in her middle dresser drawer. *I need to find something to make Sugar feel better,* thought Bailey. *I know.* Bailey dashed into her own room and grabbed her favorite stuffed bear, then hurried downstairs to the kitchen. She quickly packed everything in a brown paper grocery bag. Mr. Will called to her from the porch, "C'mon, Bailey, let's get going."

Bailey stumbled as she hurried after him to his van. She felt like nothing, not even clowns or kittens could make her laugh again—not unless Sugar was okay.

14

Worries and Waiting

Sugar was still being examined when Mr. Will and Bailey arrived at the emergency room. A clerk with hair the color of buttered popcorn and lips smeared with bright red lipstick directed them to stay in the waiting area. Bailey thought the woman was unfriendly, even when Mr. Will smiled warmly and said they wanted to see Sugar.

The woman looked at a chart. "You'll have to wait. No one is allowed in there right now, especially a child," she said. She kept typing.

Mr. Will nodded and motioned to Bailey to follow him to empty seats.

The blue molded plastic chairs were uncomfortable and there was a stupid program on the television that sat on a metal shelf near the ceiling. The magazines on a chipped table connecting the chairs looked like they were fifty years old and had been used as Frisbees.

Bailey tapped her fingers on the chair seat and looked at the woman behind the desk. *Why can't I go inside?* she fretted, clutching the creased grocery bag with her grandmother's things.

"Would you like something to eat?" asked Mr. Will. "There's a snack machine down that hallway. A package of cookies or crackers?"

Bailey shook her head no. Even if she were hungry, she didn't want to leave her grandmother. Sugar probably didn't even know they were there. She was probably worried about Bailey.

Bailey stood up and went back to the clerk's desk. Maybe if she asked nicely, the clerk would change her mind.

"Please, ma'am, may I see my grandmother now?" Bailey asked.

"Little girl, I told you later, after the doctors have finished," said the clerk. She looked at Bailey like she was just an annoying fly— like she wanted her to buzz off.

"Could you just tell my grandmother that we are here and that I love her?" Bailey could barely talk.

"Write a note," said the clerk. "I'll give it to her when I go on break." She handed a torn scrap of paper and a pen to Bailey.

Bailey wasn't sure that the woman would deliver the note, which she placed on top of her computer monitor. And besides, Sugar probably couldn't read it without her glasses. She walked back to Mr. Will, who was watching TV.

He asked, "No luck? Are you sure I can't get you a snack?" He looked at his watch.

Bailey couldn't think of anything that would taste good except Sugar's special hot chocolate. Sometimes she added mint or a dash of cinnamon, and miniature marshmallows. Bailey said, "No, thanks." She sat back down in one of the slippery, hard chairs.

"If you'll be okay for a minute, I think I'll step outside to use the cell phone. I'm sure Bekka and the boys want to hear what is happening, or *not* happening," Mr. Will said.

"Sure," said Bailey, glumly.

If Noah and Fred were here, they would think of a way to see Sugar, thought Bailey. She tried to watch the TV, but couldn't concentrate.

Soon the clerk got up to put forms in the file cabinet behind the desk. Her back was to Bailey.

This was her chance. Bailey bolted over to the double door covered with dark scuff marks and a sign that said NO ADMITTANCE. There were big shiny metal circles on the wall next to the automatic doors that doctors and nurses pushed to open them.

Sugar, I'm coming, thought Bailey as she reached for a circle.

A hand grabbed her jacket. "Where do you think you are going, young lady?" said an angry voice. "I told you that you can't go in there."

"I just want to see my grandmother," said Bailey. Her voice felt like it was in a cage.

"Well, you can't, missie," said the woman. "Sit down."

With that, the doors swung open and the emergency room doctor wearing green pants and shirt came into the waiting room.

"Are you Bailey?" he asked kindly. "Come with me. Your grandmother has been asking for you."

Mr. Will caught up with them before the doors could close again.

"Hmmph!" Bailey heard the clerk say.

They followed the doctor down the corridor. He pulled a yellow-and-tan striped curtain open so that Bailey and Mr. Will could see Sugar propped up on a high, narrow bed with rails so she couldn't fall out. Sugar was wearing a white hospital gown and was covered with a lightweight gray blanket.

Bailey threw her arms around her grandmother and asked, "Are you okay?"

Sugar said, "I'll be fine. I had ten stitches above my eye, and my knee and wrist are taped up. I twisted them badly, but they don't think they are broken. The good news is that the doctor is going to let me go home as long as I have someone to stay with me."

Bailey handed Sugar the spare glasses and said softly, "I'll take care of you."

"That's what I told them," whispered her grandmother. "I didn't tell them how old my housemate was, so don't tell." She winced when she smiled.

"And you know we'll be checking on you, too," said Mr. Will. "If you're ready, I'll go get the van."

"I was so afraid," said Bailey.

"Me, too, for a few minutes, but everything's okay now," said Sugar.

15

Home Again

Sugar insisted that Bailey go to school the next day even though they had arrived home at midnight. Bailey wanted to skip classes to look after her grandmother.

"The Keswicks will stop by to check on me," Sugar said. Bailey hurriedly made a peanut butter and jelly sandwich for each of them for lunch and added an apple to her brown bag.

"I'll make supper," Bailey promised, "and do the laundry and straighten your bed."

"I can come over and help," Emily said when Bailey told her what had happened. "If I had been with you, I would have stuck out my tongue at that mean woman." She looked so serious that Bailey had to smile.

It was hard for Bailey to focus in school. All she could think about was Sugar falling. Her teacher, Mrs. Dudlee, had to speak to her twice about paying better attention.

There were three cars in the driveway when Bailey got off the bus. She ran to the house, afraid that Sugar had fallen again. But as she opened the front door, she heard people laughing. The kitchen counters were filled with casseroles, homemade bread and rolls, pies and cakes, jellies, and pickles.

Women from Sugar's church were in the living room telling stories and offering all sorts of help while Sugar recovered from her fall.

Bailey was astonished. Usually Sugar was the one who took food to people who were sick or had a problem. Now everyone seemed to be helping her.

"Well, now that your darling granddaughter is home, we should probably go," said Mrs. Morton, who taught Sunday school to the smallest children. "You look like you are ready for a nap."

"Thank you all," said Sugar. "You're right—Bailey can handle things from here on today."

Bailey was very proud that her grandmother felt that way.

The church women weren't the only ones who stopped by. Sugar said that Justin's mother, Nora Rudd, had offered to help with errands, and Bekka Keswick had come over twice. She told Sugar that the boys said they would help with chores—for nothing. And no, Sparrow still hadn't said anything.

"So I told them about your idea for the first laugh or first word party and they thought it was a great idea. The boys clearly wished they had learned about that first," said Sugar.

Bailey did her homework while Sugar dozed in her recliner with Shadow curled up in her lap. She frequently looked at her grandmother to make sure she was still breathing okay.

I'll take care of you always, Sugar. Always, thought Bailey. Her throat tightened as she remembered how Sugar's face looked when the accident happened.

16

More Company

Miss Bekka, Noah, and Fred dropped in after supper the following day.

"More excitement at Keswick Inn today," Miss Bekka told Sugar. She plumped Sugar's pillows in the recliner. "Maven Robinson, the Phiggs' research assistant, arrived. So now all the rooms we have fixed up so far are full and we aren't even officially open yet."

"What's she like?" asked Sugar.

"She's dark-skinned like me," said Fred. "She has tiny glasses that look like they are going to fall off her nose, purplish lipstick, and her hair's combed back."

"And she has three big cloth suitcases," said Noah, "and the best part . . ."

"Let me tell," interrupted Fred. "An African Grey parrot that can sing 'Three Blind Mice' and recite nursery rhymes."

"Wow!" said Bailey.

"The parrot's name is Pinocchio," said Noah. "You should see Clover. She can't figure out what is going on when the bird talks."

"And the *really* best part," said Miss Bekka, "is that Sparrow seems quite interested in Pinocchio. She wheeled her chair near the cage so she could watch the bird."

"We'll come by when the doctor says I can drive again," said Sugar. "I doubt that I'll be homebound for more than a few days."

"Now that Dr. Robinson has arrived, the Phiggs said they might go to Jamestown for a week or so," said Miss Bekka. "I guess we'll be babysitting Pinocchio. Dr. Robinson said she would pay the boys to take care of him, as long as they promise not to teach him any bad words."

Noah gave Bailey a look that told her he had ideas he couldn't share with the grown-ups.

"Can we help Bailey take the trash out, Sugar?" he asked.

"That would be lovely, Noah," Sugar said. She had forgotten that Bailey had already done that after school.

When the boys reached the kitchen with Bailey, Noah said, "While the Phiggs are away, this is our chance to find the suitcase. Can you come over when they're gone?"

"I don't know," said Bailey, still uncomfortable with the idea of snooping. "I don't think we should. Besides, Sugar may need me."

"You promised to help," he said, scowling.

"If Sugar doesn't need me," said Bailey, looking out the window.

"Never mind," said Noah, with disgust in his voice. "I know Emily will help. *Bawk bawk bawk*. Chicken."

Bailey quickly looked at him, hating the way he said that. But Noah's eyes were smiling at her again, not glaring as she had expected.

"Bawk bawk bawk," said Bailey, flapping her arms back at him.

17

Pinocchio

Awk. I want to be a real boy. Don't bite. When
Bailey heard the commotion on the front porch,
she knew that Dr. Robinson and Pinocchio must
be outside.

"If Sugar can't come to us, we will come to
her," boomed Mr. Phigg.

"Don't get up," said
Mrs. Phigg, as Sugar
reached for a knobby
cane.

Shadow and Sallie
took one look at the
cage and the noisy gray
bird, and hid behind the
couch. They refused to
budge, even when
Pinocchio called, "Here,
kitty, kitty," and
coughed loudly.

"This is my assistant, Dr. Robinson," said Mr. Phigg. "We're off to Jamestown soon to help solve an archaeological mystery, or to at least work it into my book."

Dr. Robinson shook hands with both Sugar and Bailey.

"Welcome to the neighborhood," said Sugar.

"I probably won't be staying more than a couple of months while we do the basic research," said the woman. "Then I must return home to continue working on my books—mostly about travel."

"My mom is traveling," volunteered Bailey. "She's in Costa Rica."

"A beautiful place," said Dr. Robinson. "I know it well."

"Her mother is writing a book about Andrew Snorge-Swinson," said Mr. Phigg.

"I've met him several times," said Dr. Robinson. "Most recently at a meeting in New York. An odd duck, but very bright. I hear he has a new lady friend."

Bailey and Sugar looked at each other. "Mom?" mouthed Bailey.

Sugar raised her shoulders signaling that she didn't know.

Suddenly Bailey didn't want to talk with anybody anymore. She excused herself and rushed upstairs. She opened her special notebook and wrote: *It isn't fair. My mother better not marry bug man. I hate him.* She slammed the notebook closed.

18

Searching for the Suitcase

Bailey plumped Sugar's pillow and asked if she wanted tea or a book.

"Not now, thanks. I feel like dozing. Why don't you go see Sparrow. She's probably wondering where you've been," said Sugar.

Bailey said, "But what if you need something?"

"I'll be fine. I promise to just sit and read when I wake up," said Sugar. "Then when you get back, I'll let you fix supper. We still have lots of wonderful food to eat."

Bailey reluctantly agreed and headed through the woods to Keswick Inn.

"Sparrow's taking a nap, dude," said Noah, "so you can be a lookout again. The Phiggs have gone for a ride and Mom is upstairs sewing kitchen curtains."

Bailey hesitated.

"Bawk bawk bawk," said Noah.

"*Bawk bawk bawk,*" Pinocchio repeated from the next room.

"Okay," said Bailey, "but just for a minute." She still felt uncomfortable about helping them.

Noah and Fred, carrying window cleaner and paper towels, carefully opened the Phiggs' door. Bailey could hear them moving boxes and talking quietly. When she heard someone walking in the upstairs hall, she knocked three times on the door and hurried into the living room.

"Dang," said Noah, "the Phiggs must have taken it with them."

Bailey was secretly relieved.

"But here is something that was on the dresser," said Noah.

"I told him not to touch it," said Fred, looking very worried.

Noah opened his hand. He showed Bailey a small piece of cream-colored china with a design the color of cranberries.

"Put it back," said Fred.

"I'm going to," said Noah. "Stop being such a sissy."

Noah went back, placed the shard on the dresser, then returned to the hallway.

"You're going to get us in trouble," said Fred. Bailey nodded. She remembered how upset she became when her half sister, Norma Jean, touched her personal possessions without asking. It was the first time Bailey met her and Norma Jean handled everything in her room.

"Bawk bawk," said Noah. "C'mon, Clover. Let's play tag outside." He tapped the little dog on her back and ran for the screen door, with Clover right behind him.

Fred shook his head and picked up the cleaning supplies.

19

Another Stranger

Noah opened the screen door and Clover dashed out ahead of them. The little dog stopped at the bottom of the steps and barked.

"Hush," said Noah, but Clover barked louder. "What is it, girl?"

"Some guy is coming up the drive," said Bailey.

"I'll get Mom," said Fred. Before he could go back inside, the stranger called to them.

"Wait a minute," said the man.

Clover stopped barking and ran back up the steps to hide behind Noah.

A bald man with dark sunglasses kept walking toward them. He wore charcoal-colored slacks and a light-blue starched shirt. He held a piece of paper in one hand; his other hand was in his pocket.

"Perhaps you can help me," said the stranger. "I'm looking for something that belongs to me."

"What did you lose?" asked Noah.

"I didn't exactly lose it," said the stranger. "I'm looking for a green suitcase—a small one."

Neither Fred, Bailey or Noah said anything.

"Have you seen these people?" the man asked. He showed them a faded photograph of Elmo and Feather Phigg when they were much younger.

No one said a word.

"If you do," said the man, "please call this number. Sorry I don't have a business card with me. I really need your help. My name is Elmo Phigg."

"Huh?" said Noah, his eyes opened wide as he took a small piece of paper from the stranger. The man looked hard at their faces, as if he were trying to read their minds, then turned away. They watched him walk down the driveway and get into a dark green sedan.

"Well, dudes, what do we do now?" asked Noah.

"I don't know," said Fred.

"I think we should tell your parents," said Bailey. "What if the suitcase is his?"

"Not yet," said Noah. "We have a mystery to solve first."

20

Terrified

"So, how is Sparrow?" asked Sugar when Bailey returned.

"She was taking a nap so I didn't get to see her," said Bailey. "What do you want me to fix for dinner?"

"I feel like such an invalid," said Sugar. "Look in the fridge. I think the Dovers made a lasagna that just needs to be warmed in the microwave, and Nora Rudd dropped off a Jello salad."

"I saw a fudge cake," said Bailey.

"I saw it, too. We are blessed with such good friends and neighbors," said Sugar.

Bailey set the table while the lasagna was warming. She peeked under the tinfoil covering the fudge cake that Miss Bekka made from a family recipe. Waves of fudge frosting swirled on the round top. She put her finger in one corner and tasted the chocolate. *Delicious!*

The microwave beeped. Bailey used two pot holders to remove the lasagna pan. The cheese and sauce were bubbling on top. She heard Sugar's recliner creak as her grandmother got out. Sugar's face crinkled as she hobbled into the kitchen using her cane.

"My, my, my," she said. "You have done a splendid job. I think I'll resign as cook and let you take over."

Bailey pulled out Sugar's chair to make it easier for her to sit down.

They each had two helpings of the lasagna and salad, then Bailey cut extra-large pieces of cake.

At first, Sugar said she didn't think she could eat that much. "I'm stuffed," she said, but she finished her slice quickly.

"Now I think I'll go back to my chair to put my leg up," said Sugar.

"I have a little math to do," said Bailey, "after the dishes." She looked at the clock. It was later than she had realized. The sun was starting to go down. Bailey wondered if she should tell Sugar about the stranger who was looking for Mr. Phigg. The first Phiggs might be in danger, or maybe they were the fake Phiggs and the stranger was the real one. She knew her grandmother would be able to help figure it out.

Bailey heard Sugar turn on the TV to watch her favorite news discussion program on public television.

Bailey opened her math workbook. She liked doing the word problems. She read: "A factory can produce 206 trucks in one day. How many trucks can it produce in 175 days?"

CRASH!

A large board smashed through the window in the kitchen door. Bailey screamed as she looked up. She ran to window and saw a bearded man running towards a black pickup truck that was parked at the end of Sugar's driveway. The tires squealed as he drove away.

"What on earth!" said Sugar, hobbling into the room.

"Terrible," gasped Bailey. "A man—he looked like Justin's father—broke the window."

"Please get the broom and dustpan," said Sugar. "I will call my friend the sheriff."

Before Sugar could dial the number, the phone rang.

"Nora? Really! Oh, no. Sure, we'll look out for them," said Sugar.

Bailey swept the broken glass into a dustpan while Sugar dialed for help.

"You were right, Bailey," she said. "It was Justin's father. He escaped from jail. Nora said that he came to the house and went on a rampage. Justin tried to protect his mother. When his father took the keys to the truck, he tried to take Fern with him. Justin grabbed her and ran into the woods. Their mother is frantic," said Sugar.

"What will they do?" asked Bailey. "Fern must be so scared."

"Justin will look after her. I hope they know that they can come here until their father is caught. His trial for polluting Contrary Creek was supposed to start next month. That's probably why he's trying to scare me—so I won't testify against him."

"Are you scared?" asked Bailey. "I am!"

"Nonsense," said Sugar. "It takes more than a broken window to scare a wild woman. I am worried about Justin and Fern, though."

After Bailey swept up the biggest pieces, she vacuumed up the smaller ones. Shadow and Sallie came out of hiding when she was done.

She was still shaking when she tried to finish her math problems.

Mr. Will and the boys arrived fifteen minutes after Sugar called the Keswicks to let them know what had happened. He brought a large piece of plywood and long nails to board up the window until he could replace the glass.

Noah and Fred held the plywood while Mr. Will nailed it to the wooden door.

"There," said Mr. Will. He measured the window so that he could get the right size pane of glass the next day.

"Would you like me to stay here tonight?" he asked.

"We'll be just fine," said Sugar. "I don't think he'll dare to come back. Besides, the sheriff has promised to have someone check on us. Just keep an eye out for Justin and Fern."

"They can stay at our house," Fred offered.

"Call if you need us," Mr. Will said to Sugar. "C'mon, boys. You've homework to finish."

Bailey wished that Sugar had told Mr. Will that she wanted him to spend the night. She fastened the locks on the front and back doors and turned on the porch lights.

Sugar said she would keep Bailey company in the kitchen while she completed her homework rather than return to the library. She propped up her leg on a chair and did a crossword puzzle from the morning paper.

Bailey stared at the math problems. All she could think about was the crashing board and shattering glass. *Focus*, she thought. *Focus*.

She picked up her pencil and returned to her assignment.

21

Still Missing

It was raining when Bailey woke up. She hadn't slept well because she was worried about Fern and Justin in the woods. The rain made the leaves of the tulip tree shake as if they didn't want to be wet. She looked hard at the edge of the woods, but didn't see a sign of anyone.

"Maybe they'll show up in school," suggested Emily as she squeezed in next to Bailey on the bus seat. Her raincoat dripped on Bailey's jeans.

"I hope so," said Bailey. She didn't think they would be at school—not if they were hiding.

"Hey, can I see your answers for math?"

"Why?"

"I didn't have time to do them," whispered her friend. "It'll only take a minute."

Bailey wished Emily wouldn't ask her for answers. Emily had been watching television lately instead of getting her work done.

"I don't know. Did you study for the science quiz?"

"Sort of," said Emily, "but there was this really neat show on TV about this guy who won a million dollars and . . ."

"And you watched it," said Bailey. She did not open her book bag.

"I'm going to be on a game show someday," said Emily. "When I win a million, I'll give you some." She flashed a big smile at Bailey, who couldn't resist smiling back.

"What would you buy?" asked Bailey.

"Lots of things," said Emily. "A new big house for Mom. A monster pickup for Dad. A huge playhouse for Nannie. A roller-coaster in the backyard for Howie. And I'd take everybody, including all my friends, to Disney World. We could go see Amber, but you've got to let me copy the answers, just this once."

"No," said Bailey, surprising herself by saying it so firmly. "It isn't right."

Emily glared at her. The yellow bus joined a long line of buses in the school parking lot.

Bailey tried to ignore Emily as she scanned the faces of the younger children. She sighed when she didn't see Fern among them. She pulled the raincoat hood over her head and followed Emily down the bus steps.

Bailey stepped in a puddle. "Rats! My shoe will be wet all day."

"Serves you right for not helping me," said Emily. She dashed for the school door.

Bailey couldn't believe that Emily had just said that. Her friend didn't talk to her during lunch, either. Then, as the students lined up outside for the return ride home, Brittany yanked hard on Bailey's knapsack, pulling it off her shoulder.

"Hey, skunk, Emily got a zero on her math homework today. Now she might get a D."

Bailey spun around and grabbed her bag so that it wouldn't fall to the wet sidewalk. "That's not fair," she said to Brittany.

"Right. Not fair to your friend," said Brittany. She turned and walked back to a group of girls surrounding Emily and staring hard at Bailey.

Bailey hurried up the bus steps and decided to sit by herself, across the aisle from her usual seat with Emily. She felt as lonely as she did on the first day she rode the bus to school.

22

Visitors in the Night

The rain let up after supper, and frogs quickly peeped their pleasure. When Bailey finished her homework she looked at Sugar. Her grandmother's head nodded, as if she were trying to stay awake. Bailey suddenly felt tired. Sugar woke up when she heard Bailey putting books and papers in the knapsack.

"I don't know about you, my dear, but I'm ready for bed," said Sugar.

"Me, too," said Bailey

"We'll leave the TV and lights on around the house," said Sugar. "I don't want you to worry. Give me a big hug."

As Bailey wrapped her arms around her grandmother, they heard scratching on the back door.

"Oh, no," said Bailey, her heart pounding. She was afraid that Justin's father had returned to torment them.

The scratching continued. Then they heard whining. Bailey looked at Sugar.

"I'll open the door," said her grandmother, "except for the chain lock. That way we can see who it is without letting them in." Sugar limped across the room. Bailey followed.

"It's Ninja," whispered Bailey. Sugar unlocked the chain and opened the door, but the dog ran into the shadows.

"Justin? Fern? It's okay. You can stay with us," Bailey called in the direction of the woods. She heard rustling leaves.

Suddenly two figures holding hands dashed across the yard and hurried up the porch steps. Ninja was right behind them. Sugar pulled them inside and locked up.

Fern's cheeks were tear-streaked and her long blond hair was tangled and full of leaves. Justin's mud-covered sweatshirt was torn at the elbow and his face was hard, like when Bailey had first met him.

"I'm so glad you came here. We know what happened. I'll let your mom and the sheriff know you're okay." Sugar closed the shades and motioned to them to sit at the kitchen table.

"I bet you're both hungry after all this time," said Sugar. Without waiting for a reply, she said, "Bailey will fix you something."

Bailey put leftover lasagna back in the microwave and dished salad onto their plates.

"And we have chocolate cake—the best ever—for dessert."

Sugar called their mother. "They are safe with us," she told Nora Rudd. "Sure, they can stay here tonight or for as long as necessary. I think they want to talk with you."

Tears streamed down Fern's face as she held the phone to her ear. "Mommy," she cried. "We were so scared. Okay, we'll be good at Sugar's."

When it was Justin's turn, he took the phone into the library where he could talk in private.

"Thanks," he said when he returned, and Bailey placed the heaping plate in front of him.

Fern picked at her supper, but brightened when Bailey showed her the fudge cake.

"Yum," said Fern.

Ninja whined from under the kitchen table.

"Are you hungry, boy? I think we've got some scraps of leftover hamburger he might like," said Sugar. "Justin, look in that green plastic container in the fridge."

Justin filled a bowl with the meat and petted his scruffy brown dog.

Sugar said, "Justin, you can take the spare bedroom tonight, and Fern, I'll bet you would like to sleep on a cot in Bailey's room. I can't get up those stairs yet, so Bailey will show you the way."

Justin offered to do the dishes while Bailey helped Fern with a bath.

Sugar said, "I'll call the Keswicks. I'm sure they have clean clothes to loan us."

When Mr. Will arrived with jeans and T-shirts belonging to Fred and Sparrow, he announced, "This time there will be no discussion. I am going to spend the night on the couch."

Bailey thought that Sugar looked relieved.

Before she finally climbed into bed, Bailey looked out the dormer window. Cars and trucks with their parking lights on filled Sugar's yard, the driveway, and the road.

Bailey opened the window. She heard a neighbor say, "That creep won't bother Miss Sugar or Miss Rudd and her young'uns anymore."

"Nope," said another. "We'll come back every night if we have to."

Bailey closed the window. She knew that with all this protection, she would now be able to go to sleep.

23

Gone

Fern was still asleep when Bailey heard a clattering of pans in the kitchen. She put on her robe and hurried downstairs to help Sugar make breakfast. It wasn't Sugar scrambling eggs. It was Justin, while Sugar watched.

"You might wake Fern," said Sugar from her seat at the table. "I think my leg is well enough for me to drive her to school like her mother does. Justin wants to ride the bus."

"Sure, I'll go get her," said Bailey. "I'll ride the bus, too." She hoped Emily had gotten over being mad at her.

Fern was dressed by the time Bailey went back to the room. She brushed the little girl's hair and gave her a hug before putting on her own jeans and red turtleneck shirt.

"Your brother is fixing eggs," said Bailey.

"He's a good cook," said Fern. "He makes pancakes on Sundays."

"I talked with your mom very early this morning," said Sugar to Fern and Justin. "She said it's safe for you to come home after school. The sheriff is sure that your dad is far away by now. He and the neighborhood men will be looking after all of us."

"Can I talk to Mommy?" asked Fern, taking a huge bite of buttered toast.

Sugar said, "As soon as you finish breakfast."

"I don't want to talk to the sheriff," said Justin in a low, hoarse voice.

"You're not in any trouble," said Sugar. "He just wants to know what happened."

Bailey glanced at Justin's face. It looked tight again, like he was both angry and trying not to cry. He ate quickly, hugged Fern, and went upstairs saying he had to get ready for school.

Sugar said, "Let's go, Fern. You can help an old lady get to the car."

Bailey made tuna sandwiches for herself and Justin and looked at the clock. The bus would be at the end of the drive in six minutes.

"Justin, time to go," she called. There was no answer. She went upstairs and knocked on the guest bedroom door. No answer. She turned the knob. The window above the porch roof was open. Justin was gone. So was Ninja.

24

Friends

After school, Emily walked right past Bailey, got on the bus, and sat behind her next to Tasha. Bailey heard Emily say, "If I don't have time to finish my science homework tonight, will you call me with your answers, Tasha?"

"Sure," said Tasha, loud enough so Bailey could hear. "That's what *friends* are for."

"Thanks," said Emily, sweetly. "You are awesome, Tasha."

Grrr, thought Bailey. She looked out the bus window, wondering what had happened to Justin. There was no reason for him to run away from Sugar's house—at least none that she could think of. Maybe he had wanted to hurry home and change into his own clothes for school. Maybe he wanted to get his schoolwork done since he had missed classes.

"Want to come to my house Friday?" Emily asked Tasha. "We can stay up and watch TV or videos. You can sleep over. Mom will let us have whatever we want to eat."

"Sure, I'll call you tonight," said Tasha. "That sounds fun."

Bailey hunched in her seat so the girls couldn't see her face. She didn't want them to know that she felt hurt. She was supposed to spend Friday night with Emily, but not now. *If that's the way Emily is going to be just because I wouldn't let her copy my answers, oh well.*

Her mother, Molly, always told her to do her own work. "That's the only way to be smart," her mom said. "As long as you try your best, that's good enough for me, but promise me you won't be a cheat."

"I promise," Bailey had told her mother when they lived together in Florida.

"That's my girl," said her mom, wrapping Bailey in her arms.

Bailey's eyes stung as she thought about how her mother's thick dark hair smelled when she pressed Bailey's face into her shoulder.

"And," said her mom, leaning Bailey back so she could look into her face, "you'll always meet kids who want you to do something wrong, like cheat, or smoke or do drugs, but be strong. They are not your true friends if they pressure you."

"I know, Mom," Bailey had replied. Now she wondered if her mother knew how hard it really was to be strong and say no, especially if Emily might not be her friend anymore.

Bailey mumbled good-bye to Emily and Tasha when Sugar's yellow house came into view. She hoped Sugar would be home.

25

Still Gone

Before dashing for the bus in the morning, Bailey had left a note for her grandmother about Justin's disappearance.

"Nobody knows where he is," Bailey told Sugar after school. "Weird."

"The Keswicks haven't seen him either. I worry about that boy," said Sugar. "He's had a lot on his mind because of the way his father has treated him and the family. He's often misunderstood." She patted Bailey on the shoulder. "I also know that Justin has had a reputation as a toughie."

How well Bailey knew! The first time she met him, Justin made fun of her name and the fact that her mom had gone away.

"I hope he knows he can come back here," said Sugar. She peeled potatoes for a beef stew, then diced chunks of carrots and onions to simmer in the pot.

"Miss Bekka says that the Phiggs are returning tomorrow. She asked us to stop by for dessert to welcome them back," said Sugar.

Bailey suddenly remembered the mysterious stranger. She knew it was time to say something about him to her grandmother. Sugar might know what they should do.

"Sugar, is it possible for people to have the same name and own the same thing—?" Bailey asked, but before she could finish her questions, the phone rang. Sugar wiped her hands on a blue checked towel and answered it.

"No, we haven't seen him yet, Nora. Does he have a special hiding place?" asked Sugar.

Bailey listened as she put the silverware and napkins on the table.

"Sure, we'll call. Don't you worry. He's a smart boy." Sugar hung up. "Does Fern know where he is?"

Bailey said, "They're pretty tight."

"If she does, she hasn't said," said Sugar, looking at the clock. "You have time to review your spelling before the stew is done. I've a few calls to make."

Bailey decided her questions about the Phiggs could wait.

26

The Phiggs Return

As Bailey and Sugar climbed the steps to Keswick Inn they could hear Mr. Phigg's booming voice and Feather giggling like a little girl. *How could they be bad guys?* wondered Bailey. *They are so nice.*

The Phiggs, Maven Robinson, the Keswicks, and Sparrow were still seated around the long dining room table. Noah cleared the dishes while Fred carried in the dessert plates. Their mother had baked two strawberry-rhubarb pies, which were still warm from the oven.

"Miss Bailey and Miss Sugar, how wonderful to see you again," said Elmo Phigg, standing to greet them.

"How was your trip to Jamestown?" asked Sugar.

"Delightful," said Mrs. Phigg, but she appeared nervous. She twisted her napkin and moved her dessert fork in a circle.

Maven Robinson said nothing. Mr. Phigg cleared his throat. "Actually, we had some un-anticipated difficulties," he said.

Noah stopped in the kitchen doorway and turned around. "With what?" he asked.

Mr. Phigg looked at Feather and said, "Nothing relating to my new book. We actually accomplished quite a bit. Dr. Robinson visited the library and Archaearium at Historic Jamestowne. Then we all went to the site where the archaeologists are continuing to dig up artifacts and find evidence of the colonists' buildings and the fort."

Bailey could see that Noah wanted to get back to the issue of what had gone wrong, but his mother asked him to put the supper dishes in the dishwasher. She said the pie would taste better if eaten immediately.

Fred got the discussion back on track by saying, "Couldn't you find something you were looking for?"

Mr. Phigg cleared his throat again. "It's a long story. Perhaps some other time when things are more clear."

Dr. Robinson changed the subject. She said, a little too brightly, "I appreciate your help taking care of dear Pinocchio. His cage was clean and he seemed quite happy."

"You can thank Sparrow for keeping him company, and treating him with pieces of carrot and apple," said Miss Bekka, giving the little girl a big smile. "She sat by his cage while you were gone. They seem to be friends."

Dr. Robinson thanked Sparrow, then praised the pie as being even better than her aunt Bea made. Then she said she still had work to do. She excused herself and went to her room.

"I'll help with the rest of the dishes," said Bailey, knowing that was where she would be able to talk privately with Noah and Fred.

"What do you think happened in Jamestown?" she asked the boys when the grown-ups had moved with Sparrow to the living room to finish their coffee.

"I dunno," said Fred. "They came back with the green suitcase and hid it again."

"Don't you think we should tell them about the other Mr. Phigg?" asked Bailey, as she scrubbed a pan. "Maybe they're in danger."

"I think we should tell Mom and Dad," said Fred. "They'd know what to do."

"Not yet," said Noah. "We need more information. Besides, I can't call that man to tell him the Phiggs are back. Clover ate the paper he gave me. I don't have the dude's number anymore."

27

Basket of Bones

Sugar unfolded the *Lake Anna Guardian* on the kitchen table so she could read it while she listened for the microwave timer. She was defrosting pieces of chicken to cut up for a stir-fry that would include the first three pea pods from her garden.

Bailey put a handful of kibble in Shadow and Sallie's dish. She felt bad that she had been neglecting them lately by spending so much time at Keswick Inn.

"Look here," said Sugar. "There are two letters to the editor about my new anti-littering signs. One person thinks they are great, and the other thinks they won't make any difference because the people who litter won't care."

"I think the signs are great, too," said Bailey. "I heard kids reading them when I was on the bus. One boy said he was going to tell his father not to litter because he has seen him throw trash out of his truck window."

"Good," said Sugar. "Kids can make a difference. They can pick up trash that is in the front yards and neighborhoods. They can tell their families not to make a mess by throwing bottles, cans, and papers out the window."

"Mom e-mailed me that we have dirtier roadsides here than she has seen while traveling in poor countries," Bailey said.

Sugar sighed. "I wish people took more pride in how their communities look. It's the little things, like litter, that make a big difference."

She turned back to the front page. "Oh, my," she said. "Here's an article about Jamestown. Bones that disappeared from one of the archaeological sites many years ago were found in a small basket on a bench inside the old brick church. No one is sure how they got there or who has had them all these years. Interesting."

Bailey quickly moved to where she could read the article over Sugar's shoulder.

"Could I have the newspaper when you are done?" she asked, trying not to sound excited.

"Sure," said Sugar. "Just put the sections you don't need in the recycle bin. I'm glad you are interested in Jamestown. It's an important part of American history."

28

No Words Yet

Bailey folded the article about the Jamestown bones and tucked it in her jacket pocket. Sugar said her leg felt good enough for them to walk through the woods to Keswick Inn. She had books for the Phiggs, and a picture book, *Horace the Horrible,* for Sparrow. Even though Sparrow seemed to like to have more advanced books read to her, she looked at the picture books on her own, silently.

Bailey noticed that since that first stormy day, Sparrow had not thrown books or toys around her room. She was careful with them and piled them neatly next to her bed.

Bailey carried the books so that Sugar could pay attention to walking with her cane. They stopped to look a rose-breasted grosbeak at their bird feeder. It was black and white with a bright red spot on its throat. They admired the irises, some yellow, some purple, and the pink, white and red azaleas in full bloom. The path was fragrant with spring—the smells of mud and pine.

"It is such a wonderful time of year," said Sugar. "One of my favorites."

The azaleas that Miss Bekka had planted in the front flower bed were also in full color. Bailey saw that the Keswicks had placed three wicker rockers on their front porch. A wooden bench that Justin and Mr. Will made from split logs and a wide board was under the big hickory tree.

"Any sign of Justin?" asked Miss Bekka, as she opened the front door.

"Not yet," said Sugar. "His mother is—well, we all are—very worried. I know he's a resourceful boy. I think he'll be found soon."

Bailey saw Sparrow sitting next to Pinocchio's cage. The girl broke off a piece of her banana and pushed it through the bars. The parrot considered it carefully, and walked sideways on his perch, then used his beak to drop down to the floor of his cage. He cocked his head as if to thank Sparrow, then snatched the fruit.

"Where's Geppeto?" shouted Pinocchio. "Look at my nose grow."

Bailey thought she saw Sparrow smile.

"We brought you a new book," she said.

Sparrow looked up. Her face was still without expression even though she didn't look angry the way she had that first day.

"Would you like me to read it to you?" asked Bailey, pulling up a chair. "It's a funny story. I like the 'Daddy smaddy' part."

Sparrow gazed at Bailey for a second, put the book in her lap, and wheeled back to her room without saying a word.

Bailey said to the parrot, "At least Sparrow likes you."

Pinocchio tipped his head and blinked his eyes with white circles around them. "Have a nice day, ducky," he said. He hit a shiny gold bell with his beak. "I'm not a puppet."

"Funny bird," said Bailey.

"Don't give up on Sparrow," said Sugar.

"Give up. Give up," squawked Pinocchio. He preened his stubby red tail feathers.

29

Reading Buddies Share

Justin wasn't in school the next day, either. Bailey met with Fern, her reading buddy, at noon. Fern didn't have lunch with her or money to buy any food, so Bailey shared hers.

"What happened to your lunch?" she asked the younger girl. "Did you forget to make one today?"

"I guess I lost it," said Fern, looking away.

Bailey took a book out of her lunch sack. It was from Sugar's library. Without any help, Fern read *Little Rabbit Goes to School*. Bailey said, "You're doing a great job, Fern."

"I want to do chapter books next, like you read," said Fern. She took a big bite out of her half of Bailey's bologna sandwich. "But maybe they are too hard."

"I think you're ready for them," said Bailey. "You should try to read anything that looks good. I always do that."

"How come Sparrow doesn't ever talk or smile?" asked Fern. Her blue eyes looked concerned.

"She's very sad," said Bailey, "but we are going to have a party to see if we can make her laugh."

"Can I come?" asked Fern.

"Of course—and Nannie and Howie. Everybody," said Bailey. She wondered for a moment if Emily would want to come.

"I have a silly toy from Christmas," said Fern. "It is the Grinch dancing. That would make her laugh."

"Good idea," said Bailey. "We'll have a lot of fun."

Fern quickly ate the banana that Bailey had in her lunch bag.

Bailey said, "Do you know where Justin is?"

Fern looked away again and covered her mouth with her hand.

"Everybody's worried about him. If you know, you should tell us," said Bailey. "He must be very hungry by now."

Fern stared out the window. "I give him my lunch. I leave it by the bus stop so he can find it." Then Fern looked like she was going to cry. "I shouldn't tell. He told me not to tell."

"Is he in the woods?"

Fern nodded yes.

"Is he hiding from your father?"

Fern said, "Sort of. He's spying on him."

"Spying?" asked Bailey. "I thought your father was far away."

"He's living in the woods, too, in his truck. He has guns. Justin wants to get them away from him so we can be safe." Fern sniffed back tears.

Bailey put her arm around the girl's shoulders and said, "It'll be okay, Fern. Don't worry. Here, have my cookie."

When the bell rang, Bailey hurried to the office. She hoped the principal would let her use the phone right away to call Sugar.

30

Caught

The capture of Justin's father was the top story of the six o'clock evening news. After Bailey called her grandmother, Sugar immediately phoned the sheriff. The deputies drove down the logging road that Justin's father had used to dump the chemicals that had polluted Contrary Creek.

Just as Fern had said, they found the black pickup truck with Justin's father inside it. He shot once into the air and yelled at them, but finally gave up when he realized he was surrounded.

The TV reporter said that the sheriff had heard a noise in the woods. He turned quickly and saw Ninja, followed by Justin.

The camera zoomed in on the boy's face. Justin refused to answer questions and simply got in the sheriff's car with his dog.

"Wow!" said Bailey.

"I'm glad you told me what Fern said," Sugar responded, "or this story might not have had a happy ending. Justin is safe, and his father's back in jail."

"I hope Fern isn't mad at me," said Bailey.

"Nora Rudd said Fern is glad that Justin is home, and that he even gave her a big hug. Nobody's upset with you."

"Will you still have to go to his father's trial?" asked Bailey.

"I'm sure I will. I hope he is sent away for a long time," said Sugar.

"What if he gets out again?" asked Bailey. "He really scares me." She shivered.

"They'll make sure he doesn't escape again," said Sugar.

After three commercials and the weather forecast of sunshine and temperatures in the mid-seventies, there was also a brief story about a circus clown who had moved to Lake Anna. He was entertaining at nursing homes and planned to be in the July 4 parade.

"Sugar," said Bailey excitedly, "A real clown. Maybe he can come to our party for Sparrow."

Sugar said, "Great idea. You're thinking like a wild woman. I'll try to reach him tomorrow."

31

More E-mails

When Bailey checked her e-mails before supper she found one each from her mother, Norma Jean, and her dad.

From: mollyf2@travl.net
To: "Bailey"<baileyfish@gmail.com>
Sent: 11:06 p.m.
Subject: travel plans

Bailey dearest, Andrew and I are going to a nature farm near San Isidoro. We will cross Cerro de la Muerte, Spanish for Mountain of Death. But don't be afraid, it's safe for us and the road goes so high we will be above the clouds. Andrew said there're sodas to stop at for lunch. A soda is not a soft drink but rather what the Costa Ricans call the little restaurants along the roadside. Be good, Love, Mom

Bailey started to reply:

From: "Bailey"<baileyfish@gmail.com>
To: mollyf2@travl.net
Sent: 6:15 p.m.
Subject: hi

Have fun. Do you know the Phiggs and Maven
Robinson? They are staying at Keswick Inn.
Bailey

She decided she didn't want to know if Dr.
Robinson were correct—that she had met Andrew Snorge-Swinson and he had a new lady
friend, maybe her mother. She would rather not
think about that. Maybe bug man would get out
of the car on the Mountain of Death, see a
strange bug on the edge of a cliff and . . . or
maybe he would be carried away by leafcutter
ants. Bailey knew that these were terrible
things to think or wish for, even if they made
her feel good for a moment. She quickly
switched to Norma Jean's e-mail.

From: pjfish2005@yermail.net>
To: "Bailey"<baileyfish@gmail.com>
Sent: 4:27 p.m.
Subject: Sis

Dad is traveling around Guam this week. I'm
helping Mom decide what to sell at a yard sale
before we move. You and Sugar would like to
see what we'll get rid of. Some really good
stuff. Hahaha. Dad said Kimo and Kee may
have to stay in quarantine for a while when we
move, but he hopes they can come. I drew a
picture of them to mail to you. XXXOOO NJ

Bailey knew that Norma Jean, who was very
artistic, would draw perfect pictures of her dog
and cat. She replied:

From: "Bailey"<baileyfish@gmail.com>
To: <pjfish2005@yermail.net>
Sent: 6:35 p.m.
Subject: Hi

So much is happening. Justin is safe. He was on TV. We are planning a party to make Sparrow laugh. I wish you were here to draw the invitations. SCR

She saved her dad's for last:

From: pjfish2005@yermail.net
To: "Bailey"<baileyfish@gmail.com>
Sent: 9:25 p.m.
Subject: Hey

Hi Bailey: How's the music coming? I'm looking forward to hearing you play piano and clarinet. My jazz band is sorry that we'll be leaving Guam. I guess I'll have to start a new band once we are back in the States. I've got a lead on several jobs. I hope we can make it happen soon. Hi to Sugar, Dad

Bailey replied that she had been practicing hard, but would have more time in the summer to work on her lessons. She had lots she wanted to ask him, like what books he liked to read, and why he hadn't tried to see her since she was a baby, but her fingers wouldn't type important questions.

32

Not Sure

Bailey was looking out the open kitchen window when she saw Noah and Fred running out of the path in the woods into Sugar's yard. Clover was racing beside them.

"Bailey, come out!" shouted Noah. "Hurry!"

"Run along," said Sugar. "The dishes will wait a few minutes."

Bailey wiped her sudsy hands, grabbed her jacket, and met the boys near the clothesline.

"That weird bald guy was back again," said Fred. "He parked at the end of our driveway and whistled at us. We didn't go too close . . . ."

Noah said, "He could see that the people he is looking for are back—he saw their van—and asked why we didn't call him."

"What did you tell him?" asked Bailey.

"The truth—that our dog ate his phone number. I don't think he believed me, though," said Noah. He folded his arms across his chest.

"The man still wants us to get the suitcase for him," said Fred.

"You can't do that," said Bailey. "It belongs to the Phiggs."

"But what if it doesn't?" asked Noah.

"We've got to tell Sugar. She'll know what to do," said Bailey. "And I'm going to tell her right now. He could be a really bad guy."

"Wait," said Noah, "Phiggy stays with us, not with you. It's not up to you."

"Bailey might be right," said Fred. "It's time to tell Sugar or our parents. It's creepy."

"What if the man is from the FBI?" said Noah. "What if we don't help him with his investigation?"

"You've been watching too much TV," said Bailey. The cool wind tangled her hair and made her shudder. The clouds were moving in fast, like a train pulling a rainstorm. She zipped up her jacket and put her hands in the pockets. Her right hand felt the folded newspaper article about the bones. In all the excitement she had forgotten about it.

"Hey, I meant to give you this," she said.

"See," said Noah, after he read it.

"See what?" asked Bailey.

"Just give me a week or two, dude," said Noah. "Then if we can't figure out what's going on, you can tell Sugar whatever you want. Okay?"

Bailey still wasn't very happy with the plan. "All right, but promise that you won't steal the suitcase or get the Phiggs in trouble. I like them," she said.

"Deal," said Noah. He poked Fred's arm and said, "Let's go. I feel some drops."

When Bailey returned to the kitchen, Sugar was on the phone. Bailey rolled up her sleeves and finished washing the plates and glasses. Then she went up to her room and opened the writing book that Elmo Phigg, the first Elmo Phigg, had give her.

She wrote: *I don't know what to do. The Phiggs are such nice people. But what are they hiding in that green suitcase? Why won't they tell us what it is so we can help them?*

Bailey decided to look in Sugar's library for books on Jamestown now that she was almost finished with *The Lion, the Witch and the Wardrobe.* Maybe Sugar's history books would have clues.

She put her writing book back in a desk drawer and went downstairs to Sugar's library. There were lots of history books, but Bailey didn't see any about Jamestown on Sugar's non-fiction shelves.

Then Bailey remembered that when her grandmother was researching a topic, she often gathered all the books about it and placed them on a single shelf near her recliner. There they were—the Jamestown books—including some for kids. She picked up *Young Pocahontas in the Indian World* and read the first chapter.

33

Babo Ganoosh

"Miss Bekka thinks the First Laugh Party is a great idea," Sugar told Bailey as they rocked on the porch and sipped peppermint tea. "Sparrow is no longer looking so thin and pale. She has color in her cheeks from sitting outside in her wheelchair. She still isn't talking to anyone, and nobody has heard her laugh."

Sugar added that Miss Bekka suggested that everyone should get together for a meeting on Saturday afternoon. Mr. Will would take Sparrow with him to Fredericksburg so that she wouldn't hear the party plans.

"So, see if Justin and Fern, Emily, Nannie, and Howie would like to come to Keswick Inn at two," said Sugar.

"I'll ask them at school tomorrow," said Bailey. "This will be fun."

Bailey didn't know what to do. She hadn't told Sugar about Emily. She didn't know if

Emily would come because Bailey hadn't given her homework to copy. Maybe Emily would make fun of her again in front of their friends and would call the party a dumb idea. If she didn't ask Emily, then Howie and Nannie wouldn't come and the party would not be as much fun. Bailey sighed and stared out the window.

"I located Babo Ganoosh, the circus clown we saw on TV," Sugar continued, apparently not noticing that Bailey was only half listening. "When I called, he said his real name is Ventilatis Spitball." Sugar chuckled. "I'm not sure that is right, though. It sounds like another silly clown name to me." Her face crinkled.

"Those names should make Sparrow laugh," said Bailey.

"Babo said he can make the meeting, too. Tell your friends to bring all the funny ideas they can think of."

"Okay," said Bailey. "Do I address him as Mr. Spitball since I don't know him?" She giggled.

"If he is in his clown suit, then I think Babo Ganoosh is sufficient." Sugar smiled, then placed her mug on a side table and unfolded the most recent issue of the newspaper.

~ ~ ~

When Bailey told Emily about the party, she seemed to have forgotten that she was mad at Bailey for not giving her the homework answers. Emily said she was sure she and her brother and sister could come to the meeting. Later Bailey overheard Emily brag to Tasha that she was the only one of Bailey's school friends to be invited to a very special party.

Fern and Bailey ate their lunch before reading together the third chapter of *Frog and Toad All Year*. Fern said that Justin might have to babysit for their little sisters because their mother had to work on Saturdays, but she thought she could come if Sugar gave her a ride.

"I want to make Sparrow laugh," said Fern.

"See if you can think of silly games to play," suggested Bailey.

"I always laugh when I say rhymes and jump rope," said Fern, "but that's not something that Sparrow can do."

"No, we need to think of games she can play in her wheelchair," said Bailey.

"I know," said Fern, "how about hot potato, or passing a water balloon? We played that at Nannie's party one time."

"Those are good ideas," said Bailey. "Let me hear you read your new chapter book."

Fern removed her bookmark from page thirty-eight, and took a deep breath: "Frog hid behind a rock. He saw the thing coming. It was big and brown . . . It had two horns."

Fern smiled as she looked at the picture of Toad with upside-down chocolate ice cream cones dripping all over his head.

"Maybe this book will make Sparrow laugh," said Fern.

"I wish," said Bailey.

34

Planning the Party

Bailey boosted Fern into Sugar's pickup and fastened her seat belt. Fern clutched a book of jokes and a princess mask from Halloween.

"I hope Sparrow thinks the jokes are funny," she said, as the truck headed for Keswick Inn.

"I think they are funny," said Bailey. "Your jokes always make me laugh."

As they drove up the long driveway, they saw Mrs. Dover dropping off her children. Howie carried a stuffed frog, Nannie had a Lion King puppet, and Emily brought her trumpet.

"Sparrow would laugh if she heard me play the piano," said Sugar. Bailey smiled. Her grandmother was trying so hard to play her pieces correctly, but she kept making mistakes when she practiced for her lessons.

Mrs. Dover waved as she drove away.

Miss Bekka invited everyone into the living room where she had set up extra seats. The

Phiggs and Dr. Robinson were already settled in their favorite comfortable chairs. Pinocchio's cage was covered so he would not interrupt the meeting with his usual whistles and chatter.

Noah and Fred grabbed large pillows and leaned them next to the couch so they could sit comfortably on the floor.

Miss Bekka sat on the fireplace hearth and twisted her thick braid until it was pinned on the top of her head. She smiled. "Mr. Will and I are so happy that you are here to plan the First Laugh Party—it was Bailey's idea, you know."

Bailey beamed.

"Why won't Sparrow laugh or talk?" asked Howie, putting the stuffed frog on his mop of shaggy dark blond hair.

Sugar answered, "It's mostly because she can't walk for a year and she is living in a new home. She has sadness as hard as a snowball inside her. We need to melt it."

"Oh," said Howie. "I made a hard snowball once in preschool, but not this year in kindergarten."

"That's because it didn't snow much," said Nannie. Howie burped her name and made his frog jump on her head, then back to his.

Just then the doorbell rang and they heard the sound of a slide whistle. "Come in," called

Miss Bekka. "That must be Ventilatis Spitball—also known as Babo Ganoosh the clown."

Babo had a red bulb nose. His purple hair
stuck out like clumps of weeds, and he wore
big yellow gloves and had size thirty rubbery

shoes shaped like eggplants. As he waddled
into the room, he pretended to trip over an
imaginary object.

Howie laughed so hard his frog fell off his
head and Fern dropped her book.

"Have a seat, Babo," said Miss Bekka, wiping her eyes.

The clown first played his slide whistle,
honked a horn in his pocket, and then waggled

his hips like he was going to sit down very carefully.

"Wait, there's no chair!" shouted Howie, but the clown did a backwards somersault just before he was about to land on his butt. Clover barked in circles around him until Babo flapped his arms like a giant bird and chased her out of the room.

When Pinocchio made the sound of the slide whistle, Dr. Robinson said, "I think I'll put him in the kitchen. He picks up new sounds much too quickly."

"Hey," said Fred, "why doesn't Babo talk? He hasn't said a word."

"He's a mime," said Dr. Robinson, leaning forward in her chair. "Mimes don't talk. They act out what they want to say."

Everyone looked at the clown. He wiped his eyes and a huge tear rolled down his cheek.

"How did he do that?" asked Noah. "You know, make a big tear like that?

"It must be some kind of trick," said Fred.

"Can you do magic?" Nannie asked the clown.

Babo shook his head no, but pulled a long string of colorful silk scarves from his pocket.

"That looks like magic to me," said Nannie. "Will you teach me to do that?"

Babo clapped his hands and the scarves disappeared.

"This will be perfect," said Mr. Phigg. "I don't see how Sparrow can resist—and we all have other things to try as well."

Clover peeked around the corner to see if the clown was still there. Fred snapped his fingers and she raced to the safety of his lap where she growled like a cat's purr.

"What other ideas do we have?" said Miss Bekka.

"I will dance for her," said Feather Phigg.

"I will make pig noises," said Dr. Robinson.

"Pig noises?" Mr. Phigg looked at his assistant in astonishment.

"Yes, I'm quite good," she said primly. She folded her hands in her lap and crossed her legs.

"I thought I would sing the old camp song 'Doodly Doo.' I know all the hand motions. I can also do 'Little Rabbit Foo Foo,'" said Sugar.

"I know 'Rabbit Foo Foo,'" said Fern.

"Then we'll perform it together," said Sugar.

Fred and Noah said they were writing a play about monkeys that juggled.

Bailey said she and Emily planned to do a musical duet, but they hadn't picked a song yet.

Fern told them about her joke book and showed everyone her princess mask.

Miss Bekka proposed several games, such as Pin the Tail on the Donkey and Charades.

Babo rubbed his stomach.

"Oh, yes, I almost forget," she said. "Food. We need to have fun party food."

"And we need to decorate with balloons and streamers," said Bailey.

"And we should all make cards for Sparrow," said Emily.

Noah boasted, "She'll like our monkey play the best."

Babo shook his head and pointed to himself.

"Let's plan to have the party in two weeks," said Miss Bekka.

Babo pulled green stem out of his right pocket and it popped open, making a daisy. He handed it to Miss Bekka and everyone clapped.

"Pig noises?" Mr. Phigg, said to Dr. Robinson, at the end of the meeting.

"You'll see," she said smartly as she returned to her room.

35

A Visit with the Phiggs

Bailey and Sugar were among the last to leave. Fern followed Fred into the kitchen to see Pinocchio. Emily said, "Call me, Bailey," as she put on her windbreaker. She acted as if there had never been a problem between them.

Miss Bekka gave Babo a tour of the house. The clown seemed especially interested in reading the names on the doors of the rooms. He put his big nose close to the words and then honked the horn in his pocket, which made Clover bark again.

"Come in," said Feather Phigg. "You are welcome to see our little abode. I'm just resting before supper."

Babo took a deep bow and flapped his arms, making Bailey and Noah smile at each other. The clown examined the photos on the dresser, then sat down on a wooden chair and pointed with his yellow gloves at various things.

"Oh, that's just our closet," said Feather Phigg. She opened its door. Babo jumped awkwardly to his feet and poked his head inside. He then pointed under the bed.

"You silly thing. Of course you can have a look," said Mrs. Phigg. "The boys have done an excellent job cleaning so you won't find any dust bunnies."

Babo pretended to sneeze anyway—*ahh ahh ahh ganooooosh*. Then he pointed to a large pocket on his shirt. Bailey reached inside and found a purple handkerchief, the size of a dish towel. Babo dabbed at his big red nose, then folded the cloth in his right hand, tapped the hand with a finger from his left. When he opened his palm, the cloth was gone.

"How do you do that?" asked Noah.

Babo raised both palms as if he didn't have a clue about what just happened.

After the clown took one more long look around the room, he waddled toward Dr. Robinson's room. He didn't knock when he saw that she had a DO NOT DISTURB sign hanging on the doorknob. He followed Miss Bekka through the rest of the downstairs, and then to the kitchen where she offered him sweet tea.

Mr. Phigg was sitting at the kitchen table, helping himself to a third brownie even though

Feather told him that he would spoil his appetite if he snacked after the meeting.

"Are you doing much writing, Mr. Phigg?" asked Bailey. She sat down with him at the kitchen table. "I can't always think of things to write about."

"That's a common problem for writers," he said, licking the chocolate crumbs off his fingers. "Sometimes I just write down names that pop into my head, such as Mustard Hornberger and Horsetails Q. Lipreading. They might bring a character into my head by the next day. Sometimes I jot down what flowers are in bloom or what birds I have seen that morning. Sometimes a word or sentence leads to an entire chapter of my book."

"How is your Jamestown book coming?" asked Bailey. She realized that she and the boys had been so stuck on what was in the green suitcase that none of them had asked about his book in a while.

"Ah, better than I had hoped, and worse than I had feared," said Elmo Phigg. "I'm learning so much. Dr. Robinson told me that Captain John Smith was stung in his arm by a stingray while he was fishing in the Rappahannock River. The pain was so terrible he thought he was going to die."

"My mom stepped on a stingray at Englewood Beach. It hurt a lot and she had to go to the emergency room to have the stinger taken out," said Bailey.

"It hurt Smith, too. When we were at Jamestown, we researched the wooden boats that the colonists sailed from England to Virginia. They were very small, you know. The biggest, the *Susan Constant* was only 116 feet, as long as six or seven vans lined up in Sugar's driveway. More than seventy men and boys were crowded inside the ship for the crossing. Imagine that! The original *Godspeed* was sixty-eight feet and carried fifty-two passengers, and the smallest, the *Discovery,* crowded twenty-one people on board. We went aboard the replicas of the ships while we were at Jamestown Settlement, and saw armor similar to that worn by medieval knights, on the *Susan Constant.*"

"Really?" exclaimed Bailey.

"Speaking of boats, Smith used a shallop to explore the bays and rivers."

"What's a shallop?" asked Bailey.

"A little flat boat with oars or sails that could navigate shallow waters," said Mr. Phigg. "Here's another fascinating fact. A ship carrying about twenty Africans landed in the vicinity of Jamestown in 1619."

He rubbed his beard thoughtfully and tapped his pen on his knee. "I may write about that ship later. Meanwhile, something is missing with my Jamestown story, and I can't quite put my finger on it. And when we were in Jamestown, we came so close to . . ." He stopped short.

Bailey wanted him to finish the sentence. Then, perhaps, the suitcase mystery would be solved.

The clown put his big gloved hand by his ear.

"I think Babo wants to hear more," said Bailey.

The clown nodded yes so hard that Bailey was afraid his nose would fall off.

Mr. Phigg ignored Babo and jumped to his feet. "Oh, my, look at the time. Feather and I must take our afternoon walk before it gets too late."

Then, he reached for another brownie, a small one. "Our little secret," he whispered to Bailey and Babo, and quickly left the room.

36

The Mystery Deepens

Babo drove away five minutes before Mr. Will and Sparrow returned from town.

Mr. Will unfolded the wheelchair and carefully placed Sparrow in it.

Fern asked if she could push the wheelchair up the ramp. Sparrow shook her head no and managed to wheel it by herself. She did let Fern open the screen door. "Want to color?" Fern asked Sparrow. No answer.

Bailey offered to carry grocery bags.

"Where are my boys?" asked Mr. Will.

"I'm not sure," said Bailey. She hadn't seen them since she had gone into the kitchen with Babo and Mr. Phigg. She hoped Noah wasn't nosing around, looking for the suitcase again just because she had given him the article about the bones.

"How did the meeting go?" asked Mr. Will. He shoved the van door closed.

"Great," said Bailey. "The clown was funny, and so was Dr. Robinson."

"I find that a little hard to believe. Dr. Robinson always seems so serious," said Mr. Will, opening the screen door with his foot.

"She said she can make pig noises," said Bailey.

"Ha," said Mr. Will. "I'd like to see that."

As Bailey followed him to the kitchen, Fern met her in the hallway.

"Sparrow doesn't like me. She just wants to sit by that stupid bird all day," Fern said.

"She just doesn't know you yet."

"I want to go home," said the girl. "Now!"

"We need to find Sugar," said Bailey, but Fern was already headed out the door towards the pickup truck. She stomped down the steps and threw her princess mask at a holly bush. Bailey was about to run after her when she heard *psst*. She spun around. It was Noah.

"Did you notice anything strange about the clown?" he whispered.

She shook her head.

"Didn't you see him looking around the Phiggs' room?"

"So?" asked Bailey.

"I thought it was weird the way he wanted to see inside the closet and under the bed."

"You did, too, you know," said Bailey. "You even looked inside when the Phiggs weren't there."

"Yeah, but we were hunting for the Jamestown suitcase," said Noah.

"Well, maybe the clown is, too," said Fred.

Bailey wrinkled her nose. "Why would he want the suitcase? He's just a clown."

Before Noah or Fred could answer, Bailey heard Sugar call out that they were leaving. Bailey suddenly remembered that Fern was upset and outside.

"I gotta go," she said to Noah. As she hurried down the porch steps, she grabbed the princess mask.

"You dropped this," she said to Fern.

"I don't care if Sparrow ever laughs," said the little girl. "I don't like her anymore."

"It's hard to be patient," said Sugar. "Sparrow is like a special flower, and we are waiting for her to bloom."

Fern covered her face with the princess mask.

37

Presents from Guam

"What's that on the porch?" asked Bailey as Sugar parked the pickup.

"Looks like a package," said grandmother. "I wasn't expecting anything, though."

Bailey picked it up and examined the label. "It's for me, from Guam," she said excitedly. She ripped the brown tape and opened the box. Inside was the picture Norma Jean had drawn of the boat ride when her hair was straight behind her. There were drawings by Paulie and Sam of their house, dog, and cat, and notes from their mother, Flora, and Bailey's father. He had packed an arrangement of "America the Beautiful" that he composed for two clarinets.

Flora's note said she was looking forward to getting to know Bailey because she had heard so many good things about her. She wrote that she herself wasn't an artist or musician but liked to decorate her house. She said she had

135

been raised by her grandmother in Manila. "She did beautiful embroidery," wrote Flora. "I hope you like the enclosed dresser scarf. It is one that my grandmother made."

Bailey unwrapped the linen scarf. The edges were decorated with tiny colorful birds, flowers, and hearts.

Sugar said, "That's a very special gift."

Bailey nodded, but she felt a little uncomfortable getting a present from someone she didn't know, even if it were from her stepmother. What would her mother think? *I hope she doesn't get mad,* thought Bailey.

There was one more envelope in the box, and another wrapped gift. Her father had written in dark blue ink:

> *Dear Bailey: I hope you like the necklace and wear it often. Norma Jean helped me pick it out to match one of hers. They were made by Actassi, one of the finest local craftsmen. His name means "share the sea."*
>
> *Love, Dad*

Bailey carefully removed the tape and wrapping paper with a bamboo design, and opened the box. She studied the silver chain with a tiny sea turtle pendant clipped on it. Bailey turned it over in her hand.

"Would you like me to fasten it around your neck?" asked Sugar.

Bailey first nodded yes, then told Sugar no. The pretty necklace was the first gift she had ever received from her father. She just wanted to look at it for a while.

38

Camillo Tweed's Shop

"It's time for a treasure hunt," said Sugar when Bailey dropped her knapsack on a chair near the front door.

"What are we looking for?" asked Bailey.

"I'd like to check in a consignment store for silly things to take to Sparrow's party," said Sugar. "There are always amazing things for sale. I think we have time for a ride before the store closes. Get yourself a snack."

Bailey petted the kittens. "Good babies," she said. "I haven't spent much time with you lately. We'll play tonight, I promise."

She bit into an apple, then put her jacket back on. "I'm ready," Bailey said.

Sugar still limped from her accident, but the stitches on her forehead had been removed. The doctor told her to put a special cream on the scar so that it wouldn't show so much. Bailey was happy that her grandmother seemed a lot better and had new glasses to replace the bent ones. She was even happier that Sugar felt strong enough to go on a treasure hunt again.

As Sugar's pickup followed the road to Thornburg, Bailey was glad to hear Sugar humming—a good sign that she was feeling better.

Ahead on the left was a small building with a sign that read TWEED'S GOOD STUFF.

"What's good stuff?" asked Bailey.

"You'll see. Camillo Tweed always has astonishing things for sale, which he gets from all over," said Sugar. "Tweed's Good Stuff is one of my favorite shops."

Sugar parked near the front entrance, which was crowded with scarecrows, rusty milk cans, chipped ceramic pots, and a wooden desk that was missing one drawer. On top of it were a slowcooker and an electric frying pan that needed scrubbing.

It took a moment for Bailey to see well inside the dimly lit store. It was piled high with boxes, books, violins and guitars without strings, broken sewing machines, hatboxes, Indian artifacts, and a dusty glass case full of clown statues. Sugar headed for the back of the store to look for party favors and used books.

"Wow!" said Bailey. She knelt for a better look at the lower shelves of the display case.

There were ceramic clowns holding balloons, and clowns standing on their heads and doing somersaults. Some clowns looked happy and others sad. Bailey had never seen so many at one time.

"I wonder if Babo Ganoosh knows about this clown collection," she said to herself.

"Babo? Do you know him?" said a man's voice from behind her. Bailey lost her balance as she turned from the squatting position and sat down hard on the wooden floor.

"Kind of," Bailey said, glancing around for Sugar, but she didn't see her. She then looked up. The man's face seemed familiar but she couldn't quite place him, especially since he was wearing sunglasses in the dark store.

"Are you Mr. Tweed?" she asked, as she struggled to her feet.

"No, I'm a friend of his. I watch the store sometimes for him while he runs errands." The man's voice was too smooth, as though it were covering up something sharp.

"Babo is going to help us make Sparrow—a girl—laugh at a party we're having." She quickly wished she hadn't said anything, especially that she knew Babo.

The clerk said carefully, "Babo is a man of many disguises—a man who needs to have something returned to his possession. Perhaps you can help him."

Bailey felt like he was staring right through her. His look was chilling, like a March wind seeping through cracks around the windows. Suddenly she realized that this man must know about the Phiggs' green suitcase. "Excuse me. I need to find my grandmother," Bailey said.

"Think about helping him," said the man, slowly stepping out of her way.

Sugar was humming in the back of the shop, poking through the piles of "good stuff" when Bailey located her. She had placed several dusty books in a red woven shopping basket.

"What do you think about these?" Sugar asked, holding up a plastic bag of kazoos.

"Cool, and I think these would be fun," said Bailey. She showed Sugar two huge straw hats with artificial fruit on them that she saw perched on a manikin.

"Look at this, a windup dog." Sugar handed it to Bailey to turn the key. When she released it on the floor, the little brown dog made a squeaky bark and wobbled toward them.

"That's good enough for today," said Sugar. "We'll get balloons and streamers in town."

The man rang up their sales. He put his finger to his lips and whispered to Bailey, "Think about it." She looked away and closely followed Sugar out the door.

Bailey felt goosebumps on her arms. *I've got to tell Sugar,* but before she could open her mouth, Sugar turned on the radio to her favorite country station. She sang loudly along with the song about a woman who liked to drive a motorcycle and go dancing. As usual Sugar didn't know the words. She was making them up as she sang.

Bailey sighed. *Later.*

39

Jamestown Book

"Young lady, would you like to see the work I am doing for my book?" asked Mr. Phigg, when he saw Bailey push open the screen door with her foot. She was carrying decorations for the party.

"Sure. I guess I have time," said Bailey, checking her watch.

Mr. Phigg placed a large three-ring binder on the table next to his chair and opened it. "Here, have a look."

Bailey saw that he had made lists: dates, the names of the ships, and that the Virginia Company of London had paid for the expedition. He noted that the first two women arrived more than a year after the men and boys landed in 1607.

"I also have a list of characters. Captain John Smith, who had fought against the Turks in Hungary, was captured and briefly served as a slave before he escaped. He then sailed with the English for the new world. John Rolfe, an Englishman, is famous for marrying Pocahontas, the strong-willed and beloved very young daughter of Chief Powhatan," said Mr. Phigg. He took a deep breath.

In very neat handwriting, Mr. Phigg had jotted down descriptions, such as that John Smith had dark hair and a thick beard. He noted that Smith wanted to learn as much as possible about the natives so that he could communicate with them. Captain Smith even learned the language of Powhatan, Bailey read.

Mr. Phigg also made notes in red ink to indicate his sources of information, particularly the books he and Dr. Robinson were reading.

He listed problems that the first colonists faced, such as lack of food and the comforts of home. Many were used to sleeping on fancy beds and they grumbled about the hard ground and cold, he noted.

Mr. Phigg told her that he wanted his readers to understand both the excitement and the disappointments and hardships that came with exploring the new land. A few colonists, like Smith, tried to learn about the First People, the Indians, but others just wanted to kill them. Many colonists didn't like John Smith, either.

Powhatan, also called a "werowance" or chief, didn't trust the settlers. He resented being tricked into having a copper crown with fake jewels placed on his head to make him a subject of King James of England. Jamestown was named for the king.

"Oh, you took my idea," said Bailey. She saw that Mr. Phigg intended to tell the story from the point of view of a friend or relative of Pocahontas.

"Yes, my dear, I thought that would be different," said Mr. Phigg. "Matachanna will tell readers about her brave, adventurous half sister, what it was like to have the English arrive, and the trinkets they traded for corn. I will also tell about Pocahontas when she was imprisoned by the English. I also will write that the stories of the 'rescue' of John Smith are likely his own fabrications."

He turned the page. "I plan to add little-known history. Did you know that before Rolfe, Pocahontas was married to an Indian named Kocoum? And that when she was baptized as a Christian, her name was changed to Rebecca?"

"I didn't know about Kocoum," said Bailey.

Mr. Phigg nodded. "Well, my characters are settling in," he said. "Through Matachanna's eyes we will see the villages, the gardens, the fishing and hunting trips. She may even go with Pocahontas to England."

Bailey's eyes shone as she turned the pages. "What's this?" she asked.

"Dr. Robinson thought we should include part of the speech that Chief Powhatan supposedly made to John Smith," said Elmo Phigg. He stood up and lifted the notebook in front of him. "This part always moves me to tears," he said.

Why should you take by force that which you can have from us by love? Why should you destroy us who have provided you with food . . .

Bailey listened carefully, but his reading was interrupted by the doorbell. Emily arrived, followed by Justin on his bike.

"Run along," said Mr. Phigg. He continued to read Powhatan's speech out loud: "What is the cause of your jealousy . . ." as Bailey went to the door.

40

Party Preparations

Miss Bekka said that they would decorate for the First Laugh Party while Mr. Will took Sparrow to a wonderful children's bookstore in downtown Fredericksburg. He knew the owners would help her find something that she would like to read.

Lately, when Sparrow wasn't sitting by Pinocchio's cage, she had her nose in a book. Sometimes she pointed to the door, and Miss Bekka would say gently, "Use words, Sparrow. Do you want to go outside?"

Sparrow didn't answer. Miss Bekka said that she simply nodded and waited for someone to open the door to the porch. Then she stared sadly down the driveway as if she were expecting someone to come for her. Bailey heard Miss Bekka tell Sugar that she wasn't sure the party was going to make any difference at all.

Sugar rested her leg on a footstool as she visited with the Phiggs and Dr. Robinson in the living room. The kids decided where to hang pink and purple crepe paper streamers and yellow balloons.

Justin brought a stepladder from the shed so he could climb high to hang the streamers to the molding. Fred handed him pieces of masking tape. Bailey and Emily taped the Pin the Tail on the Donkey game on the back of the dining room door.

"Put it down more," said Bailey, "so Sparrow can reach it."

Emily lowered the donkey picture six inches.

"That's good," said Bailey. She cut out paper tails and wrote everyone's name on one— even the grown-ups'—in case they played.

Noah helped his mother decorate cookies that they had cut in funny shapes—birds, bats, boats, and bugles.

"If you don't stop sneaking frosting there won't be enough for the cookies," said his mother, pretending to slap his hand. Bailey saw Miss Bekka smile as she had a lick of frosting, as well.

Fred made a huge sign that said LAUGHING PARTY. HA HA HA HA HEE HEE HEE HEE. When he was done, Justin helped him tape it to the front door.

"Let's decorate the bird cage," said Emily. She made a bow out of a purple streamer and tied it on a hook on top where Pinocchio could not reach it with his beak. He climbed a ladder to the top to have a better look, then said, "Off my shoulder, Jiminy Cricket." He coughed several times and puffed his feathers.

"I need more help in the kitchen," called Miss Bekka. "Someone needs to mix the lemonade, and someone needs to set the party table." Emily headed for the kitchen, and Bailey followed.

"We have about an hour before everyone gets here," said Miss Bekka. "If Noah stops eating every other cookie, we'll be in good shape."

Noah crossed his eyes at his mom.

Mrs. Dover arrived early with Howie, Nannie, and Fern, who no longer seemed mad at Sparrow. Even though it was a little tight, Howie dressed in his Superman costume from last Halloween. Nannie and Fern wore their princess costumes backwards over their pajama bottoms, just to be silly.

"I guess it is time to get into our outfits," said Sugar. "Our guest of honor will be back soon." She put on a red hat with antlers.

"Oh, my," said Mr. Phigg, looking at his watch.

"Indeed," said Mrs. Phigg.

"I'm ready," said Dr. Robinson. She pulled a rubber pig nose out of her pocket and strapped its stretchy band around her head. She smirked and made a strange oinking noise—*mnunk mnunk*—in the back of her closed mouth.

"I truly don't believe it," said Mr. Phigg as he headed for his room.

41

First Laugh Party

Just before Sparrow and Mr. Will returned to Keswick Inn, the doorbell rang.

"I'll get it," said Fred. "Hey, it's Babo Ganoosh."

The clown, wheeling a large maroon suitcase with side pockets, took a deep bow before waddling through the door. He blew kisses at Sugar and Miss Bekka with his large yellow-gloved hand and sat on an imaginary chair. Clover growled.

"Shame on you, girl," said Fred. "It's just Babo. You know Babo." He rubbed her ears, but she growled again, this time more quietly.

"Hush," said Fred.

Babo looked around the room, then scratched his head. He put his right hand to his forehead and appeared to search for something or someone. Then he pointed down the hall to the Phiggs' room.

"They are getting dressed for the party," said Miss Bekka. "You can put your things in Sparrow's room for the moment."

Babo nodded yes and followed her to the bedroom. He soon returned with an orange wooden box, which he placed in the center of the living room.

"Sparrow's coming," yelled Howie.

"Get ready. Let's hide!" shouted Nannie.

"Hide, Geppetto!" shouted Pinocchio.

It wasn't easy for Mr. Phigg to get behind the couch, but he did. Mrs. Phigg wrapped herself in a curtain. Sugar stood in back of a door with Justin. Noah and Fred ducked into the hall closet, and Bailey, Emily, Nannie, Howie, and Fern bumped into each other as they tried to get behind living room chairs.

"Watch out," said Howie.

"Shhh," said Emily.

They could hear the front door open and Mr. Will say, "Why, Sparrow, look at all the decorations. I wonder what is going on."

With that Fred and Noah jumped out of the closet, and yelled, "One, two, three," the signal for everyone else to pop out of their hiding places and yell, "Surprise!"

Sparrow's eyes opened wide and Bailey thought she saw a faint smile.

"This is a party for you," said Miss Bekka. "Let's go in the living room. I think you will have a special treat."

Sparrow wheeled her chair near the fireplace and Pinocchio's cage, where she had a good view of everyone. Then, she folded her hands in her lap. Noah, dressed as a ringmaster, said, "Ladies and gentlemen, boys and girls and clown, let the fun begin. Pre . . . sen . . . ting—Babo Ganoosh."

Fred started circus music on the CD player. Babo opened the orange box and took out bowling pins to juggle. When that didn't make Sparrow laugh, he juggled hats, dishes, and floppy rubber chickens. He pretended to cry when she blankly stared at him. He gave up and took a seat on the floor near the door to the hall.

Howie was next. He burped words, including Sparrow's name, and pretended to fly like Superman.

Nannie and Fern twirled in their dresses, then read jokes from Fern's book. Bailey and Emily played their clarinet and trumpet duet of "Yankee Doodle." Mrs. Phigg danced. Mr. Phigg sang while Sugar played "Twinkle Twinkle, Little Star" on the piano.

Justin showed everyone how he had trained Clover to jump through a hoop.

Dr. Robinson, wearing her pig nose, made grunting noises. *Mnunk mnunk.*

"I still don't believe it," said Mr. Phigg. His very proper assistant smoothed her gray silk skirt and took a bow.

Everyone laughed, except Sparrow.

"Hey, where did the clown go?" said Emily.

Babo was missing.

Sparrow pointed at the hall.

42

Stranger and Stranger

"There he goes," shouted Mr. Phigg. The clown, carrying the Phiggs' little green suitcase, ran through the hall and pushed open the screen door. Justin jumped up and ran after him.

"Stop him!" called Mrs. Phigg.

"Get him," shouted Noah and he and Fred joined the chase. Justin hopped on his bike and got ahead of Babo and blocked his path.

"Out of my way, kid," snarled the clown. "Stay out of this."

"Stay out of what?" said Mr. Phigg, who huffed and puffed his way down the front walk, followed by the rest of the partygoers. "Give my suitcase back!" He grabbed at the suitcase, but the clown held on tightly.

"Give it to me!" said Mr. Phigg. He reached for Babo and yanked at his purple tufts of hair. The more he tugged, the more the clown's mask began to fall apart and pull away from his face.

"Look at that!" said Bailey in amazement to Noah and Fred.

Underneath the wig was a bald head. Under the bald head was the face of the stranger who had asked about the suitcase.

"Oh, my," said Feather Phigg. "It's Elmo Jr." She rushed to the clown and hugged him. "My son, we never thought we would see you again."

Mr. Phigg was so surprised he just looked at the wig in his hand and back at the man with the green suitcase.

"I think you have some explaining to do," he said finally. "Now give me that suitcase and we are going back inside."

The clown reluctantly handed the suitcase to Mr. Phigg, then peeled off his big yellow gloves. He glowered at Noah, Fred, and Bailey before returning to the living room.

"We haven't heard from our son, Elmo Jr., in years," Mr. Phigg said when they all sat down again. "After he graduated from college, he worked for a summer in Jamestown, helping excavate the nearby fort. He said he wanted to be an archaeologist."

"At first he wrote letters and called, but then . . ." Feather Phigg's voice faded away.

"Then we heard that artifacts were missing from the dig, and so was our son," said Mr.

Phigg. "You can only imagine how embarrassing that was for us. One of his friends told us that Junior had joined a circus."

"We went to every circus that came to town, but because we couldn't tell one clown from another," said Mrs. Phigg, "we couldn't find him."

"Then one day a green suitcase arrived in the mail. We never found out who sent it, but inside was a picture of our son from his high school graduation, a small basket of bones, blue and white beads, a green onion bottle, a bodkin, a rusty lock, and several copper coins."

"We were determined to return these artifacts to Jamestown," said Mrs. Phigg.

"They weren't yours to return," growled Babo. "You don't know the whole story."

"Then you'd better tell us," said Mr. Phigg, unaware that Emily was passing a plate of bird-shaped cookies around the room and that he had already put three in his lap.

43

Phigg Family Reunion

Babo—Elmo Jr.—took a deep breath. "I suppose I should say that I am sorry for all the trouble and worry I've caused." He looked at his hands. "I didn't really steal these artifacts, but everyone blamed me anyway. I didn't think you would believe me. You never have believed anything I said."

"Phooey," said Mr. Phigg. "You never told the truth as a child. Why should we believe you now?" They glared at each other.

Elmo Jr. continued. "Ever since I was a little boy, I wanted to be a clown, remember? So I joined the circus. I decided I would send the suitcase to you where it would be safe until I left the big top. I planned to return the artifacts once nobody was looking for me anymore. I hoped I could trust you not to open it."

"Double phooey," said Mr. Phigg. "I can't say I'm buying your story at all."

"Fess up, Junior," said Feather Phigg. "Tell us the truth. Why did you try to sneak the suitcase from us now?" She shook her finger at him.

Babo looked annoyed. "Okay, then . . ."

"His fingers are crossed behind his back," said Fern.

Babo frowned at her.

"Okay, how about this? I need money, so I was going to sell some of the stuff at the antique shop where I've been working."

"Tweed's Good Stuff," interrupted Bailey.

"Tweed's my friend," said the clown, giving her a look. "But I couldn't get the suitcase away from you. Then I found out that you'd left some of the bones at the old fort—on the brick church bench, of all places."

"I'm disappointed in you, son," said Elmo Phigg. "We'll return to Jamestown tomorrow. You'll explain yourself to those in charge of the project, and personally hand over what remains in the suitcase. And you *will* apologize."

Babo looked sullen.

"You may be a good clown, but you've made many bad choices in life," said Feather Phigg. "I want you to know I am your mother and I still love you." Elmo Jr. focused on his lap.

The room was as silent as Sparrow. Bailey was dying to have a private talk with Noah and

Fred. She could tell from the unhappy looks on the Phiggs' faces that they still didn't believe anything that their son had said about the artifacts or his life.

Sugar broke the silence. "Perhaps we should let the Phigg family have some privacy to sort things out while we play the party games. Sparrow, I'm going to blindfold you so that you can take the first turn pinning the tail on the donkey."

44

Pinocchio's Surprise

Sparrow appeared pleased that her tail came closest to the donkey's rump. Nannie came in second and Howie, third. Sugar and Bailey's paper tails missed the donkey completely. Miss Bekka had prizes for the winners: a checker set that Sparrow picked, a watercolor paintbox for Nannie, and a box of crayons for Howie.

Bailey looked at her watch. The party would be over soon and just as Miss Bekka had predicted, it hadn't changed anything. Bailey looked at Sparrow and wished hard that the she would laugh or talk like everyone else. She didn't care anymore who would make it happen—just someone. Anyone.

Nannie and Fern handed out sweets—wrapped candies—and rock salt to all the guests as good luck souvenirs.

Bailey was relieved that Emily seemed to be her friend again.

Emily helped Miss Bekka clean up the paper cups and napkins. She said her mom would be arriving soon to pick up all the younger kids, but she, however, was going to spend the night with Bailey. Sugar said she would cook something on the new old grill she had purchased for $10 at a yard sale.

Bailey watched Sparrow roll her wheelchair closer to Pinocchio's cage. The parrot preened his feathers and cocked his head, opening his eye wide. He slid down the side of his cage and strutted over to Sparrow. She put her pointer finger between the bars and Pinocchio climbed on it. He rubbed his beak against her cheek, like he was kissing her.

Sparrow closed her eyes. *She is so pretty*, thought Bailey. *If only the party plan had worked.*

Suddenly, there was a squawk and the sound of a slide whistle coming from the cage. Pinocchio climbed back on his perch.

"My name is Sparrow!" said the bird, in a little girl's voice. "Where's Geppetto?"

Bailey's mouth opened in surprise.

"Did you hear that?" asked Sugar. Her face crinkled and she leaned back in her chair.

"I don't believe it," said Miss Bekka. "Boys, hurry in here."

"I'm seven. Awk, what's your name?" said Pinocchio, still sounding like a little girl. "I can run fast."

Sparrow looked at everyone and back at Pinocchio. Her face broke into a smile. Then a giggle, like a spring brook, spilled over and flooded the room.

"She's been talking all this time to the bird?" said Noah in astonishment.

Everyone was silent—too amazed to speak. Then Bailey said, "Please talk to us, Sparrow. We want to hear you."

Sparrow looked around the room and grinned. "The party was real fun," she said quietly.

45

Missing Again

"Burgers it is," said Sugar, as she drove Bailey and Emily back to the house after the party.

Emily said, "Mom always lets me make the patties and grate the cheese for salad."

"You girls are in charge then," said Sugar. "I need to get off my feet. This old leg is still bothering me a little from the fall."

"We'll take care of you, Sugar," said Bailey.

"We'll fix everything the way you like it," said Emily, clipping back her hair so that it wouldn't be in the way when she cooked.

"I'm glad we found out what was in the suit-case," said Bailey. She opened the refrigerator and removed the package of ground beef.

"What a shame about the Phiggs' son," said Sugar, leaning against the counter. "I can't be-lieve Junior grabbed the suitcase and ran away *again* while we were all listening to Sparrow talk."

"Well, after the party Mr. Phigg told me that he thinks everything in the suitcase is fake," said Emily, "but I think it is real stuff. Valuable stuff. Maybe they will make a TV show or movie about it."

Bailey shaped the ground beef into large balls, then flattened them on wax paper. "That would be funny, if it was all fake," she said. "Everybody really wanted to know what was inside." She remembered how close the twins had come to getting into the suitcase, and how she should have told somebody about the mysterious stranger.

"I still can't get over it," said Sugar. "What a day this has been. Your party idea ended up with Sparrow talking. It's lovely to hear her voice after all these weeks."

"I heard Sparrow tell Miss Bekka that she wanted to stay with them forever," said Emily. She placed catsup and mustard on the table and took off the caps. "Do you think she can?"

Sugar said, "I think the Keswicks will certainly try to make that happen, especially now that they know Sparrow is happy with them. It does depend on whether she is available for adoption, though. You kids have all been wonderful helping her feel secure in her new home. I'm proud of you."

Later, while Emily went upstairs to take a shower, Bailey asked Sugar, "If you were thinking about doing something wrong, but didn't exactly do it, how bad is that?"

"Everyone *thinks* of doing wrong things from time to time," said her grandmother. "Thinking about doing something bad and actually doing it are not the same. Is that what you mean?"

"Sort of," said Bailey.

Sugar continued, "Unfortunately, sometimes people get caught up in lies and make bad choices. They don't trust people with the truth or to forgive them for what they've done."

"Like Babo?" said Bailey.

"Like Babo," said Sugar. "We still don't know the whole story—the truth. Let's hope the Phiggs find their son again someday and they can get things straightened out with him. It's a pity that he ran off."

Then her grandmother reached out her arm, the one that hadn't been twisted when she fell.

"Come here, girl," said Sugar. "I'm so glad you are staying with me right now. You're great company and good help."

They heard Emily turn off the shower. "Now, if there is something specific you want to talk about . . . "

Bailey leaned up against Sugar and kissed her soft cheek. "I love you, too. Can we go on a treasure hunt tomorrow after Emily goes home?"

"That was just what I was thinking," said Sugar. "Hmm. Do you think we should keep our eyes out at Tweed's Good Stuff for a small green suitcase?"

Bailey thought for a moment, then laughed. "Maybe we'd find a red clown nose and big purple shoes inside it. The mysterious clown suitcase!"

"Mysterious indeed," said Sugar, with a big smile.

Book Club Questions

1. Feather and Elmo Phigg are evacuees from the storms. Have you lived through a bad storm? When the Phiggs arrive, what do you think might happen? How does the author introduce them? What are they wearing? What device does the author use to create mystery and make you want to know more about them?

2. What makes a family? Noah and Fred are adopted; Mr. Phigg says he was raised by his grandmother; Bailey is also being raised by her grandmother. When is a mother not a mother?

3. What did you think was in the suitcase when Elmo Phigg first mentioned its mystery?

4. If you were fleeing a disaster, what would you take with you? What did the Phiggs pile into and onto their van? Having to leave Feather's cat "Poochie" behind must have been difficult. Write a story about what you think happened to Poochie.

5. Sugar says, "Sometimes people who have had bad experiences need some time before they can talk about them." Give an example of this either from the book or from your own life.

6. Emily suggests Bailey look in the suitcase when the Phiggs are not home. Noah also wants to open the suitcase. Bailey, however, says she would not because it is not hers. Do you think she is tempted? Have you ever been tempted to peek at something (like a diary, for example) that did not belong to you? Have family members or friends ever read a letter, e-mail, or diary of yours that they had no business reading? How did you feel?

7. If Emily and Bailey look in the suitcase, what might happen next?

8. Each of the Bailey Fish books introduces new characters. Mr. Phigg explains that writers often depend on their characters to create the plot. How do Feather, Elmo, and Sparrow add new events to life at Lake Anna?

9. When Sugar is in the emergency room at the hospital, the door says NO ADMITTANCE, but Bailey wants to break the hospital rules to go in to see Sugar. How is this breaking of the rules different from Noah and Fred and Emily wanting to open the suitcase?

10. What happens after Sugar's accident shows how deeply Bailey loves her grandmother. Give specific examples of Bailey's actions and thoughts that show this love.

11. Books are more interesting to read when the author "shows rather than tells." Explain what this phrase means.

12. When her friend Emily wants to copy Bailey's homework answers, Bailey says no. Do you think that is hard or easy for her? Has anyone ever wanted to copy your work? How did you feel about it?

13. What did Bailey's friend Brittany say to Bailey after school? How did Bailey feel then? What advice did Bailey remember her mom giving her about kids who pressure you to do wrong things?

14. Sparrow doesn't speak when she first arrives at Keswick Inn. Is the story more interesting because she doesn't talk? What do you think she will be like when her hips heal so that she can run and play again? What would you have done at the party to try to make her laugh or talk?

Web Sites

Jamestown

www.americanrhetoric.com/speeches/
nativeamericans/chiefpowhatan.htm

www.geocities.com/bigorrin/
powhatan_kids.htm

http://www.historicjamestowne.org/news/
archaearium_takes_shape.php

http://historyisfun.org/jamestown/
jamestownhistory.cfm

www.jamestownglasshouse.com/
Reproduction4.asp

http://www.nps.gov/colo/Jthanout/
Indianlife.html

http:/www.powhatan.org/pocc.html

www.virtualjamestown.org/Pocahontas.html

http://www.vahistorical.org

Guam

http://www.guam-online.com/people/people.htm

Alaska State flag

http://www.netstate.com/states/symb/flags/
ak_flag.htm

Sites available as of press time. Author and publisher have
no control over material on these sites or their links.

From Sugar's bookshelves

Benny's Flag, Phyllis Krasilov
Double Life of Pocahontas, The, Jean Fritz
Jamestowne's Uncovered Treasures, Judy M. Brown
Journey to Jamestown: My Side of the Story, Lois Ruby
Life of the Powhatan, A Bobbie Kalman Book
Lion, the Witch and the Wardrobe, The, C. S. Lewis
Love & Hate in Jamestown: John Smith, Pocahontas, and the Start of a New Nation, David A. Price
Pocahontas, Powhatan, Opechancanough, Helen C. Rountree
Pocahontas: Young Peacemaker, Childhood of Famous Americans series, Leslie Gourse
Treasures from Jamestown, J. Paul Hudson
Young Pocahontas in the Indian World, Helen C. Rountree
Virginia: The First Seventeen Years, 1607–1624, Charles E. Hatch Jr.

Glossary

Abode: Home.

Archaearium: A museum that contains artifacts found by archaeologists at the James Fort site and tells the story of the settlement and its relationship with the Powhatans.

Archaeologist: Someone who studies people and civilizations from earlier times by digging where cities, forts, and houses were located to see what can be found.

Artifact: Object from a certain time period. It might be found when archaeologists dig.

Baba Ghnoush: A delicious Middle Eastern eggplant appetizer.

Bodkin: A decorative silver pin that women used to hold their hair in place.

Clapboard: Boards, with one side thinner than the other, that are slightly overlapped when they are put together for a roof or siding.

Colonist: Someone who settles in another country, often while keeping ties with his own.

Evacuee: Someone who leaves his home because of a storm or other emergency and seeks safety elsewhere.

Foster child: A child who is cared for by foster parents. The length of time may vary. Sometimes foster children return to their parents, sometimes they stay in foster care, and sometimes they are adopted.

Jamestowne: Old English spelling of Jamestown has an "e" on the end of the word.

Maven: An expert or very knowledgeable person in a particular subject.

Replica: A reproduction of something. The Jamestown Settlement shows replicas of what the ships, fort and Powhatan Indian villages were like.

Onion Bottle: A short-necked glass wine bottle with a round base. Reproductions are made today at the Jamestown Glasshouse, where colonial glassmaking techniques are demonstrated.

Shard: A fragment of something, like pottery.

Wattle and daub: Woven sticks and rods are covered with mud or clay to make the sides of a building. When the mud dries, it becomes hard, like a brick.

A replica of the Godspeed *is docked at Jamestown Settlement for visitors to board.*

Replicas of the Discovery *(left) and the* Susan Constant *(pictured in upper right background).*

Historical interpreters at the Jamestown Settlement wear clothes such as the colonists or the Powhatans would have worn. This interpreter helps visitors understand life on the recreated ships.

The first two women did not arrive at Fort James until 1608, more than a year after the men and boys arrived. At the recreated colonial fort at Jamestown Settlement, costumed historical interpreters (people who help visitors understand what they are seeing) are dressed in the fashions of the time. The triangular fort includes wattle-and-daub structures representing dwellings, an Anglican church, a court of guard, a storehouse, a blacksmith's forge, a cape merchant's office (the cape merchant was in charge of merchant operations), provisioning areas (where needed supplies were stored), and a governor's house.

Visitors, such as the Phiggs, may walk through the recreated Jamestown Settlement and its Powhatan Village to see what life was like when the colonists arrived and met the Indians.

Fishnets hang from poles in the village.

Yehakins, or houses, at Jamestown Settlement's recreated Powhatan Indian village are made from sapling frames covered with woven reed mats. This interior shows a firepit at the center and animal skins on the sleeping benches.

A reproduction of a house at Jamestown Settlement's recreated colonial fort is typical of those occupied by English colonists.

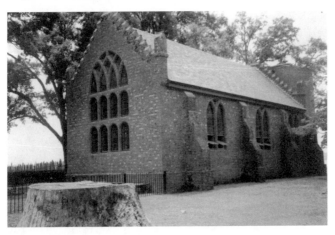

The 1907 brick memorial church at Historic Jamestowne is attached to the ruins of a 1647 tower (far right) at the site of a frame church built in 1617. The original brick and cobblestone foundations are visible under glass inside the church.

Medieval-style armor hangs in the captain's quarters of Jamestown Settlement's recreated Susan Constant, *the largest of the three ships that brought colonists from England to coastal Virginia. The armor wasn't much good for defending the colonists from cannon fire, and took too much time to put on to be practical in battles with American Indians.*

Armor breastplates and helmets are displayed and may be examined and even tried on in Jamestown Settlement's recreated colonial fort.

Archaeologists at Historic Jamestowne work on evacuating the original Jamestown fort. Below, one is screening the soil to see what objects are in it. Many artifacts are on display at the nearby Archaearium.

An archeologist's screen box like those used at Historic Jamestowne.

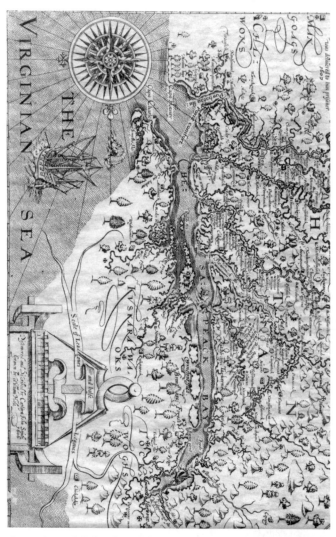

A portion of John Smith's 1607 map of Virginia. Look at a modern map of the commonwealth for a comparison. Used by permission of the Virginia Historical Society, Richmond, Virginia.

The original fort, an almost triangular shape, on the James River had wooden palisades (high fences) to protect it. Archaeologists have found remains of some of the buildings and palisades at what is now called Historic Jamestowne.

The Alaskan state flag was designed in a contest for kids in 1927, thirty years before Alaska became a state. The winner was John Bell "Benny" Benson, a thirteen-year-old Aleut orphan. The blue background represents the sky and the state flower—the Forget-Me-Not. The Big Dipper is part of the Ursa Major or Great Bear constellation and symbolizes strength. The North Star leads to the future. Alaskan schools and streets are named for Benny Benson. Sugar learned about the flag's history on a trip to Alaska with wild women.

Acknowledgments

I'm deeply grateful to many people for excellent suggestions and assistance with the Bailey Fish Adventure series including Jim Salisbury, Nancy Miller (for the discussion questions); Nancy Egloff, Jamestown Settlement historian; Tracy Perkins, Jamestown-Yorktown Foundation media relations specialist for vetting Jamestown history and information relating to Historic Jamestowne and the Jamestown Settlement; Abigail Grotke; Alexis Smith, director of elementary instruction in the Orange County, Virginia, schools; Elizabeth Madden; Lorien Cummins; members of the Mineral Historical Foundation, including A. G. Johnson, Dr. Gaynelle Whitlock, and A. P. Hall, for their memories of the Louisa and C&O railroads. Also to Hallie Vaughan, David Black and Bert and Barbara Stafford. And to Jennifer Pérez, Erin Long, Sandra Miller, and Amberlyn Freidel for special inspiration and ideas.

About the Author

 Linda Salisbury draws her inspiration for the Bailey Fish Adventure series from her experiences in Florida and Central Virginia, and as a mother, mentor, former foster mother, and grandmother.

A former newspaper editor and columnist, she writes children's book reviews and articles for various publications. Also in the Bailey Fish Adventure Series are: *The Wild Women of Lake Anna,* a *ForeWord* magazine finalist for Book of the Year 2005; *No Sisters Sisters Club;* and *The Thief at Keswick Inn.*

She enjoys boating on Lake Anna and up Contrary Creek with her husband, Jim. They share their home in the woods with old lazy cats.

About the Illustrator

 Artist Christopher Grotke of Brattleboro, Vermont, is the creative director for MuseArts, Inc. He is an award-winning animator and has been featured in a number of publications, including the *Washington Post* and *New York Times,* and his work has been seen on PBS's "The Creative Spirit."

He has done illustrations and drawings for five books. He walks in the woods with an adventurous cat.

The Do's and Don'ts of
HYPOGLYCEMIA

AN EVERYDAY GUIDE TO LOW BLOOD SUGAR

TOO OFTEN MISUNDERSTOOD AND MISDIAGNOSED!

ROBERTA RUGGIERO

President and Founder of
The Hypoglycemia Support Foundation, Inc.

Frederick Fell Publishers, Inc.
Hollywood, FL 33019
Web Site: www.FellPub.com
E-mail: fellpub@aol.com

Frederick Fell Publishers, Inc.
Hollywood, Florida 33019
e-mail: fellpub@aol.com
Visit our Web site at www.fellpub.com

This publication is designed to provide accurate and authoritative information in regard to the subject matter covered. It is sold with the understanding that the publisher is not engaged in rendering legal, accounting, or other professional service. If legal advice or other assistance is required, the services of a competent professional person should be sought. From A Declaration of Principles jointly adopted by a Committee of the American Bar Association and a Committee of Publishers.

The information in this book is not intended as medical advice. Its intention is solely informational and educational. It is assumed that the reader will contact a medical or health professional should the need for one be warranted.

Library of Congress Cataloging-in-Publication Data

Ruggiero, Roberta, 1942-
  The do's and don'ts of hypoglycemia : an everyday guide to low blood sugar / Roberta Ruggiero.
     p. cm.
Previously published: 1988.
  ISBN 0-88391-087-X
1. Hypoglycemia--Popular works. I. Title.
  RC662.2.R84 2003
  616.4'66--dc21

                          2003000277

Printed in USA
10 9 8 7 6 5 4

Design by IATPI- Miami

WORDS OF ENDORSEMENT AND PRAISE

"*The Do's and Don'ts of Low Blood Sugar* was chosen among the top best lay medical books because it covers a subject of potential interest to public library patrons in a responsible, easily understood way... A worthwhile edition to a public library collection."

—*American Library Journal*

"*The Do's and Don'ts of Low Blood Sugar* has been endorsed in our programs. Only those books that are felt to be truly outstanding selections are incorporated into our programming. It's always a personal pleasure to encounter and recommend good, conscientious work to our audience."

—*The Midwest Book Review*
Oregon, Wisconsin

"You've done a superb job after years of both personal and intellectual research on this topic. Thank you for helping so many people who will benefit from your experiences and clear writing."

—*Jeffrey S. Bland, Ph.D.*
Gig Harbor, Washington

"This is a great book. So easy and so practical. Just right for the hypoglycemic who seems to fade after concentrating for 10 minutes. You are writing for all those with a short attention span."

—*Lendon H. Smith, M.D.*
Portland, Oregon

"Congratulations on a great book that really brings the whole question of low blood sugar into an easy to read, understandable form. You certainly answer every conceivable question that a patient is likely to ask and I wish you every success."

—*Robert Buist, Ph.D.*

Sydney, Australia

"I appreciate having received your book. The focus for me was the chapter which you discussed the approach to a positive attitude. I love the way you formulated your concepts and am happy for you that the book is in print."

—*Leonard A. Wisneski, M.D., F.A.C.P.*

Bethesda, Maryland

"My first suggestion to a hypoglycemic patient is to read your book. Education and understanding of hypoglycemia, or LBS, is probably the single most important thing that one can do to deal with this condition and your book is a great place to start."

—*Douglas M. Baird, D.O., P.A.*

Tampa, Florida

"Thank you for sending me a copy of your book. The time and effort which you put into it really has paid off. You have an excellent, well written and informative book. I will be sure to show this to my many patients who are suffering with hypoglycemia."

—*Irving Karten, M.D., F.A.C.O.G.*

Hollywood, Florida

"Your latest book on low blood sugar is FANTASTIC! You have successfully distilled the essence of the subject for those that suffer from the often misdiagnosed and misunderstood condition of hypoglycemia. The information on diet, vitamins and exercise could easily be followed by anyone who is seeking health or wants to maintain their health."

—Leo B. Stouder, B.S., D.C., D.N.B.C.E.
Hollywood, Florida.

"As I began to read your book, I couldn't help but feel that I was reading my own story with all the frustrations and fears that you experienced. I would also like to say thanks for all your time and effort you put forth in getting this book published and The Hypoglycemia Foundation started."

—*Madison, Wisconsin*

"The book was a tremendous lift to my spirits and renewed my courage to keep up the pace on the road to recovery. I wish that every person who has hypoglycemia or is suffering the symptoms and doesn't know the cause could read this book. It is a great support!"

—*Selma, North Carolina*

"I believe your book, *The Do's and Don'ts of Low Blood Sugar*, could be the most helpful thing a newly diagnosed hypoglycemic could read. Its simplicity of style makes it an excellent first choice. How I wish it had been available to me in 1980."

—*Del City, Oklahoma*

"I have just finished reading your book, *The Do's and Don'ts of Low Blood Sugar*, which I picked up at the library. It is the most informative book I have found to date."

—*East Lyme, Connecticut*

"My doctor has informed me that I am 'borderline diabetic' and he has recommended that I read the book entitled, *The Do's and Don'ts of Low Blood Sugar.*

—*Summerland Key, Florida*

"...I have scoured bookstores and health food stores and every place else I could think of for information. I was quite discouraged until yesterday when I went to the library. I found a copy of your *Do's and Don'ts of Low Blood Sugar*. I was thrilled with all of the information you included in this book. From my own experience I know how much work must have been involved in gathering it. I finally feel like my husband and I will be able to get a handle on our situation and keep his condition in check."

—*Houston, Texas*

"Your book *The Do's and Don'ts of Low Blood Sugar* was a life saver. After more than 15 years I have finally found my cure: a simple diet!"

—*Poland, Ohio*

"I have read it and found it very helpful. The way it is written makes it very readable and clear and very interesting because it is written from a personal point of view."

—*Southport, Merseyside (England)*

"I read your book recently, *The Do's and Don'ts of Low Blood Sugar*. I wish I had found it before I did all my technical reading. The book made me cry. It also made me feel as if I was being hugged and comforted by a dear friend. You wrote so well about all the things I've been trying to explain to my family as well as to my doctor."

—Kew Garden Hills, New York

"I want to thank you for opening up a new world for me."

—Ft. Lauderdale, Florida

"It was like looking in a mirror to read your book."

—Ft. Lauderdale, Florida

"Since I read your book—it has saved my life-literally."

—Paris, Kentucky

"I am a 38 year-old hypoglycemic, recently diagnosed and I cannot thank you enough, Roberta Ruggiero. It was because of your book—*The Do's and Don'ts of Low Blood Sugar*, that I was able to recognize myself as a hypoglycemic, and I asked my doctor to test me. He, although skeptical, agreed, and to my delight my hypoglycemia was confirmed beyond a doubt. This singular diagnosis has finally explained a lifetime of symptoms, physical and emotional, and has helped me and those nearest to me understand that it was not nor is not my "nature" to be miserable, touchy, disagreeable, negative, etc, etc, but it is only a very controllable disorder which causes me to become that way."

—Niagara Falls, New York

"Thank you for changing my life!"

—*Holland, Michigan*

"I thank you once again on behalf of our patrons, and we look forward to utilizing your reference materials and to making good use of your help, and guidance in order to improve the care and services we provide to our community!"

May God bless you!
Thanking you for your kindness,

—*Dr. A.N. Malpani, M.D.*
Medical Director
Bombay, India

"I am a Health Educator with the Bermuda Diabetes Association. In the last few months there has been an increase in calls from people inquiring about hypoglycemia, and nearly all of them have expressed dissatisfaction with the explanation/advice they received regarding their condition."
I found your website via the Alta Vista search engine. I will recommend your book to all future callers to our Association.

Thank you!

—*Jacqui Neath-Myrie*
Diabetes Prevention Programmer Coordinator
Bermuda Diabetes Association

Dedicated . . .

To every hypoglycemic—particularly those who
have been mistakenly told that their symptoms were
"all in their head."

TABLE OF CONTENTS

The order or length of each topic does not reflect its importance or value.

Table of Contents

Please Note: The terms hypoglycemia and low blood sugar are used interchangeably throughout the book, but have the same meaning.

ACKNOWLEDGEMENTS

The best part about writing this book is remembering everyone who played a role in its creation. They not only influenced my work, but my life.

Gratitude goes to all the people who suffer with hypoglycemia and shared their stories with me as well as every professional, medical or otherwise, who said yes to an interview. Thanks also goes to the Board of Directors, Board of Advisors, and all the members of The Hypoglycemia Support Foundation, Inc. (HSF), as well as to the volunteers who gave so generously of themselves.

I would like to especially recognize the following people: Douglas M. Baird, D.O., Lorna Walker, Ph.D., Hewitt Bruce, Ph.D., Stephen J. Schoenthaler, Ph.D., Shirley S. Lorenzani, Ph.D. and the late Dr. Emanuel Cheraskin, M.D., D.M.D. Each and every one of you was instrumental to my growth. As mentors, teachers, healers, and most of all friends, your directions, reassurances, and confidences gave me the courage to continue working toward my dreams.

I would like to give special thanks to: Toni Crabtree, Marie Provenzano, Kimberly Perraud, Karen McCoy, Susan Connors, Carolyn Stein, Tomey Sellars and Dr. Phyllis Schiffer-Simon. On a professional, personal, and spiritual level, each of you combined your strength and support to spur me on during my most difficult times.

§

Acknowledgements

Special thanks go to the late Harvey M. Ross, M.D. for writing the preface; to David Kohn, Melodee Putt, and Candace Hoffmann for using their editing expertise to polish this manuscript; and to my son-in-law, Charles Stewart, D.M.D. for his valuable suggestions. My deepest gratitude goes to Don Lessne, my publisher; Elena Solis, Graphic Designer; and Lori Sindell Horton, Production Manager/Editor at Frederick Fell Publishers. Each one of you gave my book extra love and tender care from the moment it was placed in your hands.

To my children, Renee and Anthony, and my husband, Tony—your unconditional love, patience, and understanding, gave me the freedom to do my work and to make this book a reality. I am forever grateful.

To my grandchildren Krystina, Cody, Sara, and Stephen— you have made me see the world through your eyes. What more could I ask for?

Last, but definitely not least, my deepest appreciation goes to Theresa Mantovani without whom this book would not have been possible. I miss you dearly.

PREFACE

I have treated people with hypoglycemia since the late 1960s. I've learned by listening to my patients about the multiple frustrations that they experience, starting from the time they first begin to recognize something is wrong to the numerous visits to doctors over the years. Then, too, there are the frustrations experienced in their professional and personal lives right through to the confusion in treatments and difficulty in adhering to a program once it is outlined. Through her experience, first as a patient, then as an advisor who reaches out to thousands of others to help them through their difficult times, Roberta Ruggiero has learned to help people recognize this illness, find professional help and, finally, help to comply with the programs suggested for the treatment of hypoglycemia.

In *The Do's and Don'ts of Low Blood Sugar*, Roberta shares with her readers the rich knowledge of her own experience. She is able to guide, teach and support those with this problem; a problem that is, more often than not, overlooked or even scoffed at by the majority of those in the medical profession.

If you have, or even suspect that you or someone you know has hypoglycemia, this is the book for you. By following the "do's and don'ts," those with hypoglycemia will be able to reduce and even eliminate their symptoms, and start on the road to a more fulfilling life.

—*Harvey M. Ross, M.D.*
Los Angeles, California

THE DO'S AND DON'T OF HYPOGLYCEMIA:
AN EVERYDAY GUIDE TO LOW BLOOD SUGAR
Introduction to the Third Edition

The first edition of *The Do's and Don'ts of Low Blood Sugar: An Everyday Guide To Hypoglycemia* was written in 1988 with a tremendous amount of fear and self-doubt. I was writing a medical book with no medical degree and writing about a condition the medical community labeled a non-disease. Even those who recognized its existence, still called hypoglycemia the most confusing, complicated, misunderstood, and misdiagnosed condition of the 21st century.

So, why did I write it in the first place? Why a second revision in 1993? And more importantly, why am I back again in 2003, writing another updated edition? It is because of YOU, my readers. You have written to me, cried on my shoulder, begged for more answers, more information and more research.

From big cities such as Los Angeles, California to little-known towns such as Soddy, Tennessee; from Canada to Great Britain; from Alaska to Ireland, the letters pour in. And since The Hypoglycemia Support Foundation, Inc. launched its website, www.hypoglycemia.org, in 1997; e-mails arrive on a daily basis from around the world. I correspond with hypoglycemics in China, India, Africa, Pakistan, and the Kingdom of Bahrain right from my office in Sunrise, Florida. How incredible, God's plan!

Because 99 percent of those writing to me ask questions concerning hypoglycemia, I strongly believe that the word hypoglycemia should get top billing. No matter what we call it, whether low blood sugar or a blood sugar management disorder, hypoglycemia is the term most of you recognize. Thus, this edition will be called *The Do's and Don'ts of Hypoglycemia: An Everyday Guide to Low Blood Sugar.*

This book includes four new chapters. Three of them address areas of significant concern: hypoglycemia and children, hypoglycemia and alcoholism, and hypoglycemia and diabetes. Although I touch briefly on these topics in this edition, please realize that they all merit further attention and investigation. The fourth chapter provides answers to the most commonly asked questions about hypoglycemia.

Once again, the teachers, advisors, and mentors who assisted me, and The Hypoglycemia Support Foundation, Inc. for the past 22 years, have given their time and expertise to this updated edition. Their dedication and commitment have enabled the HSF to continue, to succeed, and to grow beyond our wildest expectations.

However, despite all of their support, and even though I know that this is my mission, I must admit, there have been times when I've wanted to give up. My strength, determination, and persistence would waver. I would say, "That's it! No more, I quit!" And then someone would call or write and say..."Wow, your book saved my life,"... or..."Your information saved my marriage,"... or..."I thought I was alone but now I feel as though I have an understanding friend."

Sometimes I feel very selfish. I can't tell you what these letters and phone calls mean to me. In helping others, I believe I'm really helping myself. I've grown emotionally, intellectually, mentally, and spiritually. I think that's what life is all about—living life to its fullest.

I have been blessed a hundred fold. The people I have met, been privileged to work with, share with, confide in, laugh and cry with—my family, friends, brothers, and sisters of this incredible universe—you are among my greatest blessings.

INTRODUCTION

If you think you may be going crazy; if you have thoughts of suicide; if you're constantly exhausted, anxious and depressed; if you go for weeks without a decent night's sleep; if your personality changes like the flip of a coin; if a counter full of munchies doesn't satisfy your sweet tooth; and if your doctor thinks you must be a hypochondriac because medical tests don't show anything physically wrong with you—don't despair, there's hope!

You may not need a psychiatrist, or even pain pills, tranquilizers or anti-depressants. Surprisingly, a simple DIET may relieve your symptoms!

This condition, which is confusing, complicated, misunderstood and too often misdiagnosed, is hypoglycemia, or low blood sugar. According to leading medical authorities, it affects one-half of all Americans, including celebrities Burt Reynolds and Merv Griffin. It is most frightening because most people who have it, don't know it. Often, the myriad collection of symptoms are blamed on other causes.

I know because I've been there. I suffered with hypoglycemia for ten years. Numerous medical specialists, dozens of tests, thousands of pills, and even the administration of electroconvulsive shock therapy (ECT), did nothing to eliminate my symptoms.

A simple glucose tolerance test (GTT), proper diet and strong determination finally led me down the road to recovery. Unfortunately, it took years. If only I had had the knowledge that lies between the covers of this book, my journey would not have been so traumatic.

To help others avoid what I experienced, to bring to them the causes and effects of hypoglycemia, and to give support, encouragement and enlightenment to those suffering this insidious disease, I formed The Hypoglycemia Support Foundation Inc. (HSF) on June 6, 1980.

Through the HSF, I have had the opportunity to speak with thousands of "searching" hypoglycemics. They all are looking for the best doctor, diet, book or miracle cure. They are asking the questions that I once asked: What should I eat? Should I take vitamins? Should I exercise? Why isn't my diet working? Why doesn't my family understand? Can I ever eat out again? More serious questions commonly asked are:Why doesn't my doctor recognize hypoglycemia? He says it's just a "fad" disease. Is the glucose tolerance test necessary? How can I find a physician sympathetic to a hypoglycemic's needs? The list is endless, and so, sometimes, is the pain.

During this time, as I was trying to educate hypo-glycemics, they in turn, educated me. They told me what they needed and wanted and, above all, what they were not getting. I learned of their pitfalls, anxieties and fears. Coupled with my own feelings, everyone I encountered seemed to respond with the same universal phrase, "If only I had known . . ."

There are many good books out on the subject of hypoglycemia. However, when I insisted that a patient get a book to read about his or her condition, I began to realize that most of the people were in the first stages of hypoglycemia, a time when the mind is confused, the body is weak and concentration is difficult.

When I found myself repeating the same guidelines over and over again, I realized that these patients first needed simple, concise and comprehensible guidelines to help them handle their condition. They needed a prerequisite, a book to read BEFORE all the other books on hypoglycemia. They needed a book with specific do's and don'ts written in layperson's vocabulary before grasping for medical definitions and explanations.

This is what I hope to achieve with *The Do's and Don'ts of Hypoglycemia*. Use it as a key to education, interweave it with commitment and then, love yourself enough to take the final step—application! Are you ready?

"To be sugar free in a sugar coated
world is a nightmare!"

Donna 1990

 # Chapter 1

LETTERS FROM OUR MAILBAG

W hy devote a chapter strictly to letters and e-mails that I have received? The answer is quite simple. I am hoping the following correspondence will have the same effect on you as it had on me. I am hoping that the connection that was formed, the bond that was cemented and the feeling that flowed between the writer and me will be passed on to you, my reader. I want you to benefit by gaining inspiration from the challenges and triumphs experienced by other hypoglycemics and learn from their mistakes and their successes.

Together, let's shed more light on hypoglycemia which it needs if the sting is to removed from it's tail. The following letters will speak for themselves.

Dear Roberta:

THANK YOU, THANK YOU, THANK YOU!
The information you have been kind enough to share with me has been the key link enabling me to return to a normal life.

Several months ago, I began growing faint and was, on about half a dozen occasions, taken to the emergency room of a local hospital. In every instance, I was told there was nothing wrong and that I was probably just hyperventilating. After consulting several doctors without any success at all, I was properly diagnosed by a local physician who recommended a glucose tolerance test. Once it was determined that I had hypoglycemia, I was referred to the Cleveland Clinic for dietary planning.

The staff at the Cleveland Clinic were enormously helpful but referred me to you and your organization for additional help. The materials you have supplied me have helped me understand my problem and do what is necessary to return to a normal life. I am saddened by my own experience with the many doctors who were unable to determine what was wrong with me. I am frightened for the many thousands of patients throughout the country with similar problems who are no doubt experiencing the same kind of difficulty with their diagnosis. I hope for their sake that they will be as fortunate as I was to be directed to you and your wonderful, caring organization.

Please let me know if there is anything I can ever do to repay the enormous debt I owe to you.

Sincerely,
Fort Lauderdale, Florida

Dear Roberta,

Thank you...Since I read your book (it saved my life, literally) about three years ago, I've been on again, and off again the diet. I usually go back on my diet after a very bad episode, such as my pancreas killing me, or I start blacking out again.

Only those who have had this devastating illness can understand how one understanding person who writes a book (you & your book) can save so many people from unnecessary reactions such as suicide.

I wrote to you once before several years ago crying my eyeballs out. Finally, after my entire life and several doctors telling me everything but, hypoglycemia, it was good to know I was not nuts.

Thank You!
Paris, Kentucky

Dear Roberta,

I have just finished reading your wonderful book for the second time and I can't tell you how much it helped me. It's such a terrible disease to have, it was the most trying time of my whole life, I thought I was going insane for sure. It started out for me about seven months ago, I got out of bed one morning and started to have a panic attack, (which I had never experienced one in my life), and thought I was having a heart attack. My husband was at work and my children, ages seven and three, were still asleep, so I called my neighbor and she took me to the hospital. They told me it was my nerves, gave me a shot and sent me home. After that I kept having panic attacks, anxiety, and severe depression. I went to my doctor and he gave me nerve pills and said that it had to be something in my subconscious that was triggering all of my symptoms. I just knew that it was something physical because I started to develop a lot of other symptoms after that. I would go back to my doctor and tell him that the pills weren't helping, about the other symptoms I was getting and he almost acted mad because I wouldn't take his word for it. I feel that God really had his hand in all of this because my family and friends were all praying for me and my neighbor (who took me to the hospital), her daughter has hypoglycemia and she thought that I could have it, because she had the same symptoms that I was having. So, I went back to my doctor again and I asked him if he thought I could have low blood sugar. He sort of laughed and said that most people who have panic attacks think they have that or else a brain tumor.

I feel that he just agreed to give me a five hour GTT to humor me, I think it really offended him because I was right and he was wrong. My blood sugar level went down to 46 in the third hour of my test, when I called his office to get the results, he didn't even talk to me on the phone, his receptionist told me I had low blood sugar and made an appointment for me to see a dietician at the hospital. She, (the dietician), was very helpful and she even said she couldn't understand why doctors don't recognize and check people for hypoglycemia more often. Three days later I called a different doctor and made an appointment and had all of my medical records transferred over to him. Well, I am so happy that I switched doctors. My new doctor took a complete family history and said that I am a prime candidate for hypoglycemia with having diabetes in my family, and I also had diabetes with my first pregnancy. He felt that 46 on my GTT was no doubt low and he's following up on everything, too. He wants to see me every six months to check for diabetes and to see how I am doing.

I am so thankful that I didn't have to suffer a real long time, like you or some of the other poor people in your book, before I found out what was wrong. I am thankful that I now have a lot more good days than bad ones. It is so nice to have a doctor who is understanding and recognizes how dreadful it is to have this disease. I just don't understand why all doctors don't recognize hypoglycemia. It is really a shame to think that there are so many people out there who are having terrible mental and physical problems, and they probably have low blood sugar, I might never know that they can feel better just by following a diet!

Thank you for writing your book and sharing your story with so many others, I'm sure it has been very helpful to everyone who reads it, and thank you for forming the HSF.

Thank-you
Saginaw, Michigan

Dear Ms. Ruggiero:

I recently came across your book *The Do's and Don'ts of Low Blood Sugar* and would very much appreciate any information (nutritional or otherwise) you may have regarding hypoglycemia. As I began to read your book, I couldn't help but feel that I was reading my own story with all the frustrations and fears that you experienced. I would also like to say thanks for all your time and effort you put forth in getting this book published and The Hypoglycemia Foundation started.

After 10 years of being treated as a manic depressive, 20 electroconvulsive shock therapy (ECT) treatments, and being placed on every anti-psychotic and anti-depressant medication on the market, I was finally diagnosed as hypoglycemic. Since I have changed my diet accordingly, I feel

100% better the majority of the time.

Thank you for your time and attention you have given this letter. I have suffered quite extensively these last 15 years and have no desire to repeat this experience! Therefore, any information that you can provide me with will be most helpful.

Sincerely,
Madison, Wisconsin

Mrs. Ruggiero,

I was so happy to have found your book, *The Do's and Don'ts of Low Blood Sugar.* I'm 26 and have known for several years that I had hypoglycemia but knew little more than to stop eating sugar. I followed the "sacred diet" faithfully for years but never seemed to get much better. When I asked about what to do I was given another copy of that diet, patted on the back and was told that I would be just fine if I left the sugar alone. When I called the office confused and wilted, I was told to get a candy bar and that would bring my sugar up and I would be fine. The confusion mounted. That was when I decided I would find out on my own what I should do. So, I hit the libraries, and that is where I found your book. I felt like you had written the book after spending a few months watching me. It really was nice to finally know that I was dealing with something conquerable.

Your book marks the beginning of my quest for information on this quiet culprit, who sets up camp in the corner of your life, and robs you of your senses. Even though I still find myself in unexplainable tears or wrapped in a blanket in 90 degree weather, I finally feel hope. I feel sure that God has His hand in this matter. Thank you for writing and sharing your experiences and knowledge.

God Bless You,
Milford, Michigan

Dear Mrs. Ruggiero,

I can't tell you how enlightening your book, *Do's & Don'ts of Low Blood Sugar*, was for me. My daughter was diagnosed with hypoglycemia in August of '91. We had been having problems with our daughter since around puberty, she is now 17. Her grades were slipping, she was always in a strange mood and her temper seemed to flash out of the blue. She just didn't seem like a happy adolescent. My daughter has always been independent and a handful but I thought these changes were just part of puberty.

When we would get on her about school she would tell us she was studying but found it hard to remember what she read. My husband and I would just shake our heads and say she just wasn't putting enough effort into her work. We even had her tested for LD problems but the test proved negative. By the time she entered high school she was having headaches, first thing in the morning, which I figured could be a migraine but she never liked school, was doing poorly, so I figured most times it was a ruse to get out of school. Then we started with dizziness and she was complaining of almost passing out. At this point we took her to the doctor. She had the Glucose Tolerance Test (over 5 hours) and was diagnosed. We were given a diet, told this was common in teens and she would probably outgrow the problem. It seemed no big deal. The doctor said to keep her on the diet for three months then start reintroducing foods—looking for the dizziness as a guide. Artificial sweeteners were fine, and natural fruit juices were also acceptable, no restricted amounts.

By this time I had talked my husband into family counseling. It seemed what I thought was a family was disintegrating around me. I was an emotional mess. It never dawned on me to read up on her hypoglycemia. I could only concentrate on one thing at a time and counseling was it.

Counseling seemed to be helping out but we still had periods of uneven behavior. I had read an article in the paper about behavior problems with hypoglycemic kids and asked the doctor if this was   true. He said, "No way, don't give her that handle to use." I believed him. Why? I can't answer that, not even now. After a year almost, all of the foods had been reintroduced. She has reported no dizziness but erratic behavior, even worse than before. Our counselor had her evaluated by a psychiatrist who diagnosed a long term depression. When she was arrested for battery last week I called our counselor and asked for his help. His first thought was a reevaluation. His supervisor overruled this and they had a staff meeting instead. In the meeting was the supervisor, our counselor, the psychiatrist and a psychologist. They concluded that she had a "Personality Disorder" and we had to accept her as is and we were on our own and then they wished us good luck.

Two days after this verdict my daughter brought home your book. (My daughter works at a library.) I can't even describe how I felt as I read this book. The pain, the guilt, the unbelief that I could be unaware of this for so long. That I had put my daughter through hell because I didn't do my job as a mother. I tried calling the counselor. I didn't even know if he told the staff that my daughter has hypoglycemia. We had told him when we first started the sessions. He was honest with us. He told us he knew nothing about it, we explained what we knew from the doctor and promptly forgot about it.

I don't know how to pull this together. I can't let this diagnosis stand as is if the hypoglycemia wasn't taken into account, which I feel it wasn't. I know that my daughter will not miraculously turn into Mary Poppins but if LBS accounts for even a small percentage of her problems I feel it should be reevaluated.

I need advice. I've set this trap by my own ignorance but I don't want my daughter to pay for my mistakes.

Sincerely,
Mokena, Illinois

Dear Mrs. Ruggiero,

Thank you for writing your book, *The Do's and Don'ts of Low Blood Sugar.*

In 1980 I was diagnosed as hypoglycemic by an alert and caring physician. Bless him! Even though I was not subjected to many of the horrors most hypoglycemics experience when they first realize 'something' is wrong I well remember the feeling of having been transported to some twilight zone where nothing made sense as I struggled to understand my condition. My own experience convinced me it takes two people, a knowledgeable doctor and an informed patient, to manage this condition. In my attempts to understand hypoglycemia, what it is and how to treat it, I read most of the literature available to the average person. Given my belief that education is essential to the hypoglycemic, it is still my policy to read everything available on the subject. I believe your book, *The Do's and Don'ts of Low Blood Sugar*, could be the most helpful thing a newly-diagnosed hypoglycemic could read. Its simplicity of style makes it an excellent first choice. How I wish it had been available to me in 1980.

Sincerely
Del City, Oklahoma

Dear Sirs,

I was thrilled to find Roberta Ruggiero's book, *The Do's and Don't of Low Blood Sugar*, and find out about your organization! My symptoms of hypoglycemia began in 1984 after the birth of my daughter. I knew there was nothing physically wrong with me so I thought I must have been going crazy. My mood changes were too frequent and drastic to be normal. I knew we could not afford a psychiatrist so I made an effort to cope with the problems on my own. It may have been a blessing in disguise, however, because I was not given tranquilizers and other drugs and therapy about which I've heard horror stories. My symptoms grew to include sudden hunger, weakness, dizziness, nervousness, fatigue, confusion, depression, etc. I suffered for four and a half years until finally a sympathetic doctor agreed to give me a glucose tolerance test. It was then that my suspicions were confirmed and I discovered that I was definitely hypoglycemic.

It has been almost a year since my GTT and I am finally beginning to feel that I am making progress. My doctor, sympathetic though he was, gave me the wrong advice about my diet telling me that I needed more sugar. As a result I spent about five months eating the wrong things, and my symptoms got much worse instead of better. A friend recognized what was happening to me and put me on the right track. I am doing much better now, but am still not as well as I would like to be.

That is the reason I was so glad to find Mrs. Ruggiero's book. I was beginning to lose ground and get depressed about my condition again, feeling that it was a never-ending battle. The book was a tremendous lift to my spirits and renewed my courage to keep up the pace on the road to recovery. I wish that every person who has hypoglycemia or is suffering the symptoms and doesn't know the cause could read this book. It is a great support!

Thank you so much for such a helpful book and for letting me share my story with you, though I'm sure you've heard it hundreds of times from others! Thank you for all you are doing to help others with hypoglycemia!

Yours truly,
Selma, North Carolina

Dear Mrs. Ruggiero:

I read your book recently *The Do's and Don'ts of Low Blood Sugar*. I wish I had found it before I did all my technical reading. The book made me cry. It also made me feel as if I was being hugged and comforted by a dear friend. You wrote so well about all the things I've been trying to explain to my family, as well as to my doctor.

Sincerely,
Kew Garden Hills, New York

Dear Roberta,

Thank you so much for your call. I can't tell you how honored I felt. Since I got over the shock that my condition was "nutritional" and not "mental," I always felt that there was something I should be doing so that others would not needlessly have to go through what I went through. You took that step and I hope that I can contribute to help spread the word!

Sincerely,
Topeka, Kansas

Dear Dr. Ruggiero,

"My name is Kate and I am a hypoglycemic. I would like to share my story. I am 18 years old, and I was recently diagnosed with the condition about three months ago. Up until then, the doctors didn't know what was wrong with me. When I was 14, I suffered three concussions (from soccer) and ever since then I've had a non-stop headache. They wrote it off as a post concussive syndrome, but little did they know that it was really all from my low blood sugar. I've had a non-stop headache since November 2, 1997. I had other symptoms that related to the symptoms of hypoglycemia. The doctors put me on every medication you can think of, ranging from anti-depressants to anti-seizure medication. I never saw any change, nothing made the pain stop, only certain things made it worse (stress). Throughout the whole four years I was never depressed though, it was strictly for the use of stopping the headache, which it never did. Hypoglycemia is in my family, but I never knew I had it, until I gave up soda for lent this year, 2002, and when I had a small little piece of candy, my headache tripled. So then I asked my doctor what was wrong and he had no clue, he said I might have an allergy to sugar, and so I asked him how we find out, and then I proceeded with the five-hour glucose testing. It was a real shock when the tests came back positive for hypoglycemia. If I didn't stop the soda, I never would have figured it out.

The doctors always threw medicine at me and never once thought to check my blood. From that day on I started seeing a nutritionist and my health has dramatically changed. For the first time in four and a half years I actually felt like I had hope and that I knew I was going to get better. I've been on an amino acid drink, which has helped me so much, and I'm currently trying to get off my medication. I've seen such a difference, that I wish the doctors would have figured it out back then."

Sincerely,
Kate

⚶ Chapter 2

MY PERSONAL EXPERIENCES

There was no turning back. After years of trying to hide my deepest secret, I was now sharing it with what seemed to be the world. Tallahassee's "Capitol News" quoted me verbatim on May 9, 1978: It stated that Roberta Ruggiero, a former shock treatment patient from Cooper City, called the therapy "barbaric" saying she would "rather die than go through electric shock again."

The trail from private mental patient to public notoriety started out rather innocently. After my first child was born in 1961, I went into a deep depression. I couldn't stop crying. I had heard of postpartum depression, but mine was a deluge of tears that had no end. My family physician kept assuring me that my reaction was normal, and that it would go away. When it didn't, he introduced me to my first tranquilizer—Valium.

Then the headaches started. The pain was there in the morning when I woke up, and persisted through my waking hours, and sometimes through the night. The pounding got so intense it felt as though my heart was actually throbbing inside my head. I was then given pills to reduce the pain.

I began having difficulty sleeping at night. Trying to get up in the morning was even more of a task. I became tired and weak. Cooking and cleaning the house, which I had always enjoyed, became a dreaded chore. I began to skip breakfast, hardly eat lunch and just nibble at dinner, if I had the energy to cook.

In 1963, I gave birth to my second child. All of my pre-vious symptoms were compounded by dizzy spells and blurred vision. My nerves, needless to say, were hopelessly frazzled. My hands and feet were constantly cold to the point of feeling frostbitten. Even with medication, my symptoms got progressively worse. My doctor put me in the hospital for a multitude of tests: laboratory, x-rays, spinal taps and electroencephalogram. All the tests came out negative. There was nothing physically wrong with me. I began to think beyond a doubt that I was going crazy. I withdrew into a shell, avoiding contact with my family and friends because I was too embarrassed and ashamed to face them.

It was at this point that my doctor recommended psychotherapy. I spent several months with the first psychiatrist. He thought that perhaps the strain of getting married at an early age (18) and having two children 16 months apart, were the major contributing factors to my illness.

Maybe a "contributing factor," but not THE reason. When the psychiatrist put me on heavy doses of anti-depressants, I went to psychiatrist number two. It was a repeat performance.

My pain and symptoms were being drowned with strong medication. I was given pills to calm me down, pills to help me sleep and pills to relieve pain. That was the order of the day. But since medication and therapy were not enough to relieve the symptoms, much less stabilize them, a third psychiatrist suggested electroconvulsive shock therapy, (ECT) known simply as shock treatments! By this time, I was desperate and would have tried anything. The year was 1969, and in addition to all of my physical and emotional pain, I began to feel guilty about what I was putting my husband through. I agreed to go away and have what I believed was the "cure"—my last hope.

I was wrong. I had not anticipated that my hospital room would have bars on the windows and doors. I didn't know that my clothing, wedding ring and "Miraculous Medal" would be taken away. And even more frightening were the screams, stares and glassy eyes of the patients who had already received treatments. I'll never forget the cot and its leather straps that bound my hands and feet, the electrodes that were put on my temples, and the rubber gag inserted in my mouth. The memories haunt me to this day.

After my first treatment, while I still had some faculties intact, I begged to go home, or at least speak to my husband. If he knew what I was going through, he would stop them. They said no. I had signed the papers for a series of electric shock treatments, and that's what I was going to get.

I had eight treatments in eleven days. The results were horrifying. I am thankful I don't remember all of them. I do remember feeling like I was in a state of limbo. My mind was functioning, but not in coordination with the rest of my body. Despair, shame, guilt and thoughts of suicide remained. Approximately ten months later, I reluctantly agreed to another series of treatments, but this time on an out-patient basis. It was at the end of this series, that I swore I would rather die than ever be subjected to electric shock treatments again. The physical pain was nothing compared to the feelings of isolation, embarrassment and humiliation they caused.

With no solution in sight, we took the advice of our family physician who suggested that a change of scenery or a move to another state might offer some relief. It would be like a fresh start. Therefore, when my husband had an opportunity to move to South Florida, we didn't hesitate.

Our move was exciting. I began to feel a little better. The pain in my head began to go away. Just having the sun shine every day seemed to promise a future where none had existed for so long. Then, suddenly, it happened again. This time, though, a new symptom assailed me. I began having fainting spells. I agreed to go for one last medical consultation. Dr. Arthur Ecoff, an osteopathic physician, examined me, reviewed my records and suggested a glucose tolerance test. I had never had this test before and was skeptical that a diagnosis could be reached. At this point, I would have settled for any diagnosis!

The GTT was taken and I was told I had a severe case of functional hypoglycemia. I was ecstatic! At last, I had a diagnosis, a name and a cure! But, to both my bewilderment and surprise, instead of a bottle of pills, injections or vitamins, I was given a DIET! Good-bye Yankee Doodles, Devil Dogs, hot fudge sundaes and apple pie. Hello chicken, fish, fresh vegetables, whole grains and fruits. I thought, "This is going to be a cinch."

Unfortunately, what I hoped would be an "overnight" remedy turned out to take several years of sorting through a mass of confusing and complicated information. Due to the unfamiliarity with the stages of recuperation, the controversy surrounding its treatment, and non-acceptance from many in the medical community, I found myself with the feeling of being the only person in the world suffering from this baffling disease.

Eventually, success did come, but alleviating my symptoms was a long and slow process. It would have been quicker if only I had understood the importance of individualizing my diet, the necessity for vitamins and exercise, and the role a positive attitude plays in the healing process. Above all, if there were other hypoglycemics to lend support and encouragement, the road back to health would not have been so rocky. Faith, patience, determination and the boundless love of my family were the cornerstones to my recovery.

Consequently, I didn't hesitate for a moment when I came across an article in <u>The Miami Herald</u> appealing to anyone who had experienced devastating effects of electric shock treatments. A committee for patients' rights was lobbying in Tallahassee and, after listening to my story, was eager to have me testify before the state legislature on behalf of mental patients. My hope was to convince the lawmakers to put severe restrictions on the use of ECT and, better yet, give the glucose tolerance test before its administration.

Little did I know that my life would never be the same. My story appeared in newspapers and on radio stations. I was immediately inundated with phone calls and mail from all over the state.

Letters, like the following, became all too familiar.

"Please send information. I had undiagnosed hypo-glycemia for 23 years, and during that time, I ran the whole gamut—depression, weight gain, weight loss, anxiety, psy-chiatric therapy and institutionalization—until the proper diagnosis was reached. The glucose tolerance test revealed that I had a blood sugar level of 35! Since that time, I am like a new person. I follow the proper diet, enjoy life and have no apprehension about blacking out without notice."

"I was ecstatic to see your article. My case was diag-nosed approximately four months ago by my chiropractor. My internist had written me off as either psychotic or a hypochondriac, or both."

This feedback was the inspiration for my decision to start speaking to both hypoglycemics and members of our community.

When I couldn't handle the flood of letters and phone calls, and when I realized I needed medical and professional guidance, the idea to form a support group became a reality.

And so, the formation of The Hypoglycemia Research Foundation, Inc., became official on June 6, 1980 and renamed The Hypoglycemia Support Foundation, Inc. on December 13, 1991. I am proud to say that I believe that no other organization has accomplished so much with so little.

23

When I say "little," I refer to practically no money, secretarial services, office equipment, supplies, private phone or office space. How did we survive? Through positive people, positive thoughts, endless hours of hard work, dedication and prayer—plenty of prayers.

For seventeen years, from 1980 to 1997, the HSF held monthly meetings. We had medical or professional speakers share their knowledge of hypoglycemia, whether it was from a medical, nutritional, psychological or holistic point of view. We participated in health fairs and seminars while I personally brought the message about hypoglycemia to local organizations, schools and hospitals.

In 1984, I was proud and honored to be coordinator of a research project studying the correlation between diet and behavior in juvenile delinquents. It was under the direction of Stephen J. Schoenthaler, Ph.D., a professor of criminal justice at California State University, Stanislaus. With the help and guidance of Dr. Douglas M. Baird, Dr. Lorna Walker, and Nutritional Biochemist, Jay Foster, the study was conducted at The Starting Place in Hollywood, Florida. The participants were 35 juvenile delinquents willing to find out if there might be a nutritional and physical cause to their behavior.

We tested them physically, psychologically, nutritionally, and chemically. The results, though not conclusive due to lack of a placebo control group, are published in the book *Nutrition and Brain Function* (Craiger Press, Basle, Switzerland, 1987) Future studies using control groups and other scientific criteria are absolutely necessary in this area.

In 1988, I wrote the first edition of *The Do's and Don'ts of Low Blood Sugar: An Everyday Guide To Hypoglycemia.* It was the core of all that I had learned since finally being diagnosed. I wanted to share it in the hope of sparing other hypoglycemics from the pain and suffering I went through.

In 1993, a revised edition of my book came out with two additional chapters. "Letters From Our Mailbag" was a hit with our readers. Hypoglycemics, sharing their experiences, convinced my readers that they were not alone and there was indeed help at hand.

For the last five years I have kept a low profile with the HSF. I needed time to find out exactly what role my organization should play, and what course of action I must take. During this time of re-assessment, I took a leap of faith and launched the HSF's first website, www.hypoglycemia.org. What a journey it has been. I've seen our visitor numbers climb to almost 1,000,000 as of this writing, over 5500 have responded to our hypoglycemia/diabetes survey, and e-mails and requests for information have come from 25 countries!

Take a look at what an impact we are having!

- We are guiding families of hypoglycemic children in the city of Kuwait.
- We are providing hope to teens afflicted with low blood sugar in Marshall, Missouri.
- We are supplying libraries in India with our books and tapes to aid mothers dealing with the frustration of hypoglycemic babies.
- Businessmen in the Philippines are improving their stamina and focus through the application of our information.
- We are lecturing to medical students, encouraging them to recognize and accept hypoglycemia.

Now, this book is in its fourth printing with a revised edition and a new title. It was written with the same hope of sparking your enthusiasm and planting the seeds of determination, strength and persistence. You need it all in order to learn every single thing about controlling hypoglycemia before it controls you!

⚬⟨ Chapter 3

DEFINITIONS OF HYPOGLYCEMIA

I've read and re-read the definition of hypoglycemia at least a hundred times. I've been asked repeatedly, what is hypoglycemia, and, in turn, have asked the leading authorities in the field of preventive and nutritional medicine. Their answers, although similar, are varied. Some are more technical than others. One thing is for certain—the definition of hypoglycemia can be as diversified and complex as the condition itself, or as simple and easy as some of the steps to control it.

In simple layman's language, hypoglycemia is the body's inability to properly handle the large amounts of sugar that the average American consumes today. It's an overload of sugar, alcohol, caffeine, tobacco and stress.

In medical terms, hypoglycemia is defined in relation to its cause. Functional hypoglycemia, the kind we are addressing here, is the over-secretion of insulin by the pancreas in response to a rapid rise in blood sugar or "glucose."

All carbohydrates (vegetables, fruits and grains, as well as simple table sugar), are broken down into simple sugars by the process of digestion. This sugar enters the bloodstream as glucose and our level of blood sugar rises. The pancreas then secretes a hormone known as insulin into the blood in order to bring the glucose down to normal levels.

In hypoglycemia, the pancreas sends out too much insulin and the blood sugar plummets below the level necessary to maintain well-being.

Since all the cells of the body, especially the brain cells, use glucose for fuel, a blood glucose level that is too low starves the cells of needed fuel, causing both physical and emotional symptoms.

Some of the symptoms of hypoglycemia are:

Fatigue, insomnia, mental confusion, nervousness, mood swings, faintness, headaches, depression, phobias, heart palpitations, craving for sweets, cold hands and feet, forgetfulness, dizziness, blurred vision, inner trembling, outbursts of temper, sudden hunger, allergies and crying spells.

After reading a list like this, one can see why hypoglycemia can be misunderstood and easily misdiagnosed. Don't be alarmed if you read other books that I recommend and see that the list is, in fact, even longer. Don't be confused and frightened when you read other definitions that range from a paragraph to several pages in length.

For the beginner, it is important that you first recognize that most often hypoglycemia is the result of a diet high in sugar, alcohol, caffeine and tobacco.

Before going any further, look at your dietary habits and/or any addictive traits. Start adding up the sodas, coffee, cakes and cigarettes you consume in one day. Keep track of how many meals you miss. Are you under a tremendous amount of stress with your spouse, children, boss, etc. . . ? All of these circumstances can give birth to a case of low blood sugar that can plague you for the rest of your life. Don't take your body for granted. Neglect it, and you'll pay a high price. Take care of it, and low blood sugar becomes an inconvenience that you can manage by yourself.

"Please don't tell me I can never, ever eat a hot fudge sundae!"

Helena 2001

~ᗞᑕ Chapter 4

IS THERE A DOCTOR OUT THERE?

The phone rang and I didn't want to answer it. I was going to be late for an appointment 20 minutes away. Reluctantly, I picked up the receiver and a woman's voice said, "Is this The Hypoglycemia Support Foundation?"

"Yes. May I help you?" I asked. She proceeded to tell me her story. It was one that I had heard hundreds of times before, but the tone of her voice was more despondent.

Usually, I can listen attentively, but this time my mind was on my appointment. "Please give me your name and address, and I'll send you some literature."

But the frail voice continued to speak. "Please, please help me. I'm begging you—find me a doctor immediately. I'm anxious and depressed. I can't sleep at night and I can't get up in the morning. I have an incredible craving for sweets. I read an article on hypoglycemia and believe that could be my problem. When I asked my present physician to give me a glucose tolerance test, he refused. He prescribed Valium. Please, before I get hooked on tranquilizers, I want to see a doctor who will listen to me."

I shuddered, and my heart sank. An overwhelming feeling of helplessness set in. I forgot about my appointment and listened to the tortured voice of a person in distress. I wondered to myself, as I had many times before, how many more stories like this one will I have to hear? When will hypoglycemia be accepted as a genuine and serious illness? My own experience and the experience of thousands of others demonstrate that hypoglycemia is real. It does exist. When will the medical profession take it seriously?

In 1980, when I formed the HSF, I wrote to about 50 local physicians looking for help and guidance. I was desperately seeking to arrange places to send the numerous patients who kept asking me where to go for treatment. No one responded. Discouraged and disillusioned, I decided to move beyond my local sphere of influence and contact physicians around the country who knew about hypoglycemia. Astonishingly, a number of them answered.

Emanuel Cheraskin, M.D., D.M.D., Harvey M. Ross, M.D., Jeffrey Bland, Ph.D., E. Marshall Goldberg, M.D.,

Carlton Fredericks, Ph.D. and Robert S. Mendelsohn, M.D., all responded, offering encouragement, support, guidance and hope. Although I was optimistic that I would hear from them, I think deep down inside I was surprised. Probably, because I knew the recent history of hypoglycemia. In the late 1960s and early 1970s, hypoglycemia was written up in a large number of lay publications. The disease suddenly became trendy. It was used as a way to explain some of the worst ills of humanity with little or no scientific backing, and a number of people proclaimed themselves to be hypoglycemics without bothering to consult a doctor or get a glucose tolerance test. The backlash in the medical establishment was swift. In 1949, the American Medical Association (AMA) awarded Dr. Seale Harris its highest honor for the research that led to the discovery of hypoglycemia. After the flood of quackery and self-diagnosis began, the AMA, in 1973, did a 180 degree turn and labeled hypoglycemia a "non-disease."

Don't let this discourage you. There are doctors out there. As the HSF started to gain recognition, acceptance and credibility, doctors from all fields of medicine volunteered their services. From general practitioners in the medical field to osteopaths, chiropractors, nutritionists, and dietitians, they all came. They lectured at our meetings, held seminars, wrote articles and served on our board of directors.

So, don't give up so easily. Take your time, have a positive attitude and follow the HSF's simple guidelines in your search for that special "healer."

Do.......... choose a physician carefully but preferably NOT during an emergency situation.

Do.......... ask for physician referrals from friends, neighbors, family, business associates, hospitals and organizations.

Do.......... read the chapter in this book on the glucose tolerance test, then call the office of someone you are considering and ask the following questions:

a. Do you treat hypoglycemia?

b. How do you test for it?

c. If you administer the glucose tolerance test, how long does it take and how much does it cost?

d. Do you provide nutritional counseling?

e. What is your consultation fee?

f. Are you available by phone if I need to reach you?

g. Will you have time to answer any questions I may have?

h. If I am having financial problems, will you take payments or will you accept my insurance? (ask only if applicable)

Do.......... have someone go with you on your first visit. Sometimes, the first visit is an emotional one and you may be nervous or apprehensive. Consequently, questions and/or answers may be misinterpreted or misunderstood. Having a second party along usually helps.

Do.......... bring a written list of symptoms, past medical records and personal recollections relating to your present problems. The importance of your past history and the sequence of events leading up to your present condition, cannot be overemphasized.

Do.......... bring in a diet/symptom diary (example in back of book). It should include a list of everything you have eaten, including any medication you may have taken in the previous five to seven days. Try to list the time eaten and any symptoms or reactions following consumption. This is important and can be a useful tool for the physician in diagnosing hypoglycemia. However, if you are physically and emotionally unable to do it, DO NOT PANIC—a diagnosis can still be made without it.

Do.......... bring in your list of questions. Ask them one at a time and make sure you understand the answer before going on to the next.

35

Do.......... tell the physician about any medication you may be taking at the time. Certain medications cannot be tolerated by hypoglycemics.

Do.......... write down instructions of any kind, or take along a tape recorder.

Do.......... discuss in detail your feelings or concerns, not just your symptoms. If you have fears you are not expressing, your treatment will be longer, more difficult and far more expensive.

Do.......... be specific and to the point. The more prepared you are, the better equipped the doctor will be to make a proper diagnosis.

Do.......... find out if your physician is associated with a hospital in case of an emergency.

Do.......... discuss costs and insurance information. Insurance companies differ on their policies and willingness to pay for various tests and procedures. Is your doctor willing to work out a payment arrangement and/or accept whatever the insurance company pays?

Do.......... get a second opinion, especially if you are not completely satisfied with the first physician.

Do.......... check the office procedures and staff. Do they overbook? Are they friendly? Are they helpful? The last thing you need is a doctor too busy to listen or makes you feel uncomfortable.

Do.......... choose a competent, caring, and trustworthy physician who respects your individuality. The doctor-patient relationship is crucial. If your doctor doesn't have your complete confidence or isn't meeting your special needs, then it's definitely time to change.

Do.......... notify the physician's office, preferably in writing, if you are upset with the conduct or services of either the physician or the staff.

Do.......... discuss a complete prevention program. You need to know how to avoid future health problems, not just how to eliminate the ones you now have. Your current problems are not the only issues that need to be addressed.

Do.......... be leery of alternative or new treatment that promises or claims to be a cure-all.

Do.......... carry a Health Emergency Card if you're experiencing many LBS symptoms; especially if you've recently blacked-out or fainted. You can keep your card in your purse, car or briefcase — any place that can be seen in case of emergency. To order a Health Emergency Card, please check the back of the book for details.

CRRGDO

Don't...... call your physician after listening or reading an article on hypoglycemia and DEMAND a glucose tolerance test. Instead, take this information, and a list of your symptoms and the reasons why you feel the test is necessary. Make an appointment to see your physician and present him with all the information. If he appears inattentive or cannot give you a seemingly justifiable reason why you should not have the test, look for another physician.

Don't...... stay with a physician you cannot communicate with or feel confident about. It will only complicate existing problems.

Don't...... call your physician unnecessarily. If your questions can wait, write them down and save them for the next visit. The physician will likely have more time then to give you a better explanation.

Don't...... wait to call your physician if you're in pain, your symptoms are persistent, or last several days.

Don't...... continue to be a patient of any physician who just listens for a few minutes and says your symptoms "are all in your head." If you are given a prescription for Valium, get a second opinion as soon as possible.

Don't...... withhold any medical history out of fear or embarrassment. It is necessary for a proper diagnosis.

Don't...... seek the advice of a physician and then not follow the instructions issued to you. It's a waste of time and money.

Don't...... run from one doctor to another. Give each one at least two to four visits to help you.

Don't...... avoid going to a physician. If your symptoms persist after you've put yourself on a hypo-glycemic diet, seek medical advice.

Don't...... avoid a physician because you lack insurance or money. Ask a family member or friend for financial assistance. You can't afford not to. If it is hypoglycemia, the faster you are diagnosed and treated, the sooner you'll recover.

Don't...... demand to be unnecessarily hospitalized.

Don't...... hesitate to speak up—ask questions. If you're too timid or embarrassed to communicate with your doctor, then he/she won't be able to adequately meet your needs.

Don't...... compare your program or progress with someone else's. Each person's emotional, physical and spiritual make up is unique. A competent physician will tailor a program to fit your individual needs.

Don't...... forget, there ARE many caring, sensitive, trustworthy physicians out there. If at first you don't succeed in finding one—try, try again!

⁓ℂ Chapter 5

THE IMPORTANCE OF INDIVIDUALIZING YOUR DIET

One of the HSF members called to tell me she was feeling terrible, particularly after eating breakfast. She started to shake, her stomach was nauseous and she felt jittery throughout the morning. She didn't understand why her symptoms were getting worse even though she was staying on a strict diet—no sugar, white flour, caffeine, alcohol or tobacco.

I suggested that we go over her diet but she emphatically said, "It can't be my diet. I eat only what my doctor told me to eat and what the books I read suggested." However, upon my insistence, she started to give me an account of her daily intake of food. First thing every morning, she drank an eight-ounce glass of orange juice. Even though the book she read said to take four ounces, she figured eight should be twice as good.

I didn't let her continue any further. From my own personal experiences, there is no way I can handle orange juice on an empty stomach first thing in the morning. An 8-ounce glass of orange juice, although it is "natural," contains six teaspoons of sugar. For me and many hypoglycemics that I have spoken to, orange juice causes the same reaction as a strong cup of black coffee. The results are the shakes, butterflies in the stomach and an overall feeling of wanting to "jump out of your skin."

At first, it was difficult for this hypoglycemic to understand that if she had this "nervous attack" every morning after eating the same breakfast she should begin to question her diet; not continue to abide by it when she suffered adverse symptoms. We are individuals and thus must tailor every diet to our own bodies when a given diet proves troublesome.

As I mentioned before, there are many books on hypoglycemia. If you've read some of them, by now you're aware that many disagree on what type of diet to follow. It's indeed confusing if you read one book and it tells you to eat a high protein/low carbohydrate diet, while another book says to consume low protein/high carbohydrate foods. Where does that leave you, the confused and bewildered hypoglycemic?

First of all, I am sure that each author has enough confirmation and evidence that his or her diet is successful. Most likely, they all are. Probably, this is due to the fact that the big offenders (sugar, white flour, alcohol, caffeine and tobacco) are eliminated and six small meals are consumed instead.

But the key to a successful diet lies in its "individualization." Each one of us is different. Each one of us is biochemically unique. Therefore, every diet must be tailor-made to meet our individual nutritional requirements.

The list of foods your physician gives you or the list you may read in your favorite book on hypoglycemia, even the suggested food list in the back of this book, are basic guidelines. **Variations come with time and patience, trial and error.** Don't be afraid to listen to your body. It will send you signals when it cannot tolerate a food.

So, basically stick to the suggestions in the following do's and don'ts, and hopefully, with just a few adjustments during your course of treatment, a new and healthier you will gradually appear.

Do.......... Do keep a daily account of everything you eat for one week to ten days. In one column, list every bit of food, drink and medication that you take and at what time. In the second column, list your symptoms and the time at which you experience them. Very often you will see a cor-relation between what you have consumed and your symptoms. When you do, eliminate those foods or drinks that you notice are contributing to your behavior and note the difference. DO NOT STOP MEDICATION. If you believe that your medication may be contributing to your symptoms, contact your physician. A diet diary is your personal blueprint: a clear overall view of what you are eating, digesting and assimilating. It can be the first indicator that something is wrong and, perhaps, a very inexpensive way of correcting a very simple problem.

Do.......... start eliminating the "biggies"—those foods, drinks and chemicals that cause the most problems: sugar, white flour, alcohol, caffeine and tobacco.

Do.......... be extremely careful when and how you elimi-nate the offending substances. Only YOU, with the guidance of a health care professional, can decide. Some patients choose to go at a steady pace. If you drink ten cups of coffee a day, grad-ually reduce consumption over a period of days or weeks. The same is true for food or tobacco. If you are heavily addicted to all of the afore-mentioned, particularly alcohol, then withdrawal should not be undertaken unless you are under the care of a physician.

Do.......... replace offending foods immediately with good, wholesome, nutritious food and snacks as close to their natural state as possible. Lean meats, poultry (without the skin), whole grains, vegetables and allowable fruits are recommended. We want to prevent deprivation from setting in, especially the "poor me, I have nothing to eat" attitude. There is plenty to eat.

Do.......... eat six small meals a day or three meals with snacks in between. Remember not to overeat.

Do.......... drink plenty of water. Most physicians say eight glasses of water a day is best.

Do.......... be aware that when you start on a hypogly-cemic diet, you might experience migrating aches, pain in your muscles and/or joints, headaches or extreme fatigue. This is normal when eliminating refined foods. Call your physician if they persist.

Do.......... be prepared to keep your blood sugar stabilized at all times, whether at home, office, school or traveling. At home you should always have allowable foods ready in the refrigerator or cupboards. Always keep snacks in your car or where you work.

Do.......... package food in Tupperware or air-tight containers. Aladdin's insulated thermos jar is handy for cold food and snacks. Aladdin also sells wide-mouth insulated bottles for hot foods, like soups or cut up meat and vegetables. Packaged nuts, seeds, and cheese can be easily carried or stored in a purse or in jacket pockets. You can buy almost everything you need at a supermarket.

Do.......... rotate your foods. Eating the same foods over and over again for consecutive days can result in food sensitivities or allergies.

Do.......... read labels. Avoid ALL sugars—dextrose, fructose, glucose, lactose, maltose and sucrose. Read labels in health food stores too. Just because you buy something in a health food store, does not necessarily mean you can tolerate the ingredients.

Do.......... avoid artificial sweeteners, additives, preservatives and food coloring. Monosodium Glutomate

(MSG) is a big problem for many hypoglycemics —avoid it completely.

Do.......... watch your fruit consumption. If you are in the early or severe stage of hypoglycemia, you may not be able to eat any fruit. Some patients can eat just a small amount. Your diet diary will help guide you. Avoid dried fruits completely.

Do.......... be careful of the amount of "natural" foods or drinks you consume. Even though juices are natural, they contain high amounts of sugar. Whether or not the sugar you consume is natural, your body doesn't know the difference. Sugar is sugar, and your body will react to an excess of it.

Do.......... dilute your juices, using about 2/3 juice to 1/3 water. If that's still too strong for you, try 1/2 juice and 1/2 water. Drink small quantities or drink them after you have eaten something, especially if you find that taking them on an empty stomach causes you problems.

Do.......... be inventive. Introduce new, unprocessed foods that have no preservatives, additives or chemicals. Look especially for whole grains and vegetables.

Do.......... arrange food to look palatable.

Do.......... broil, bake or steam food.

Do.......... attend some natural cooking classes. You will be taught to reduce sugar, salt, saturated fats, cholesterol and allergenic foods from your diet and still enjoy eating. Call your local schools, libraries and health food stores, or scan the local papers to find out what is available in your area.

Do.......... understand the meaning of "enriched." It does not mean extra amounts of vitamins. It means a small amount of some of the vitamins that were processed out of the food have been replaced.

Do.......... have your family stick to some of the basic principles of your diet. The big NO's for a hypoglycemic (sugar, white flour, alcohol, tobacco and caffeine) are detrimental to anyone's health.

Do.......... change your attitude about what constitutes a snack. We tend to think of snacks in terms of goodies or sweet treats. A good snack can be a half-baked potato with broccoli, half-stuffed tomato with tuna fish, some steamed zucchini and onions on a half cup of brown rice, a chicken leg or a slice of turkey.

48

Do.......... seriously consider going to OA (Overeaters Anonymous) or AA (Alcoholics Anonymous). Many HSF members found these meetings to be extremely helpful in controlling their addictions to sugar and food in general.

Do.......... be aware of the fact that some medications contain caffeine. If you're having reactions to the following medications, bring this matter to the attention of your physician: Anacin, APC, Caffergot, Coricidin, Excedrin Fiorinal, Four-Way Cold Tablets and Darvon Compound, etc.

Do.......... weigh yourself every day. Be aware of weight gain and weight loss. This is vital information in maintaining good health.

Do.......... check into other areas if you don't make progress with dietary changes. Hypoglycemia has been linked to allergies, hyperactivity, schizophrenia, juvenile delinquency, learning disabilities and candida albicans. Read the books recommended in the appendix for additional information.

Do.......... invest in the *Low Blood Sugar Cookbook*, by Edward & Patricia Krimmell. It can be easily purchased at www.amazon.com

Do.......... start a library of cookbooks. They don't necessarily have to be for hypoglycemics. Many good books with no or low sugar recipes are available.

Do.......... try at least one new recipe a week. At the end of the year you'll have tasted 52 new dishes, thus, ensuring that you are not tied to eating the same dull fare. It will help you look forward to mealtime and you won't feel so limited with your diet.

Do.......... store your food properly to avoid contamination and spoilage resulting from bacteria and molds.

Do.......... wash your fruits and vegetables thoroughly to reduce or remove the amount of pesticide residue.

Do.......... be aware that chemical sensitivities can aggravate LBS and induce reactions in vulnerable people. Paints, pesticides, solvents, gas stoves, smoke, even perfumes and hairsprays can make some people sick.

Do.......... know the seriousness of smoking cigarettes, especially for the hypoglycemic. According to our past Surgeon General, C. Everett Koop, "It is clear that nicotine in cigarettes and other forms of tobacco makes them addicting in the same sense as heroin and cocaine."

Don't...... panic when you first hear about all the foods that you must eliminate from your diet. Keep repeating all the foods that you CAN eat—there are plenty.

Don't...... stay on a diet that is not supervised by a professional, whether it's a physician, a nutritionist, or a holistic health practitioner. It should be someone with a degree or some training in nutrition.

Don't...... forget that being PREPARED with meals and snacks is the key to a successful diet and a healthier you.

Don't...... be apprehensive about eating out. Many restaurants now have salad bars, making it much easier for the hypoglycemic (just be sure to use either oil and vinegar or lemon juice for dressing). Lean meat, fish, vegetables and salad can be ordered at almost any restaurant.

Don't...... skip breakfast. It's the most important meal of the day for a hypoglycemic.

Don't...... worry unnecessarily about weight gain or loss at the beginning of the diet. As long as it is not severe and you are being supervised by a health care professional, it's common to have a weight fluctuation when the body is experiencing dietary changes.

Don't...... compare your results or progress with anyone else's. Each body's metabolism is different.

Don't...... take over-the-counter drugs or diet pills unless you have discussed this with your physician. They can have an adverse effect on hypoglycemics.

Don't...... be obsessive about your diet. The CONSTANT focus on what you can and cannot eat will only instill more fear, stress and frustration.

✿C Chapter 6

GLUCOSE TOLERANCE TEST

So you think you may have hypoglycemia. You have all the symptoms. After discussing it with your physician, he agrees to give you a glucose tolerance test (GTT) to confirm the diagnosis. A test for three or four hours is requested when diabetes is suspected, but a six-hour glucose tolerance test is by far the most reliable method to detect low blood sugar. You should settle for nothing less.

The night before having the GTT, you will be asked to fast after your evening meal. You are to eat or drink nothing until the time of the test. When you arrive at the doctor's office or laboratory, still fasting, a tube of blood will be drawn and you will be asked to give a urine specimen.

Then, you will be given a very sweet beverage called "Glucola" to drink. This drink contains a measured amount of glucose. Your blood will be drawn in 30 minutes and once again in one hour after drinking the glucola. For each hour after that, you will give a blood sample until five or six hours have passed. A urine specimen is given each time your blood is drawn.

Each tube of blood and each urine specimen is tested to determine the amount of glucose it contains. When the report is sent to your doctor, he or she will be looking for glucose levels above or below normal at any time during the test.

During the test, you may start to sweat, get dizzy, weak or confused. If you experience these symptoms to the point of being extremely uncomfortable, or you get a headache or your heart starts beating quickly, ask the doctor's staff to draw your blood IMMEDIATELY. Any of those symptoms could be a sign that your blood sugar has dropped to a very low level, and you want your doctor to have the lowest readings possible. If you wait until the next hour, your blood sugar may go back up and your doctor will be deprived of information essential to making an accurate diagnosis.

The interpretation of the GTT is just as critical as its administration. Because individuals have different body chemistries, what is a normal drop or curve for one patient may not be for the next. Do not forget that laboratory tests are only aids to a diagnosis, not the final word.

Remember, too, that the test is not for everyone. Children and the elderly, in particular, frequently require another method. Dr. Carlton Fredericks, author of *Carlton Fredericks' New Low Blood Sugar and You*, frequently used "therapeutic diagnosis." "This means putting the suspected hypoglycemic on the correct diet and watching the response. If, after a month or two, the symptoms are significantly reduced, the diagnosis has been established." This procedure can be a less expensive, more convenient and less stressful method for diagnosing low blood sugar.

In conclusion, if you've read the basic facts about the glucose tolerance test, discussed it thoroughly with your physician and both of you have decided that this test is necessary, read the do's and don'ts first.

Do.......... understand the purpose, procedure and instructions BEFORE you have the glucose tolerance test administered.

Do.......... make sure the test is scheduled first thing in the morning (no later than 9:00 a.m.).

Do.......... ask the doctor or nurse to repeat instructions if you do not fully comprehend what you are or are not supposed to do.

Do.......... tell your physician, if he/she is not aware, if you are on any kind of medication. Some medications may affect blood sugar levels.

Do.......... use the "therapeutic diagnosis" for children and the elderly.

Do.......... bring someone with you, especially if you are experiencing severe symptoms.

Do.......... bring a book, newspaper or magazine of your choice to help overcome the boredom. Sitting five or six hours is not something we're used to doing. Consequently, restlessness often sets in.

Do.......... have a pen and paper available to write down all the symptoms you are experiencing and at what time.

Do.......... bring a sweater with you. Very often, a patient will experience chills during the GTT. It is best to be prepared.

Do.......... arrange beforehand to have someone pick you up if you go alone for the test. Sometimes, afterward, you may be weak and driving could be difficult.

Do.......... bring a snack to eat immediately after the test, particularly if you must go home alone. Eating some protein (nuts, seeds, meat, cheese, etc.) will bring your blood sugar up, allowing you to feel good enough to get home safely.

Do.......... set up an appointment before you leave to go over your test results.

Don't...... demand a glucose tolerance test. It is not always necessary.

Don't...... accept a three or four hour glucose tolerance test for diagnosing hypoglycemia.

Don't...... demand to have the glucose tolerance test if you have a fever or infection. It could affect the test results.

Don't...... be shortchanged. Go over the results of your GTT with your physician thoroughly.

Don't...... be fooled by the terms "borderline" or "mild" in the case of hypoglycemia. Too often when patients hear these terms, they don't take their

57

diagnosis seriously. This could eventually cause grave consequences.

Don't...... dismiss the fact that you may still be hypo-glycemic even if the GTT doesn't confirm the diagnosis. Laboratory tests are not always con-clusive. The conditions under which the test is given may alter the results. The best rule to follow is: don't treat the results of the test, treat the symptoms.

⚚ Chapter 7

EDUCATION A MUST

Let's pretend it's your husband's birthday and you want to surprise him with his favorite meal; veal cordon bleu. It has been a while since you last made it. You have all the ingredients but just don't remember how to make the stuffing. Now you did have an excellent cookbook—in fact, that's where you got the instructions the first time. You'd better find it.

Your anniversary arrives and you can't believe your eyes. You're overwhelmed by the gift your family bought you—the food processor you always wanted. You just can't wait for a special occasion or holiday so you can show off your culinary skills. However, after you open up the box and see all the pieces, you wonder, "Will I ever learn to use them all? Does this food processor come with a book? It must have directions."

It doesn't matter whether you're whipping up a gourmet meal, fixing a car, planting a vegetable garden or sitting down to learn how to operate a new computer, you need all the information and complete instructions BEFORE you begin.

You need to take the same kind of care with hypoglycemia. Read every book you can get your hands on that discusses the subject. Some will contradict each other, others will be confusing and difficult to understand. No matter, you will learn something from each of them. Remember, too, you don't have to read the thick books all at once, you can read them a chapter, a page or a few paragraphs at a time. Just do it consistently. Learning takes time, energy, patience, and commitment. Don't give up. Just do it gradually and consistently. Don't say you don't have the time or ability, you do.

I wish I could personally introduce you to two HSF members who have taken "don't" out of their vocabulary. First there's Walter. Speak of determination! Here is a man who traveled for more than two and a half hours—EACH WAY —to attend our meetings. Walter was not sure how many miles he traveled because he had to drive very slowly. Otherwise, his 1970 Ford pickup truck might not made it. When I asked him why he made the trip every month, he didn't hesitate to respond, "Because I want to get better. I believe the meetings help me just like Weight Watchers helped my wife. Also, I have a lousy memory, so it's a reminder of what I have to do."

Then there's Hazel. I think she attended almost every meeting the HSF held.

I asked Hazel to share with you why she attended almost every meeting. "I was in terrible condition," she replied, "almost ready to commit suicide. In fact, at one point, I had a knife to my wrist. I threw it down and cried to my husband. . . he had to get me a doctor. I was confused, depressed, shaky. I was so angry because I couldn't do what I wanted to."

"I found a doctor in Beverly Hills. He took a glucose tolerance test but stopped it in the fourth hour because I was passing out. He was the first to tell me I was hypoglycemic but that I shouldn't worry. He recommended that I just eat candy, hard sour balls every hour, and go to see a psychiatrist. He also handed me the usual one-page diet. I locked myself in the house for a month. I didn't get off the couch. Then one day I read your article in The Miami Herald. Since the diet the doctor gave me wasn't working and I was desperate, I attended the first HSF meeting."

I asked Hazel what the meetings had done for her. "They gave me the courage to stay on the diet," she said. "When I missed a meeting, I found that I would slip off my diet. I also learn something new every time I attended, even if it was only one thing. Sometimes I think I'm well and can do it alone, and then realize that I need support. You not only learn from each other, but you realize you're not alone."

It's not so important what method you use. Books, tapes, lectures — they all give you the opportunity to learn, listen and share. Both Hazel and Walter can attest to this. I hope that one day you will, too.

Do.......... educate yourself about hypoglycemia. It is a MUST in order to control your symptoms and make the healing process as painless as possible. I cannot stress enough that KNOWLEDGE AND UNDERSTANDING OF THE CAUSES, EFFECTS AND TREATMENT OF THIS CONDITION ARE IMPERATIVE.

Do.......... start by getting a small library of books—at least three—by leading authorities in the field of hypoglycemia. (See the list of recommended books in the appendix). Then make it a habit to re-read them occasionally. You may find it more enlightening and informative on the second or third reading.

Do.......... buy yourself a marker and, while reading, mark any sentence that you feel applies to you and that you want to remember for future reference. Perhaps there is a sentence or paragraph that upsets or confuses you, mark it and discuss it with your physician or a health care professional working with hypoglycemic patients. Usually, just a simple explanation clears the way to a healthier you.

Do.......... realize that NO book will supply ALL the answers. Some, in fact, will be contradictory. Do take the information you feel you understand and apply it to yourself individually.

Do.......... consider tapes. For those who abhor the idea of reading, or who cannot read, for whatever reason, there are tapes available on hypoglycemia. These, fortunately, can be played any where at any time that's convenient.

Do.......... you suspect that your child, husband, wife, co-worker or friend is hypoglycemic? Are they reluctant to read any books or listen to tapes? If so, get some brief articles on the subject and leave them around the house, office or in their room. The bathroom mirror or the refrigerator door is an excellent place to start.

Do.......... attend meetings, lectures and seminars NOT ONLY on hypoglycemia, but on any health-related subject. Since most illnesses, such as heart disease, cancer, arthritis, diabetes, schizophrenia, are now being linked to improper diet, you are likely to get nutritional advice at any meeting you attend.

Do.......... your homework. Find out about such meetings through your local newspaper, radio stations, TV (some early morning shows will list meetings), cable television, library, physician, health food store, hospital and Chamber of Commerce.

Do.......... contact your hospital, library or school. If no health-related meetings are scheduled, particularly on hypoglycemia, request that they consider the subject. This will alert your area to the needs and wants of the community.

Do.......... write down the date and time of the meeting, put it on your calendar, make arrangements with baby sitters, drivers and family members. Explain how important your attendance is at these meetings and prepare to swap services so that feelings of guilt or imposition do not arise.

Do.......... take your spouse or an immediate family member with you. It will take some of the pressure off the relationship if they understand the causes of your symptoms.

Do.......... use this time to share. If at first you're uncomfortable, try again at another meeting. Sharing experiences often relieves tension and fear, two emotions that can impede progress.

Do.......... have questions ready. Most meetings are followed by a question and answer period. Take advantage of this opportunity to gain invaluable information.

Do.......... consider attending OA (Overeaters Anonymous) or AA (Alcoholics Anonymous). Even though they may not provide nutritional information per se, they will help you deal with addictive behavior. As hypoglycemics, we are addicted to certain foods—white sugar and white flour are the biggest culprits.

Do.......... form your own support group, if nothing else is available. Two, three or four people gathered together, sharing and offering hope, can be the best medicine any doctor could prescribe.

Don't...... pass up any opportunity to help make the journey back to health through information obtained at meetings, lectures and seminars.

Don't...... give repeated excuses such as: I can't drive at night, it's too far, I can't get a baby sitter, etc. Perhaps the first time these excuses might be valid, but you should prepare for the next time.

Don't...... surround the speaker before or after the program and try to get a diagnosis. Not only is it unfair to the speaker, but it can do you harm. It is impossible to make a diagnosis without a complete medical history and list of symptoms.

⁓ℭ Chapter 8

ARE VITAMINS NECESSARY?

I n 1984, I decided to leave my business partner, Marge, to give more time to the HSF. Our business was at the peak of its success. She and my husband were appalled that I would bow out, but I knew it was something I had to do.

When we were at the lawyer's office to sign the final papers, she seemed unusually upset. Her speech became slurred, she couldn't concentrate and she appeared lethargic. Her problems got worse and I became more alarmed. Although Marge was only in her mid-30s, she had suffered a stroke two years earlier, and I was worried that it might be happening again.

Questions poured out of me—"Marge, why are you so nervous? Are you angry? Did you take a tranquilizer? Did you have a drink before you came here?" After throwing dozens of questions at her, I discovered the real culprit. Marge suffered from Premenstrual Syndrome (PMS) and was taking vitamin B-6 because she had heard that it could help control her symptoms. She bought a bottle of vitamins and, without knowing the proper dosage, began popping them into her mouth like gumdrops. She was overdosing on her vitamins.

In her effort to relieve pain, Marge, like so many of us, didn't bother to ask questions. She didn't take into consideration the proper dosage, the risk of allergic reactions, and the possible side-effects of combining medications with other vitamins or food. So desperate in her attempt to find a fast and easy cure, she did not even consider the potentially harmful consequences. Marge's poor judgment and inadequate information left her with an apprehensive and fearful decision about ever taking vitamins again.

This story is not unique. Situations similar to Marge's occur much too often. They breed controversy. Therefore, for every published article you read recommending the use of vitamins, be assured you will find a contrary view that discards them as nonessential.

The American Medical Association and the American Dietetic Association claim that if one consumes food from the four basic food groups and obtains the Recommended Daily Allowance (RDA), then the use of vitamins is unnecessary. But, who always eats a balanced diet?

Both associations feel that most Americans can and should get all the nutrients they need to be healthy from food rather than supplements. I don't think any advocate of supplements would disagree. However, what most Americans CAN and SHOULD do are not necessarily what they ARE doing. In fact, due to certain circumstances which I'll soon discuss, most Americans are nutritionally STARVED!! How? Read on.

Many of you have asked the question, "Do I need vitamins?" only to be told to just eat balanced meals. According to television commercials, one would tend to believe that a balanced meal consists of a hamburger, french fries and a coke.

Most of us are on a merry-go-round. Not the one for fun, but a merry-go-round of life; one that leaves us too busy and tired to get off and catch our breath. Many of us are faced with job and financial insecurities, family and marital difficulties, sickness, casualties and even death. It's no wonder that little time is spent on learning about the effects of poor dietary habits. Consequently, the diet of the 21st Century often consists of fast foods, heavily fried, sugar-laden, canned, frozen or leftover meals. Here lies just one of the many reasons why most people do not get sufficient amounts of vitamins and minerals in their diets.

69

Let's take into consideration some of the other vitamin "robbers:"
air pollution
alcohol
caffeine (coffee and soft drinks)
food additives, preservatives and food coloring
food processing
medication (Diet pills, diuretics, laxatives)
menstruation
soil depletion
stress (mental or physical)
tobacco

Examine the above list and review your dietary habits to see if you are eating a variety of fresh foods. Does your list include fresh vegetables, lean meats, whole grains and fiber?

What cooking methods do you use? Do you broil, steam or bake? How do you store your foods, particularly fruits and vegetables? All of these factors play a role in determining the amount of vitamins and minerals one actually consumes.

So, now, where does all this leave the hypoglycemic? Every book I've read on hypoglycemia and every doctor I've worked with over the past 26 years recommends vitamin and mineral supplementation for hypoglycemics. Vitamin therapy in conjunction with proper diet, exercise and reduction of stress has a positive, supportive and therapeutic effect in the treatment of hypoglycemia.

However, before you swallow that capsule, pill or liquid, read the following do's and don'ts:

Do.......... be informed and seek professional advice before starting any long-range, extensive vitamin therapy.

Do.......... check out your local osteopathic physician, chiropractor, nutritionist or dietician if your present medical physician cannot supply you with this information. The aforementioned professionals are more likely to incorporate vitamin therapy as an adjunct to the healing process. Make sure the person you consult is licensed. Also try to speak to someone who has already used the practitioner's services and thus can give you insight as to their ethics, reputation and success.

Do.......... inform your physician if you are taking vitamins, especially if you are under that doctor's care for a particular disease or condition and/or are taking medication. Some vitamins and medications don't mix well and destroy or weaken each other's effects.

Do.......... check out the reputation of the vitamin store where you purchase your vitamins, especially if you're purchasing them without professional guidance. Ask questions about the vitamin or vitamins you are considering, such as: What is the vitamin supposed to do? Should you expect side effects? How long should you take the vitamin? Is there any literature available on the product?

Do.......... make absolutely certain that the salesperson's first interest is in your health and safety and not in making a sale. If the salesperson has a forceful approach, leave and look for another store.

Do.......... check the price of vitamins. Once you know what you have to take, shop around for the best price.

Do.......... double check the dosage you are to take, the time of day it should be taken and any other instructions.

Do.......... check vitamin interaction. Avoid taking vitamins with alcohol or medication.

Do.......... make sure the vitamins you purchase haven't been tampered with. Check that the label hasn't been broken.

Do.......... throw out any bottle whose label you are unable to read, either because it's faded or damaged.

Do.......... make sure the vitamins you purchase are not made with any fillers. There should be NO sugar, corn, wheat or starch.

Do.......... keep all vitamins in a cool place and keep them out of reach of children.

Do.......... take vitamins with meals, unless otherwise directed.

Do.......... remember to take your vitamins with you on vacation and business trips. This is usually a time of increasing stress, strong activity and change of diet, and therefore not a good time to discontinue any program you are on.

Do.......... STOP taking vitamins if you suspect them to be a cause of nausea, diarrhea, constipation, etc. You can introduce them at a later date, always one at a time. If there is still a reaction, STOP immediately.

Don't...... take vitamins indiscriminately! They can be just as harmful as medicine if taken without knowledge and caution.

Don't...... double up on vitamins, thinking that if one is good, then two must be better. This is not necessarily so. Too many vitamins can be just as harmful as too much medication.

Don't...... follow anyone else's vitamin program. You should have your own. REMEMBER: everyone is a unique individual with different needs. This individuality includes vitamin therapy of any kind, and therefore should be supervised by a professional.

Don't...... run out and get the "vitamin of the month." Educate yourself before experimenting.

Don't...... stop any medication abruptly because you start taking vitamins. Seek professional advice about combining the two.

Don't...... stock up on vitamins. Your needs may change. Buy vitamins as you need them.

74

～ C Chapter 9

HOW IMPORTANT IS EXERCISE?

H ave you ever made a list of things you wanted to accomplish? I don't mean just a to-do list for next Monday, but a laundry list of goals that you want to achieve in your lifetime. I've written at least a dozen of these lists. At one point, I was adding one lifetime goal every day. I soon felt overwhelmed and frustrated because I knew I could not complete them all. I had to stop because I felt oppressed just thinking about the three dozen things I HAD to achieve in my lifetime.

No matter how ambitious my lists became, exercise was hardly ever on them, or if it was, it was near the bottom. This is probably because I was never athletic. I was born in Brooklyn, New York, in a six-family tenement house with no lawn or backyard. The nearest park was miles away. Skating was the only sports activity I participated in. There were plenty of schoolyards, sidewalks and empty streets around, but that was the extent of my exercise as a child.

Some of my friends are still shocked when they hear I don't know how to ride a bicycle.

My attitude about exercise changed many years ago when I attended a health seminar at which Covert Bailey, author of *Fit or Fat?* was one of the program speakers. After hearing him talk on the importance of exercise, I was totally convinced that I had to add exercise to my existing hypoglycemic regimen. I was controlling my hypoglycemia through diet and vitamins, but I knew I could fine-tune my physical condition, improve it, tone and strengthen my body if I incorporated specific daily physical activity into my life.

Now, you mention it and I've tried it—aerobics, yoga, stationary bike, mini-trampoline, jogging, swimming, jumping rope—I've done them all. It was not until May 19, 1986, that I started walking. At first, I walked just a quarter of a mile, then a half mile and then, within a month, I was walking two miles a day, four to six days a week. This was a milestone for me. Walking has since given me more energy and flexibility, relaxes me better than any tranquilizer, suppresses my appetite and rejuvenates me both emotionally and physically.

Hopefully, it won't take you years of procrastination before you incorporate an exercise program into your daily life. Perhaps you can't do it now; you may be experiencing too many hypoglycemic symptoms. However, try making that list of goals as soon as you can. Just don't put exercise at the bottom.

The do's and don'ts of exercise are as follows:

Do.......... get your physician's approval before starting any exercise program. Most likely you will be given a complete physical, including an EKG and stress test, depending on your age, medical history and present symptoms.

Do.......... seek alternative advice from a health and fitness expert if you choose to ignore the above.

Do.......... choose your exercise carefully. The best exercises for hypoglycemics are: walking, swimming, dancing, jumping rope or riding a stationary bike. Walking is the most effective exercise, in addition to being the most compatible with normal daily activities. Depending on the stage of illness you are in, walking is the least stressful exercise for a hypoglycemic. Running, jogging or strenuous aerobic classes should be held off until most of the physical symptoms are controlled.

Do.......... seek a non-strenuous aerobic exercise program as an alternative to or in conjunction with walking.

Do.......... make sure the class you choose has an instructor who is qualified through both training and experience.

Do.......... check for information about time and date of classes, particularly free ones that are advertised in newspapers or community news bulletins.

Do.......... find a private instructor who will give you personalized lessons if you are afraid to start your exercise program with a group. Use the instructor until you are ready to join a group, which should be in a relatively short period of time. Yes, a personal instructor is expensive, but you will only be using that person for a short time. It is well worth the added expense.

Do.......... stretch before doing any exercise.

Do.......... switch exercises occasionally. It avoids over-development of certain muscles.

Do.......... a slower version of an exercise to warm up or cool down.

78

Do.......... be properly fitted with the appropriate clothing, depending on the exercise and climate. Avoid anything too heavy and tight in summer and too thin and flimsy in winter.

Do.......... be properly fitted with shoes.

Do.......... check the floor or exercise area for anything hazardous. For example, if you choose to skip rope, make sure the floor is not slippery or wet.

Do.......... consider a therapist who does body manipulation or deep muscle massage (osteopath, chiropractor or massage therapist) if sore muscles, malignment of your body or torn ligaments prevent you from exercising. A massage therapist can produce better results than medication, a frequent foe of hypoglycemia.

Do.......... consider a "buddy system" if you need support or motivation to start a program. Grab your spouse or friend and begin together to reap the benefits of an alternative method to achieve good health and fitness.

Do.......... use every opportunity to increase your activity. Examples: Park in the far corner of the parking lot (during the day only) when shopping or going to work and walk those extra steps; pass up the elevator and take the stairs; and use a stationary bike while watching television.

Don't...... set high expectations. If you are leading a sedentary life, it would be unrealistic to walk one or two miles at first. You have to build up your stamina SLOWLY.

Don't...... think you can lose weight quickly by pushing yourself to exercise too frequently. You'll only hinder any program you are on.

Don't...... push yourself to exercise if you are too fatigued or are experiencing severe symptoms of hypo-glycemia.

Don't...... exercise on a full stomach or exercise on a completely empty stomach, either. Eat an hour before exercising to avoid a blood sugar drop. Remember: don't eat a big meal; you should instead be eating several small meals throughout the day.

Don't...... walk in hot sun, severe cold, or other undesirable conditions, such as rain, snow or strong winds.

Don't...... wear tight clothes, especially zippers or buttons if you're in an exercise class where you must lie on your back or stomach.

Don't...... buy inexpensive shoes In the long run they'll cost you dearly .

Don't...... compare your progress with someone else's. Each body is unique; therefore, length and success of each program is different.

Don't...... give up too quickly on any program where you don't see results. Be PATIENT some programs don't result in a visible improvement for weeks or months.

"I don't want to die. Can I die from hypoglycemia?"

Dave 1996

≈ℭ Chapter 10

THE BENEFITS OF THERAPY

Y ou found a doctor, took the glucose tolerance test and it's confirmed—you have reactive or functional hypoglycemia. You begin to read about your condition, follow a diet, start on a vitamin program and, to your surprise, have enough energy to begin exercising. Even though your pace and timing may be slow at first, it's something you've never done before.

The severity of your symptoms starts to disappear. You're able to function—go to work, attend school and/or handle home situations. You should be thrilled. But you're not. You're full of fear, guilt and anger, and the loneliness is unbearable. You cry frequently. Discussing your feelings with family and friends only makes matters worse. Too often you hear remarks such as, "You should be grateful you only have hypoglycemia. Luckily, it's not cancer or a disease you could die from."

No, hypoglycemia will not kill you but, according to Dr. Harvey Ross, in his book, *Hypoglycemia, The Disease Your*

Doctor Won't Treat, it's a disease that will make you wish you were dead.

Is there anything you can do? Yes. Maybe it's time to consider psychotherapy.

Although the attitude about seeking therapy is somewhat better, there are still many myths associated with this approach. At one time, it was considered only for people who were totally out of control, or for the severely mentally and emotionally ill. Consequently, people were afraid to open up, to share their inner most thoughts and secrets. If they did, perhaps some therapist would label them as "crazy," take control of their lives, put them away or do something else equally as bad.

Some people believe that nobody else ever has these feelings so therefore, no one else understands what they are going through. They fear exposing themselves and leaving themselves vulnerable.

Fortunately, for many, this thinking has changed. Today, it's not "Are you going for therapy?" but "Who are you going to?" Therapy, and there are many different types to choose from, has reached a level of acceptance. Some are seeking counseling to prevent minor problems from becoming major ones, some are seeking direction as to where they want to go in life, while others are trying to reclaim their lives entirely.

If you feel mentally and emotionally lost, if the physical problems of hypoglycemia are too much to bear, if you're ready to open up and discover the "real" you, and if you're ready to deal with all of those emotional issues in your life that you have put on the back burner, then therapy may be for you. Therapy does for the mind what diet and exercise do for the body. It's an investment that will pay dividends for the rest of your life.

Do.......... have a physical evaluation and any necessary tests to rule out a physical disease or condition before beginning extensive therapy.

Do.......... consider seeking therapy when the feeling of "I can't cope" arises. Waiting until an emergency or crisis, may force you into impulsive, short-sighted decisions.

Do.......... look at therapy as a way to explore and discover yourself, especially if you are depressed and despondent.

Do.......... look into the different types of therapy available from psychiatrists, psychotherapists, social workers, hypnotherapists and the clergy. Use the same criteria outlined in Chapter three on choosing a physician.

Do.......... be aware that therapists DO NOT have the answers to your problems. One of the things a therapist can do is to help patients trust in their own thoughts and feelings, explore them and follow through in what they really WANT to do and not what they think they SHOULD do.

Do.......... search carefully for a competent therapist. Talk to friends. You'll be surprised to find that many are seeking their advice and guidance. Then, without prying into their problems, ask questions: What do they like or dislike about their therapist? Was he or she helpful, and in what way? What beneficial qualities did the therapist possess?

Do.......... evaluate the therapist, just as the therapist evaluates you.

Do.......... find out:

1. where the therapist was trained,
2. the therapist's attitudes and points of view,
3. how the therapist plans to help you.

Do.......... see if you can develop a rapport with the therapist. A trusting relationship between patient and therapist is crucial to the healing process. Ask yourself, "Do I like this person? Am I comfortable? Can I relate freely?"

Do.......... realize that the spouse or significant other of the hypoglycemic is under tremendous stress and often needs therapy themselves. According to Dr. Hewitt Bruce, a psychologist in West Palm Beach, Florida, that I have had the privilege of working with both personally and professionally, "No one understands the stress of the spouse or significant other. I believe that more than the patient, the spouse or significant other needs a lot of emotional support. They're not considered sick. They're not considered ill. They're healthy. They are strong. For the spouse it's sometimes a job to care for the hypoglycemic, yet there's no pay, no bonuses, no pat on the back and sometimes no appreciation. So many are suffering emotionally themselves and therapy of any kind could be of great value."

Do.......... consider group therapy. Many hospitals have programs to help patients deal more effectively with their emotions.

Do.......... remember that in any kind of group therapy confidentiality is crucial. It is the only way TRUST can be established, thus ensuring necessary success.

Do.......... check out the new holistic health centers for alternative methods if orthodox treatment fails to help. But be cautious of cultists or quacks.

Do.......... check your local papers for support groups that deal with mental or emotional problems.

Do.......... be fully aware of all the drastic effects of ECT (Electroconvulsive Shock Therapy), especially memory loss. If you're a computer expert, pharmacist, mathematician, etc., even a slight memory loss can deleteriously affect your life, endangering your livelihood.

Do.......... get a second opinion if ECT is prescribed or even suggested. Ask about other forms of treatment and give consideration to there use. Remember—educating yourself about any treatment is crucial.

Do.......... realize that the end of therapy is, not only as important, but, sometimes more important than its beginning.

Do.......... read *When To Say Goodbye To Your Therapist,* by Catherine Johnson, Ph.D. It will help you determine whether you are treading water in therapy or whether you can strike out on your own.

⊘⧭⧬⧭⊘

Don't...... look upon therapy as a sign of weakness. Remember, it takes more strength and courage to admit that you have problems and need help than to ignore the situation.

Don't...... continue therapy if you feel you're not accomplishing something, even if it's only a small change or a little insight at each session.

Don't...... blame yourself if:
1. you feel extremely uncomfortable with the therapist,
2. you feel intimidated,
3. the therapist seems judgmental.

Don't...... go back if the above feelings persist. Don't give up and keep on looking.

Don't...... stop therapy too suddenly. Give yourself sufficient time for treatment to become effective and gradually, as you grow more confident, wean yourself slowly from the therapist.

Don't...... become so dependent on your therapist that you won't make a move without his/her direction.

Don't...... panic if your therapist terminates the relationship. Sometimes, because of a sudden transfer, career change or ill health, your therapist must change his/her venue. Your present therapist should however assure you that they will put you in touch someone just as professional and caring.

⚞ Chapter 11

POSITIVE ATTITUDE:
IT WON'T WORK WITHOUT IT

Wheneen I first began dreaming about forming the HSF, I was constantly plagued by my own insecurity. I wasn't a doctor, a nurse, or even a college graduate. What made me presume that I could start an organization to help sick people? I didn't have an answer to that question. Yet, there I was trying to form an advocacy group for a disease whose existence medical doctors didn't recognize, whose name most people couldn't pronounce and even fewer could understand.

What was worse, it wasn't even a disease with a lot of drama. It wasn't associated with children or death, and it wasn't even considered life-threatening. As a result, the media covered it only occasionally. How, I kept asking myself, can I make people realize that low blood sugar is real, that the food/mood connection is real, that people can suffer severe emotional problems because their diet has thrown their body's chemistry out of balance?

I despaired of ever starting an organization which could have the kind of impact that would make people pay attention, especially because I didn't have any fancy titles or letters, such as Ph.D., after my name. Then, I started to read and re-read. My attitude started to brighten. I found out that many other lay people had contributed to the medical field. People such as Nathan Pritikin, founder of The Pritikin Longevity Center; Jean Nidetch, founder of Weight Watchers; and Barbara Gordon, who wrote *I'm Dancing As Fast As I Can* and told the world about the dangers of Valium in a way no medical textbook ever could.

I knew there was hope. I began to visualize my dreams for the HSF. I wanted support groups in every state, a hypoglycemia hotline, visual aids in schools to warn children about junk foods, and proper testing for people being admitted to state mental hospitals, prisons, juvenile detention centers and jails.

What kept me going, and still does, is enthusiasm, positive thinking, positive people, faith, trust and a firm belief that this is a job that I have to do. It wasn't simple, not at first and not now. But it is getting easier, and it can get easier for you too. The tools, the people, the places, are all there to help. You just have to be ready to receive them. If you can't cope any longer with depression, guilt, fear and denial that a hypoglycemic confronts every day, then do something to replace these negative feelings with positive, uplifting ones.

Start by opening your hearts and minds to Dr. Wayne Dyer's books on positive thinking; Dr. Norman Vincent Peale's on enthusiasm; Norman Cousins' on laughter; and Dr. Leo Buscaglia's on love. Mix them all together and let them be the cement that holds all the other necessary building blocks of good mental health together.

Do......... have a support group of people who won't step on your dreams, who will encourage you, and support you emotionally when you're feeling good AND when you're not.

Do......... have a good selection of positive reading material or tapes. Replacing bad feelings with positive ones is an arduous task. These tapes and books will help do the job when you need an ego boost and no one is around to give it to you.

Do......... put up positive quotes around your house or office. They will lift your spirits and, as a bonus, they'll help lift the spirits of those around you.

Do.......... use positive words. Say "I can," "I will," and "I shall." Use only positive phrases, such as "This diet is working. It is the best I've ever had." Repeat these affirmations throughout the day.

Do.......... take 15 to 30 minutes every day for meditation or prayer. It refreshes the spirit.

Do.......... see happy, uplifting and funny movies. Laughter is terrific medicine.

Do.......... try yoga. It lowers blood pressure and relieves stress.

Do.......... consider listening to inspirational music, whether it's Bach or the Beatles.

Do.......... occasionally treat yourself to something special, whether it is lunch with a friend, a day on the golf course, a manicure, a massage, or a walk in the park.

Do.......... put your goals in writing. Read them over each day to instill a sense of purpose and direction. This way, you can check your progress and see that your goals are continuing to be met.

Do.......... stop procrastinating. If you've put off writing that letter, calling a friend, cleaning out your desk or closet or starting a project, do it NOW.

Do.......... seriously consider a job change if you've said more than once—"I hate my job." Look into other fields than the one in which you are presently engaged. Learn what the requirements for employment are and take the necessary steps to get the training that's needed for this transition.

Do.......... seek intellectual stimulation. It enhances the body's immune function and helps increase your vitality. Try reading and/or attending workshops and seminars on varied topics— health, beauty, environment, business, etc. Broaden your horizons and increase your mental acuity.

Do.......... try to find a teenager, or use your own children, to do extra work around the house or run errands. Remember, you don't have to be Super Mom or Dad! You don't have to do it all—or do it all alone. Share the load of responsibilities. You'll be surprised at how well someone else can do these tasks!

Do·········· volunteer work. Many times in helping others, we end up helping ourselves.

⌒⌒⌒

Don't······ surround yourself with people who have nothing but negative things to say about the world and what you are trying to achieve. They'll only make reaching your goals more difficult.

Don't······ use the words "can't" and "won't " Negative words produce negative thinking.

Don't······ watch depressing movies or listen to sad music when you feel depressed It will only make you feel worse.

Don't······ see problems as obstacles. See them as a way to learn and grow.

Don't······ worry so much about the future or dwell on the past that you miss out on "living" today.

∼✺ Chapter 12

HEALTH AND BEAUTY:
YOU CAN'T HAVE ONE
WITHOUT THE OTHER

I'd like to mention a special someone who, because of her faith and trust in my work and reputation, chose me to assist her for a once-in-lifetime assignment. Carolyn Stein, president of Carolyn Stein & Associates, is a media image consultant. Through her workshops, seminars and keynote speaking engagements, she teaches people how they can create an image of success and develop top communication skills.

Every four years, for the past twenty-four years, Carolyn has been given a very special assignment—media image consultant to the Republican National Convention. For the past three conventions, I went as her assistant.

Carolyn and I met through the Florida's Speaker's Association, of which she and I were both directors. She soon became aware of my previous work in the beauty industry and that I now devoted most of my time and energy to the HSF. It didn't take much persuasion though, for

Carolyn to convince me to go along as her assistant on what was indeed going to be the ultimate "special assignment."

The Republican Conventions I took part in with Carolyn were held in August 1992, in Houston, Texas; August 1996, in San Diego, California; and August 2000, in Philadelphia, Pennsylvania.

Looking back, it's mind boggling to think I had the honor and pleasure of meeting four Presidents and First Ladies, including the Vice President, the Presidents' Cabinet members, Senators, and Representatives from all over the country. Added to that list were stars such as Tanya Tucker, Wynonna Judd, Gerald McRaney, the Gatlin Brothers, Roger Staubach, and Lee Greenwood. At the last convention in Philadelphia, the Rock, Bo Derek, and Rick Schroeder headed the star-studded list.

But it wasn't just our country's leaders or the star-studded list of celebrities that I found so intriguing. It was the participation of today's youth, a large number of very young individuals who weren't home "trying to find themselves" or just hanging out with friends. They were here in force, with a statement. They wanted to get involved.

Equally impressive were the senior citizens that turned out. Rather than sitting home in front of the television, complain about what is happening in the world, they too took a stand for what they believed and joined in.

So, these two generations along with everyone else, shed their jeans for overalls, for dresses, slacks, shirts, and ties. They put on the outfit to suit the occasion and dove in.

This feeling is beyond politics. It's the very essence of being involved in life and your surroundings. When you commit yourself to life, health and beauty follows. You'll accept nothing less.

I have so many memories and stories of this time. However, one stands out. One evening I was standing in a corridor and I heard a group coming towards me, they were Secret Service Agents, and President Ronald Reagan was with them. Before I knew it, President Reagan was standing in front of me and I was shaking his hand and talking to him! Don't ask me what I said and what he replied. I don't remember, I was so awe-struck. But I do remember his presence, his stature, and his demeanor—a giant in history.

Here I was, Roberta Ruggiero. Whether I was meeting leaders of the world, applying make-up, re-doing a hairstyle or straightening out a jacket or tie, I was taking part in American history. It was phenomenal!

However, I kept asking myself, "Why me? Why had I been chosen for this assignment?" Particularly, since most of my work is in the health field. Well, ask a question, and if you stop long enough to listen, there's always an answer.

I have repeatedly said health and beauty go hand and hand. You can't have one without the other. So, there I was, right smack in the middle of proving my theory correct. Everyone with whom I came in contact had a "glow."

I saw skin, hair and nails — all the picture of health. I felt energy, vitality and excitement emanating from everyone. It was evident that the health, beauty, honor, and pride of each individual present would be a contributing factor to the success of these conventions.

The experiences I have had in Houston, San Diego and Philadelphia confirm what I have been saying all along— diet ALONE does not control low blood sugar symptoms. Besides individualizing your diet to meet your particular needs, you must look into a vitamin program, exercise regimen, and stress reduction techniques. You need to maintain a positive attitude, associate with positive people, and look to meditation and prayer for an inner source of peace and fulfillment.

And last, but not at all least, you must look at your physical beauty. It's all there ready to shine. Enhance it a bit with a new hairstyle. Give yourself a facial or a manicure and pedicure. Be daring. Spruce up some old outfits with scarves, pins, fashion earrings or belts. Buy that wild tie you've always wanted or the boots you felt too embarrassed to wear.

Health and beauty walk hand in hand. It's so important to look it, feel it, and be it. Combine the two and you never know where it will take you. It took me to three conventions!

Do.......... remember this chapter is to spur you on; to start the wheels going and your enthusiasm flowing. It is just a prerequisite for you to look further into whatever area sparks your interest.

Do.......... set a special "beauty" time aside each week just for you. A time to focus and enjoy the art of taking care of your personal needs. A time to pamper yourself from head to toe. You've been worried about what you put INSIDE your body; it's now time to take care of your outward appearance.

Do.......... buy some books or magazines on beauty. They will give you more in depth explanations of the areas I've highlighted in the following do's and don'ts. If money is a problem— spend some time at your local library—they usually have the most up-to-date beauty publications.

Do.......... start your beauty session with a long, relaxing bath. Light some candles, burn some incense and put on some soft music. Let this be some private time just for you.

Do.......... try some aromatherapy in the bath. According to aromatherapist, Gerri Whidden, "Aromatherapy is the use of natural plant essence to produce health, beauty and well being. A few drops of the essences called Essential Oils can be used for inhalation in a bath or as massage oil to stimulate, sedate or uplift."

Do.......... try a loofah scrub brush, and use it after soaking in the bath. Wet the loofah with soap and, using a circular motion, massage your skin. It'll remove dry, dead cells and make your skin feel soft as silk. The loofah scrubs are inexpensive and can be purchased at your local beauty supply or drug store.

Do.......... give yourself a manicure after a bath or shower. Your cuticles will be soft and easier to push back. First, file your nails GENTLY with an emery board. Take your time to acquire the shape you desire. Make sure that you don't file too much into the nail corners. This weakens the nail.

Do.......... push back your cuticles GENTLY and do not use a nail file. Use an orange wood stick. It is even better to cushion the end of the stick with a little cotton.This will allow you to put pressure on the cuticle yet not cause any pain or injury.

Do.......... invest in a pumice stone especially designed for the tip of the nail. This will smooth the nail and give you a better looking manicure. Again, this is inexpensive and can be purchased at your local beauty supply store or drug store.

Do.......... trim excess cuticles and hangnails CAREFULLY with a cuticle nipper.

Do.......... massage your hands with cream. Wipe off the cream that is on the nails. This can be done by using a cotton ended orange wood stick which has been dipped in polish remover. Go over the nail gently, and remove any excess cream or polish.

Do.......... apply a base coat. This is absolutely necessary for the nail polish to adhere to the nail. Otherwise, your polish will start to wear off immediately. Then apply two thin coats of your desired color of polish. WAIT as long as you can before applying a top coat. If all these coats of polish are put on without allowing them time to dry between coats, your polish will NEVER fully set.

Do.......... apply a soft new shade or try a wild romantic color to your nails, even if you've never done it before. I promise it'll perk you up!

Do.......... give yourself a pedicure using the same steps as above.

Do.......... treat yourself to a professional manicure and pedicure. Your birthday or anniversary is the perfect time to indulge yourself.

Do.......... treat yourself to a professional facial by a licensed aesthetician at least once or twice a year. In between, a minimum of once a month, give yourself a home facial.

Do.......... start by choosing the best facial products for you. It's very hard to recommend a product but, again, a licensed aesthetician would be able to help you decide what's best for your skin type and tone. If an aesthetician is not available in your area, go to a cosmetic counter at your nearest department store.

Do.......... start with a cleanser that will remove all residue as the first step of your facial.

Do.......... follow it with a deep pore cleanser. Remember to be very gentle with your skin. Don't pull or push it.

Do.......... use a gentle mask specially chosen for your skin type. Rinse thoroughly. The rinsing process is extremely important. Gently pat dry and use a protective day or night cream.

Do.......... remember that consistency is of the utmost importance. Continually starting and stopping any program on health or beauty is most deleterious to your body. It sends mixed signals and can cause undue stress.

Do.......... seriously consider a make-up session with a professional cosmetologist. It will enhance your appearance and do wonders for your morale.

Do.......... be aware that according to research, cosmetic allergies can also lead to hay fever and asthma. Discuss this with your physician if you feel this may apply to you.

Do.......... consider a hair removal process, either waxing or electrolysis, if excess facial or bikini hair a source of discomfort or embarrassment.

Do.......... consult a licensed aesthetician in your area for a professional evaluation.

Do.......... consider a professional massage. Massage Therapist, Judith McBride, R.N., L.M.T., says, "It is my experience that massage therapy is an excellent way to help nurture and heal others. I have found that by restoring balance through the physical being, the mental, emotional and spiritual self are positively influenced. As a Nurse Massage Therapist, I have effectively blended several disciplines to serve as a natural method for wellness by facilitating healthier lifestyle choices and illness/injury prevention."

Do.......... be aware that the benefits of Massage Therapy include: deep relaxation and stress reduction, relief in muscle tension and stiffness, increase in circulation of both blood and lymph fluids and an over-all increase in flexibility and coordination.

Do.......... consider a new hairstyle—sometimes a new look is a great image booster and morale energizer. However, remind your hairstylist that you want a hairstyle that is simple, uncomplicated and requires light maintenance.

Do.......... talk to your hairstylist about a permanent. This can add fullness, body and manageability to fly-away, baby-fine or coarse hair.

Do.......... consider cosmetic dentistry—bonding or veneer covering if the appearance of your teeth is causing you shame and embarrassment—or even if you just want to improve your appearance. Seek out professional advice from your local dentist.

Do.......... buy a new item for your wardrobe— a shirt, a blouse, a new tie. Be daring—buy and wear what you've always wanted to wear but were too afraid or ashamed to try. Do it—do it now!

Do.......... put sleep high on your priority list. It's extremely imperative to get a sufficient amount of sleep. It is during the sleep period that the healing process is accelerated.

Do.......... try stress reducing techniques when falling asleep is difficult—deep breathing, meditation, yoga, stretching, or a hot bath. Put on soft music, read a book—whatever kind relaxes your mind, have sex—only if consensual.

107

Don't...... sit in the sun and bake because you think a tan will make you look healthy. You'll pay a price— dry, wrinkled skin, plus an increased risk of developing skin cancer.

Don't...... pull, push, poke or squeeze your skin at any time, especially if you have a blemish on your face. You could cause permanent scarring or accelerate the stretching and aging of the outer layer of your skin.

Don't...... wear tight clothing, especially belts, shoes or pants. Avoid any unnecessary discomfort.

Don't...... underdress in winter or cold weather or over- dress on hot summer days. Again we want to avoid severe changes in body temperature.

Don't...... continue using any make-up or skin care product if you experience any allergic reactions. Consult an aesthetician or dermatologist for advice and direction.

Don't...... take too hot a bath or soak too long. It could leave you weak. If you're experiencing many hypoglycemia symptoms it is best not to take a bath unless someone else is at home with you in case an emergency arises.

Don't...... use a sauna, hot tub or jacuzzi unless you use precaution. Please follow posted instructions. If you are experiencing a host of symptoms do NOT use prior to consulting your physician.

Don't...... have hair removal done—whether waxing, electrolysis or even tweezing—during your menstrual cycle. The outer layer of the skin is very sensitive during this time and often contributes to more pain and sensitivity than usual. If you must tweeze eyebrows—try applying some baby Oragel first—it'll slightly numb the skin and help to lessen the pain. This is an excellent tip for teenagers having their eyebrows done for the first time.

Don't...... attempt a manicure or pedicure if you have difficult or fungus nails. See a licensed manicurist, pedicurist, or licensed podiatrist.

Don't...... think for a moment that all of the above do's and don'ts apply only or mostly to women. Today, many men are removing the barrier of "for women only" and enjoying and benefitting from the combination of health and beauty techniques. Be brave men—give some of this a try!

"I can't believe my three-year old was just
diagnosed as having hypoglycemia.
I can't stop blaming myself."

Natalie 1999

⚶ Chapter 13

CHILDREN & HYPOGLYCEMIA: AREA OF GROWING CONCERN

Since the HSF's website premiere in 1998, I received an alarming number of e-mails from parents, teenagers and teachers who openly shared their fears, frustrations, and concerns about hypoglycemia. I am including a few of the most notable here so you too can read what these children have been going through. Some of their names have been changed to protect their privacy.

Although their messages are similar, one from Sandra of Cumming, Georgia stands out. Dated October 25, 2000, it opened with this warm acknowledgement of the support we are providing and a request for more information. "Thank you so much for sharing your knowledge and providing a superb web site. There is an area, however, that I found extremely little information and education on and perhaps you can provide enlightenment for those in need. It's in regards to children and hypoglycemia.

"My ten-year-old daughter is intelligent, bouncy and happy most of the time. But over a period of several months, she began to experience significant mood swings, excessive grumpiness, lack of concentration, headaches, etc. Her teacher, my adult friends, and my family related her behavior to "a phase," a lack of sleep, or to the onset of puberty. I finally understood she had hypoglycemia while we were on vacation. One episode in particular was a telltale sign. She was having a major emotional breakdown, which was completely out of character and unsolicited, but within ten minutes of BEGINNING to eat, she turned into a person. Suddenly, the light bulb went off in my head! I am so grateful that I did not simply brush her complaints and symptoms as just life stress or her maturing process."

Sandra had already ordered my book—a good place to start since it is easy to read and understand even for someone as young as her daughter. I stressed the importance of keeping a diet/symptom diary and working with a healthcare professional knowledgeable in treating hypoglycemia and sympathetic to her daughter's needs. I suggested several other books, particularly, *Feed Your Kids Right* by the late Dr. Lenden Smith and *Is This Your Child? Discovering Unrecognized Allergies in Children and Adults* by Dr. Doris Rapp. Both of these authors, leading pediatricians, talk extensively about children, diet and behavior in these books. I also recommended *Food & Behavior: A Natural*

Connection by Dr. Barbara Reed Stitt and *Lick The Sugar Habit* by Dr. Nancy Appleton.

Sandra continued to keep me informed about her daughter's progress over the past year and a half, and she has provided insight into what it's like to be a parent struggling to deal with a child who has hypoglycemia. She sent me the following e-mail on March 17, 2002. No book or author on hypoglycemia could have worded it more poignantly, for this comes from the heart and soul of a mother.

"My daughter is doing very well. We are extremely grateful for discovering the root of her problems. There are children struggling physically, mentally and emotionally, and parents are not aware that their food intake is the cause. I grieve to think off all the children being misdiagnosed or medicated that are truly suffering from a blood sugar disorder. I personally believe that because America is addicted to carbohydrates and refined foods, there exists a huge mass of the population that suffers from intermittent or permanent blood sugar disorders. I encourage parents to modify their child's diet as the first line of action to correcting any physical or behavioral problems they see in their children. It may not be the only answer, but will most certainly have a positive affect."

Looking at this problem from an educator's perspective, Janet of Seattle, Washington, wrote, "I am a high school teacher and have a student diagnosed with hypoglycemia. I have a note from her mother asking that high protein snacks be allowed in the classroom to help treat her condition. However, she eats big bags of chips, drinks soda, and yesterday had a big cinnamon roll from the vending machine. She told me, "I need it because I don't feel good." Is this junk food snacking permissible or is it something I should alert her mother to? She has been absent quite a bit this semesters because she has not felt well?"

I commended Janet for her concern and for caring enough to seek a solution. And, of course, my response to her question about junk food snacking was—"No, protein snacks do not consist of bags of chips or a big cinnamon roll. This junk food is exactly what got your student in trouble in the first place."

Fifteen-year old Randy, from Topeka, Kansas, wrote, "I recently found out that I have hypoglycemia. A few days ago I was at school and I just passed out. I was dazed and after I got up, I couldn't see anything for at least fifteen minutes. Should I have more tests? Should I take vitamins? Please send me additional information. I'm just curious about what can happen."

Randy's curiosity is justified. What if he was just a few years older and driving a car when he passed out? What if he felt lightheaded and dizzy while crossing the street or at the top of a flight of stairs? The possible scenarios are endless and most frightening.

I told Randy that I didn't know why the doctor had not insisted on more testing. This was something he and his parents had to ask the physician personally. However, I did explain that reactive hypoglycemia is a result of improper diet, what you are or are not eating. Stress and lifestyle can also exacerbate it. This is the kind of hypoglycemia that the HSF addresses and it sounds like this is exactly Randy's problem. I questioned his eating habits. "Do you have a diet high in sugar? Do you skip meals?" I then recommended that he revisit our website and reread *How To Individualize Your Diet*. I also gave him a list of suggested reading material and told him he could call me if he needed to talk or wanted further direction.

So, where do we go from here? Not every child has hypoglycemia nor should all children be subjected to a glucose tolerance test. However, one in five children in the United States is overweight. That's six million American children! Yes, hereditary, lack of physical activity, and unhealthy eating habits are all contributing factors. But consider this: Americans consume over one hundred and eighty pounds of sugar per person per year! SUGAR and a high sugar diet are the biggest culprits in hypoglycemia. Soda, fruit juices, candy, ice cream and high sugar coated cereals are the norm for today's children. With preteens and teenagers, parents must also consider alcohol and tobacco experimentation. These two substances, when combined, can be very volatile.

If your child is experiencing any of the symptoms that Sandra's daughter, Janet's student, or Randy described, they too may be suffering from hypoglycemia.

A quick recap...mood swings, severe fatigue, insomnia, sudden outburst of temper, failing grades, sleeping in class, and fainting spells are all possible warning symptoms or signs.

The message is loud and clear. Parents, teachers, and community leaders must all band together to help our children. To understand and learn more about the food/mood connection, start with the following simple do's and don'ts.

Do......... open up lines of communication with your child concerning their food habits and possible associated signs & symptoms. Let them know also that wrong choices, even in diet, may produce negative consequences.

Do.......... EDUCATE yourselves! Parents, it is your responsibility to be educated in this correlation between diet and behavior. What your child eats and doesn't eat directly relates to how he thinks, feels, and acts.

Do.......... search the Internet, local library, bookstores and attend any seminar on this or related subjects. The more you know the better you will be to make an informed decision.

Do.......... work with a health care professional that is knowledgeable with hypoglycemia and sympathetic to your child's needs. Re-read the chapter, "How To Find a Physician."

Do.......... work with local schools, teachers, counselors and community leaders. Share the information in this chapter with all of them.

Do.......... cultivate an on-going relationship with your child's teacher concerning diet and behavior. Open, honest communication is crucial.

Do.......... review your child's dietary habits before administration of any medication, especially, Ritalin. Share your finding with his/her physician. Often a change in a high sugar diet will eliminate the need for such hyperactivity medications or minimize the dosage required.a few weeks or months of trying a diet change first could save years of unnecessary medication.

Do.......... monitor the amount of junk foods you child is eating. A parent said that his child hid candy wrappers all over the bedroom—under the beds, in his dresser draws, and pants pockets. This is a sure sign of a junk food/candy addict.

Do.......... evaluate your child's eating habits, keep a diet/symptom diary and eliminate the big offenders: sugar, caffeine, tobacco and alcohol. A good place to start is by reading the chapter "How To Individualize Your Diet."

Do.......... make shopping for food, planning meals, and cooking a family affair.

Do.......... read labels carefully. Eliminate any foods or drinks with a high sugar and caffeine content.

Do.......... opt for organically grown and pesticide-free products, especially if your child is known to have food allergies. You can even help children start their own vegetable garden. If you live in a city or an apartment, encourage an herb garden, which is smaller and much easier to keep.

Do.......... encourage your child/adolescent, or teenager to share any physical symptoms with you. Naturally, if you have a family physician, he/she should also be the first person that should be made aware of severe fatigue, insomnia, panic attacks, fainting spells, etc.

Do.......... realize the importance of carrying your Health Emergency Card with you (or your Child) at all times. This card is available from HSF; the order form is at the back of the book. This is especially crucial if anyone has a history of fainting spells. This card includes the emergency telephone number of parent or close relative/friend and physician. Most importantly, it explains that one is hypoglycemic, so paramedics or other health professionals can quickly administer the appropriate medical treatment.

Do.......... encourage your child to share any emotional symptoms with parent, physician, close adult, teacher or school counselor, especially depression and suicidal thoughts. If this is not possible, let him/her know that there are anonymous hot-lines available. Check your local yellow pages.

Do.......... eat breakfast. It is the most important meal of the day.

Do.......... be aware of the harmful dangers in water fasts or diet pills, especially if the latter is taken without a doctor's supervision.

Do.......... exercise. Take advantages of opportunities at work or school to join a sports team, take part in gymnastics. If this is not possible, walk or do yoga to relax, anything that gives you some exercise each day.

Do.......... forget the soda, go for bottled water. Each 12-ounce bottle of soda has 10 teaspoons full of SUGAR!!

Do.......... choose broiled or baked chicken and salads if you must opt for fast foods.

Do.......... experiment with high protein bars and shakes, especially if you skip meals. Be aware however, that many bars contain a high amount of sugar. You must read labels.

Don't...... ignore lack of self control, angry outbursts, hysteria, inability to handle changing or stressful situations. This applies to both adults and children.

Don't...... assume that children's junk food habits are something they will outgrow.

Don't...... assume that children understand the importance of good dietary habits. They learn from what they see and hear from other family members.

Don't...... forget to include a daily multi-vitamin/mineral as part of your child's daily regimen.

Don't...... put your child on any medication for behavior, particularly for Attention Deficit Disorder (ADD) or Attention Deficit Hyperactivity Disorder (ADHD) without talking to a healthcare provider, evaluating their eating habits, checking for food allergies and food sensitivities.

Don't...... STOP ANY MEDICATION WITHOUT THE ADVISE OF YOUR PHYSICIAN.

Don't...... tolerate any doctor who ignores your concerns or your child's symptoms.

Don't...... forget to be supportive and HUG your children. Let them know that their problems are important to you and that you will always be there to help.

Especially for teachers:

Do.......... have information about diet and behavior available for your students and parents including specific organizations, support groups, and toll free numbers.

Do.......... in-house educational programs that include students, parents, and teachers.

Do.......... evaluate the food, snacks and soda that is available to the children, whether in the school cafeteria or vending machines. Challenge their presence and lobby to have any offending food or drink product changed!! Involve other parents and teachers.

Do.......... be sympathetic if a child and his/her parent inform you that they have a blood sugar management problem and need to have a snack at certain times of the day. Please don't dismiss this request. A snack can be something as simple as a few almonds or a protein bar. This shouldn't disturb the class or other children. You could even use this as an excuse to explain proper diet and nutrition to children. No one, hypoglycemic or not, needs sugar and refined foods and junk food.

Do.......... get a written note from a health care professional if you suspect a child may be having a sugar management problem. Or request a parent conference and share what you know. They may be at their wits' end and this information could help them immensely.

"My doctor told me to just eat the candy bar
to raise my blood sugar.
I'd rather have gumdrops."

Suzanne 1998

⚜ Chapter 14

HYPOGLYCEMIA & ALCOHOLISM
IS THERE A CORRELATION?

Alcoholism. No one is immune to it. It doesn't discriminate on the basis of race, religion, gender, or socioeconomic status. Sadly enough, there are also no age barriers. Whether it is used as a chemical, drug or food, 23 million Americans are under its influence.

From the womb to the grave, alcohol's effect on the body can be devastating. Its physical and emotional effects can range from upsetting the metabolism and nutritional state of the body to increasing the risk of cancer, liver and heart disease, high blood pressure, and diabetes. It can cripple the emotions with low self-esteem, and promote feelings of isolation, rejection, loneliness, hopelessness, and fear.

There is an abundance of literature that indicates that alcohol consumption during pregnancy can put the unborn child at risk for numerous health problems. Even if the child appears unscathed by a pregnancy where alcohol was used, this "healthy" child still has a 30 percent chance of trying alcohol by the time they are nine years old!

Children, who make it through high school without experimenting with alcohol, may not resist the temptation though college. And along with the risk of alcoholism, consider these alarming statistics from the National Institute on Alcohol Abuse and Alcoholism, a division of the National Institutes of Health (NIH). "An estimated 1400 college students are killed every year in alcohol-related accidents, drinking by college students contributes to 500,000 injuries, and 70,000 cases of sexual assault or date rape. Also 400,000 students between 18 and 24 years old reported having unprotected sex as a result of drinking."

Information on alcoholism and treatment options is available just about everywhere—in newspapers, magazines, on the Internet. The problem is so pervasive and devastating that individuals, communities, and businesses have come together to try to combat and educate people about the disease. Three organizations—Business Against Drunk Drivers (BADD), Mothers Against Drunk Drivers (MADD), and Students Against Drunk Drivers (SADD)—are involved with educating the public about the deadly combination of drinking and driving and advocating for harsher laws for offenders. And of course, the most well known organization helping people cope with alcoholism is Alcoholics

Anonymous, which has been providing education and assistance for years.

It would seem that all the information we want about alcohol use/abuse is right at our fingertips. Unfortunately, most of this information fails to acknowledge the connection between hypoglycemia (low blood sugar) and alcoholism. Fortunately, I have managed to compile a small library of texts establishing a correlation between these conditions.

In *Dr. Atkins' New Diet Revolution*, Dr. Atkins writes, "Experience shows that, when an alcoholic succeeds in getting off alcohol, he usually substitutes sweets. This is because almost all alcoholics are hypoglycemic, and sugar provides the same temporary lift that alcohol once did."

Dr. Harvey M. Ross, in *Hypoglycemia: The Disease Your Doctor Won't Treat*, Dr. Ross states "What is most important is the plethora of doctors and counselors who ignore the results of the research that prove that the alcoholic has a blood sugar problem."

According to Dr. David Williams, author of *Hypoglycemia: The Deadly Roller Coaster*, "To combat alcohol and other drug abuse, abstinence, proper diet, nutritional supplementation, and education about abuse and hypoglycemia must be part of the program."

Dr. Joan Mathews Larson, author of *Seven Weeks To Sobriety:The Proven Program to Fight Alcoholism Through Nutrition*, has a phenomenal website: www.healthrecovery.com. Acquainting yourself with this incredible resource is a must! Both in her book and website, you will be introduced to Dr. Larson's Health Recovery Center and her in-depth explanation of hypoglycemia and its relationship to alcoholism.

The biggest contributor though to my education on the hypoglycemia-alcoholism connection has been Dr. Douglas M. Baird, Medical Director of the HSF. In our meetings and seminars, Dr. Baird has often reiterated, "I have never, ever seen an alcoholic who was not hypoglycemic. It just doesn't occur, it's the same problem."

Dr. Baird's interest in the treatment of alcoholism dates back to the late 1970's, when he became intrigued by the withdrawal symptoms that many times accompany the cessation of drinking—tremor, weakness, sweating, increased reflexes, gastric symptoms and seizures. In extreme cases people withdrawing from alcohol might even experience visual or auditory hallucinations. These symptoms, he said, often prevented alcoholics from quitting or caused them to replace alcohol with sugar, high carbohydrates, caffeine and/or tobacco (nicotine).

Working on the premise that alcoholism, like hypoglycemia,

was related to a faulty metabolism, Dr. Baird set out to design a program to meet the recovering alcoholic's needs. Preliminary physical and dietary evaluations are completed as well as blood and sugar testing. The chemical imbalance created by years of poor dietary habits is then brought back into alignment with implementation of an individualized diet and vitamin therapy. Dr Baird has been using his program for over 20 years and has a 75 percent success rate in helping alcoholics cope with their disease and not fall into hypoglycemia. His program works, he says, because, "it stabilizes the alcoholics blood sugar and thus makes it easier for the alcoholic to maintain abstinence."

The following e-mail was sent to Dr. Baird from a recovering alcoholic:

"I was diagnosed with severe hypoglycemia in the late 1960's. I am afraid to say that I never really took this condition very seriously until now and only followed the recommended diet for about a year. I have to confess that while I was on the high protein/low carbohydrate diet, with the elimination of sugar & caffeine, I never felt better in my entire life. A new relationship and lifestyle change is what triggered my old eating habits.

"I happened to notice in your bio that you seem to suspect a direct correlation between alcoholism and hypoglycemia.

I also am a recovering alcoholic. While I was in rehab, this was a question that I presented to the doctor attending me. He did not give me any concrete answers.

"I suppose the logical portion of my brain would conclude that, of course alcoholism is related to hypoglycemia. How could one drink all that sugar and not have "reactive" hypoglycemia? I do know that while in the grip of a heavy drinking binge, I could almost sense that I'd reach for more alcohol in a desperate effort to stabilize my sugar level and it became a viscous cycle. Try to drink more to keep the sugar level from falling too dangerously low and steady myself from shaking so violently.

"I am struggling right now, desperately trying to get myself back on the right path, but seeming to lack the necessary self-discipline. I have even had talks with myself trying to convince myself that this is very, very serious and in order for me to feel better, I have got to muster the determination to give up all the junk that is making me so ill. I have struggled (especially the past three years) with depression/anxiety/insomnia and I am tired of dragging myself through every day feeling exhausted."

It took great courage to write and share the above experiences. It's clear that in this case, hypoglycemia was not taken seriously. Doctors often don't have the answers to the questions we ask and many times we have to find the answers within ourselves. Even with self-discipline and determination, this writer struggled every day. I wonder if she/he had the information contained in this chapter, plus the following do's and don'ts, would the road to recovery had been easier and less painful. I truly believe so.

Do.......... EDUCATE yourself thoroughly on the correlation between hypoglycemia and alcoholism by reading *Seven Weeks To Sobriety: The Proven Program to Fight Alcoholism* by Dr. Joan Mathews Larson and *Under The Influence* by Dr. James Mylam.

Do.......... look into the work by Dr. Barbara Reed Stitt, author of *Food and Behavior*. Stitt, a former Chief Probation Officer, writes about her years of research and experience with correcting behavior by modifying diet.

Do.......... set an example if you are a parent. We cannot tell our children to "just say no to drugs," if we ourselves are not role models.

Do.......... make sure your children are supervised, the greatest risk occurs when children are left alone.

Do.......... get your child involved with after school activities.

131

Do.......... recognize the warning signs of alcohol and drug abuse in children: decline in grades and school attendance; discipline problems; changes in attitude, friends, and physical appearance; and most importantly, physical conditions such as loss of appetite, excessive fatigue, and sleeping habits.

Do.......... recognize the warning signs of alcohol abuse in adults: personality changes, high absenteeism on the job, low productivity, confrontations at work and home, and increase sleeping habits.

Do.......... recognize that most, if not all, alcoholics are hypoglycemic and unless both are addressed, recovery is severely hampered.

Do.......... realize that recovering alcoholics often replace addiction with some form of sugar, caffeine and/or tobacco (nicotine).

Do.......... find a physician, mental health provider, support group (facility if needed), or buddy system that encourages proper nutrition and supplementation with vitamins and minerals.

Do.......... insist on appropriate testing (glucose tolerance test, vitamin/mineral analysis, etc.) to determine if you have hypoglycemia.

Do.......... reread chapters on "How To Individualize Your Diet," keep a diet/symptom diary, evaluate dietary habits, and eliminate offending foods.

Do.......... reach out and ask for professional help. Medical and psychological assistance may be needed more than tough love.

Don't...... think you can solve your problem ALONE if you are both hypoglycemic and alcoholic. Medical and nutritional therapy and/or guidance are needed.

Don't...... be fooled by the temporary high that alcohol gives you. A drop in blood sugar will soon follow this quick-energy feeling resulting in the high/low scenario very familiar with hypoglycemia and alcoholism.

Don't...... be ashamed about your addiction. Both hypoglycemia and alcoholism are medical disorders compounded by chemical imbalances and nutritional deficiencies.

"There are 39 people in my family with sugar
problems. Some have diabetes,
some hypoglycemia.
It will be a blessing to get help."

Ramona 2002

~❦ Chapter 15

HYPOGLYCEMIA:
A PRELUDE TO DIABETES

It is rare that I have a conversation about hypoglycemia that the subject of diabetes doesn't come up. The thousands of letters and e-mails I've received over the past twenty-plus years confirm that this is a major concern.

One such e-mail, sent in mid-1998 gives you an indication of what I mean. A full time college student at Tulane University in New Orleans writes, "I feel like I'm going to die from this thing that grossly interferes with my life...I want to know everything...I don't understand much. Should I just eat everything when I have an attack? Tell me what to eat when I'm freaking...I also want to know how this affects my metabolism? How does it differ from diabetes? Is it the predecessor? What are the long-term effects? Can this kill me? Because sometimes I want to die or just be able to stick an insulin needle in my arm and feel better. Perhaps it is because I am uneducated on the issues, but it seems to me that diabetics have it easier. They can just "get a fix" so to speak. I don't really like needles but I could get used to them if it would make me feel better, feel normal."

On March 16, 1999 the following came from DM, "I was just diagnosed with hypoglycemia. Can you explain in plain language that I can understand how hypoglycemia is pre-diabetic? Please tell me this isn't true and if so how could I become diabetic?"

It was difficult to respond to these two e-mails. What do you say to someone who sounds so desperate and helpless? Is information enough? In both these cases however, information is THE only answer. When fear and panic sets in because of the unknown, every physical symptom becomes magnified. If only they read *Lick The Sugar Habit* by Dr. Nancy Appleton, *Hypoglycemia: The Classic Healthcare HandBook* by Jeraldine Saunders, or *New Low Blood Sugar and You* by *Dr. Carlton Fredericks*. Each of these books would have answered all the above questions! It saddens me that this information isn't readily available through the medical community. Maybe it is because hypoglycemia and diabetes are neatly separated as health conditions—one is accepted while one is virtually ignored. Hypoglycemia is often only spoken of in the context of insulin and blood sugar level management for people with diabetes.

Just scan your local newspaper and magazines, diabetes (high blood sugar) definitely takes center stage in medical headlines. Right now, Type two diabetes, like obesity, is at epidemic proportions in the United States and the world. Seventeen million Americans have diabetes with 800,000 new cases each year. Is there any wonder why this disease is the fourth leading cause of death? Diabetes also increases the risk of heart disease, gangrene and limb amputation, kidney failure, and blindness. As a leading killer, it also decreases your life expectancy. The saddest part is that 50 percent of those affected may not be aware that they have this deadly disease.

Hypoglycemia (low blood sugar) on the other hand has taken a back seat. There may be an article here, a book there, but seldom do you see statistics. Too bad, for maybe if we had numbers, more Americans would stand up and take notice of its alarming rise. One book I read estimates that 100 million Americans are hypoglycemic. Unfortunately, there are few formalized studies on hypoglycemia as a stand-alone condition. Therefore, it is very difficult to substantiate these numbers. Often, the only research to be found on hypoglycemia is within the context of other diabetes studies.

Because of this however, we may never know how many Americans are suffering, needlessly, from hypoglycemia. Do we need numbers to show that there is a connection between low blood sugar (hypoglycemia) and high blood sugar (diabetes)? Or do we just need to read more of the e-mails that the HSF receives?

"I was diagnosed with borderline hypoglycemia in 1999. My doctor told me not to worry and handed me a single sheet of paper with some diet instructions. Since he didn't seem concerned, I left with the feeling like my condition was "no big deal." I kept eating all my chocolate chip cookies and gave in to all my cravings. I am now dealing with the consequences. I feel terrible. My symptoms are worse and I was just diagnosed (2002) with diabetes. Both my mother and grandmother had diabetes. Why didn't I take this more seriously? What can I do now?"

"I desperately need to find a doctor that knows how to treat my hypoglycemia. My present one told me all I had to do was carry a candy bar with me. My Dad is severely diabetic and I don't want to end up with that disease. I live in the Cincinnati, Ohio area, please help me."

"Can uncontrolled hypoglycemia result in diabetes?"

I asked Dr. Lorna Walker, the HSF's nutritionist, to answer the last question. This was her response. "Hypoglycemia is a blood management disorder in which the pancreas reacts to a rapid rise in blood glucose levels by secreting too much insulin. While in diabetes, when blood sugar gets abnormally high, the damaged pancreas is unable to bring it down by secreting too little. In some cases, this hyper-insulinism is the precursor to adult onset diabetes (type 2 diabetes). The hypothesis is that the overactive pancreas, when predisposed by genetics, diet, and lifestyle finally begins to wear down and the end result is diabetes."

No letter, e-mail or explanation can be as profound as the simple black and white facts. So, in 1998, I added a hypoglycemia/diabetes questionnaire to our website. Due to the increase of questions and concerns about a possible connection between hypoglycemia and diabetes, I wanted to find out if this association could be observed. The goal was to determine whether untreated hypoglycemia is a pre-cursor to diabetes. The survey was also designed to gather information on how and by whom hypoglycemia had been diagnosed and what type of treatments, if any, were found to be beneficial. As this book goes to press, the HSF has received over 5500 responses (3,752 confirmed hypo-glycemics) from 25 countries!

We are in the process of sorting through this extensive volume of information to categorize and evaluate the results. Below, however, is a brief synopsis of what we've discovered so far.

Sixty-four percent of confirmed hypoglycemics (diagnosed by a physician with a glucose tolerance test) indicated that one or more family members had been diagnosed with diabetes!

With this information, we can alert hypoglycemics to the seriousness of this condition, as diabetes will almost certainly be the next stage if left untreated. It is also critical for diabetics to share this information with other family members as a preventative measure.

When we asked those surveyed what kind of symptoms they experienced, the most common were:

Heart Palpitations	80%
Dizziness	79%
Mood swings	77%
Headaches	74%
Depression	67%
Addiction to sweets	62%
Extreme fatigue	52%

When diagnosed with hypoglycemia, only 59% changed their diet. That number is high considering only 48% of physicians who diagnosed hypoglycemia, through a glucose tolerance test, recommended treatment. A little more than 50% of the participants incorporated vitamins and exercise while only 25% changed their mental attitude towards the illness. Unfortunately, 23% considered candy the cure-all for their low blood sugar problems.

Check out our hypoglycemia/diabetes survey on our website, www.hypoglycemia.org. It will give you an idea of what we are looking for and how this information will help future treatment of these conditions. This survey of course isn't the answer, as it cannot take the place of medicine or well-structured clinical trials. However, it is actually giving us the questions we need to encourage more scientific research into this condition that is so often not taken seriously.

Before the future, let's look one more time at the present. Diagnosing and managing hypoglycemia is one of the key determining factors in the subsequent development of adult onset (Type 2) diabetes in later life. Diet, lifestyle, age, pre-disposition, and insulin and tissue resistance are all variables that need to be addressed concerning this issue. To date, there is nothing we are able to do to counteract the effects of either aging or genetic pre-disposition. The remaining elements, however, can be managed. If one is successful, there is a good chance that Type 2 diabetes can be prevented or delayed.

Look carefully at the following do's and don'ts. Hopefully, they will encourage you to take action. Making smart dietary choices can make all the difference between staying healthy or becoming chronically ill. In this case, it may prevent hypoglycemia from turning into diabetes. Know that hypoglycemia is real, "it is not a fad disease" as some physicians states it is. It is a blood sugar manage-ment disorder and not just a complication of diabetes.

Do.......... evaluate your dietary habits if you experience any of the following symptoms:severe fatigue, depression, insomnia, heart palpitations, crying spells, craving for sweets, cold hands and feet, etc. See the chapter "Definition of Hypoglycemia" for complete list of symptoms.

Do.......... eliminate the big offenders: sugar, white flour, alcohol and tobacco. See chapter on "How To Individualize Your Diet".

Do.......... find a health care professional that is knowledgeable with hypoglycemia and sympathetic to your needs.

Do.......... know the definition and warning signs of Type 2 diabetes, the kind that we are addressing here in this chapter. This type of diabetes is usually a result of diet and lifestyle. Common symptoms are unusual thirst, frequent urination, blurred vision and fatigue.

Do.......... learn more about diabetes; its causes and effects. Visit the American Diabetes Association's website at www.diabetes.org.

Do.......... follow the basic diet guidelines for hypoglycemia if you have been diagnosed as diabetic: NO sugar, white flour, alcohol, tobacco and caffeine.

142

Do.......... work with a nutritionist or diabetic counselor. However, be leery if anyone says that sugar and white flour are OK to eat.

Do.......... monitor your blood glucose closely. This is absolutely necessary for diabetics. Some hypoglycemics also feel that this is helpful and necessary. The medical community hasn't advocated it for the latter.

Do.......... increase physical activity.

Do.......... control your weight. This is most important since excess weight makes the body less sensitive to insulin, the hormone needed to control glucose levels in the blood.

Do.......... take diabetic medication if diet, weight control and exercise don't lower your blood sugar levels to normal range. Of course, this is strictly under the care of a physician

Do.......... keep blood pressure and cholesterol under control since people with diabetes are more prone to heart disease and stroke.

⌦⌫

Don't...... make any changes in diet and medication if you are diabetic. Changes must be made under the supervision of you physician.

Don't...... delay notifying your physician if you feel your diabetic medication has unpleasant side effects.

Don't...... STOP any medication without the your physician's approval.

~⟨ Chapter 16

ASK THE EXPERTS

W hile moving in the summer of 2001, I found myself with 48 boxes labeled "HSF." Since the fall of 1977, I collected over 400 files including hundreds of books and tapes relating to hypoglycemia and The Hypoglycemia Support Foundation, Inc. The cry for help was overwhelming. The boxes contained handwritten cards and letters, lengthy e-mails, notes about desperate telephone calls I had received. Parents, teenagers, boyfriends, wives, husbands; they all had questions they hoped and prayed the HSF could answer.

And answer we did! Dr. Douglas M. Baird, the HSF's Medical Director, and our Nutritionist, Dr. Lorna Walker, addressed the medical questions. Their dedication was extraordinary, their unselfish donation of their time and expertise went above and beyond anything I expected. I responded by sharing my own experiences and what I had learned over the past years.

The information contained in these archives is so valuable that I am including it here. I asked other members of our Medical Board to share their thoughts on the questions posed to us: Dr. Herbert Pardell, Dr. Nancy Appleton, Dr. Stephen J. Schoenthaler, and Nutritional Biochemist Jay Foster. Dr. Nancy Scheinman, a psychologist at Miami Heart Institute, also shared her expertise. Without their dedication, caring and concern, this chapter would not have been possible. We extend a very special thank you to all of them.

(The opinions expressed by the experts should not be construed as a specific diagnosis or treatment recommendations. These answers are offered to provide a framework of information concerning commonly asked questions. Likewise, the HSF does not endorse specific products, tests, or protocols. The HSF encourages each person to take the individual steps necessary to establish the correct diagnosis and treatment regimen.)

Q. What is the difference between functional and reactive hypoglycemia?

A. Functional hypoglycemia refers to decreases in blood sugar that cannot be explained by any known pathology or disease. It's a nice way of saying, "Your glucose regulating mechanisms aren't functioning normally, and we don't know why." Reactive hypoglycemia refers to hypoglycemia resulting from the body's abnormal response to rapid rises in blood glucose levels caused by diet or stress. The terms are now frequently interchangeable. *Dr. Douglas M. Baird.*

Q. What should I eat when my low blood sugar hits? Orange juice? A candy bar?

A. The worst thing you can eat when your hypoglycemia "hits" is sugar in any form! It may make you feel better temporarily, but soon afterwards your pancreas will over secrete insulin, which caused your blood sugar to drop in the first place. Eating small, frequent meals that are low in fat and carbohydrates and contain moderate amounts of protein is the best way to control your blood sugar. Over time, you will learn what works best for you to keep your sugar within a reasonable range. *Dr. Douglas M. Baird.*

Q. Will hypoglycemia go away?

A. Not really. Blood sugar management disorders are hereditary, and as of this writing, we are not advanced enough to change our genetic code. However, hypoglycemia can be managed and controlled. What this means is that with dietary therapy and lifestyle changes, the number and severity of low blood glucose occurrences can be reduced or even eliminated over time. If a hypoglycemic returns to his/her old eating habits and lifestyle, symptoms will quickly return. Also, when we find ourselves under increasing stress, we are more apt to develop symptoms in those areas where we are weakest, with blood sugar abnormalities being no exception. *Dr. Douglas M. Baird.*

Q. Diabetes runs in my family. Will I have the same sort of problems?

A. Not necessarily. From a genetic standpoint, your predetermined diseases are largely a function of the luck of the draw. Whose genes you inherit determine your susceptibility to many diseases. It must be remembered that genetic predisposition does not necessarily guarantee that you will develop the disease. Blood sugar management abnormalities, which often manifest themselves as hypoglycemia, need not degenerate into full-blown diabetes. These disorders can be managed so that one can minimize the effects of one's genetic inheritance. *Dr. Douglas M. Baird.*

Q. I get heart palpitations, and extensive testing confirms that nothing is wrong with my heart. My diet is not perfect, but could this be the problem? Could hypoglycemia be the culprit?

A. Heart palpitations can be caused by a number of conditions, and many times, we cannot pinpoint the cause. If primary cardiac conditions have been ruled out (and I assume that the usual suspects-stimulants, allergens, etc., particularly caffeine-have been eliminated) but the symptoms are bothersome enough to warrant additional investigation, hypoglycemic episodes could be triggering palpitations and/or tachycardia (rapid heart rate).

Since dietary management is the cornerstone for the management of hypoglycemia, I would suggest that one way for you to determine if there is a connection is to change the way you eat. Remove all refined sugars from your diet, and eat small, frequent meals high in low-fat protein and moderate in complex carbohydrates. Try eating a small protein snack before retiring, but do not overeat.

Remember, dietary manipulation, vitamins, minerals and lifestyle changes are almost always part of an overall treatment program necessary to achieve control of any hypoglycemic symptoms, heart palpitations included. *Dr. Douglas M. Baird.*

Q. My husband quit drinking and now craves chocolate.

A. This is not an uncommon response. Alcohol is simply a very refined sugar. When one quits one form of sugar, they many times substitute another. I have never seen an alcoholic that was not hypoglycemic. Alcohol and sugar are different forms of the same fuel. The inability to properly manage blood sugar levels in the bloodstream may cause a variety of problems, especially with brain function. This can be quite serious. The problem of proper and adequate fueling of the brain must be managed on an ongoing basis if an individual is to function optimally. *Dr. Douglas M. Baird.*

Q. Can having severe hypoglycemia give a false (high) blood alcohol level with a Breathalyzer?

A. When one's blood sugar gets too low, the human body has a number of compensatory mechanisms that will try to correct this condition. One of those processes is called gluconeogenesis, literally "making new sugar." One of the byproducts of that process is acetone. This is the reason why people with blood sugar problems and those on calorie restrictive diets have what the medical profession calls "acetone breath." Law enforcement personnel often confuse this smell with alcohol.

Now, whether the Breathalyzer can discriminate between acetone, other ketones, and alcohol is the critical question. Your attorney will have to contact the manufacturers of that technology to see whether that discrimination can be made by the available technology. I do not have a definitive answer to that question. *Dr. Douglas M. Baird.*

Q. I must have surgery and I'm hypoglycemic. I'm not concerned about the procedure, but I am worried about the intravenous glucose. Is there anything else the doctors can give me instead?

A. Yes, there are other IV fluids that can be utilized in a hospital setting that will not affect your blood sugar. Ask your doctor. The stress of the surgery itself, however, may adversely affect your ability to manage your blood sugar. While this is a nuisance, it can be brought under control once you are back home. *Dr. Douglas M. Baird.*

Q. I have most of the symptoms of hypoglycemia, especially depression and mood swings. My doctor wants to put me on antidepressants. How can I convince him to take a glucose tolerance test first?

A. Depression and mood swings can certainly be a part of the symptom complex associated with hypoglycemia. They can also be symptoms of other disorders. The common work-up to begin to identify some of the underlying causes of these symptoms includes general chemistries, blood count, thyroid function testing and, if the symptoms warrant, glucose tolerance testing. If your doctor is unwilling to make the effort to eliminate the causes for your symptoms (for whatever reason), it may be time to consider seeking a second opinion. *Dr. Douglas M. Baird.*

Q. Can hypoglycemia affect one's vision, and how?

A. Blood sugar abnormalities can affect (and probably do) almost any tissue in one's body. The most dramatic effects are observed with brain function because the brain does not store readily available fuel. Other tissue areas are affected to a greater or lesser extent based on their individual susceptibility to blood sugar fluctuations as well as their fuel storage capabilities. The eye is an extension of the brain. It is a neutral tissue, does not store fuel and is susceptible to damage caused by reduced availability of fuel and/or oxygen. *Dr. Douglas M. Baird.*

Q. I am 29 years old and have just been diagnosed as having hypoglycemia. I have been under a lot of stress and was wondering if this could have triggered the condition.

A. To understand how stress can adversely affect this condition, a little physiology lesson might be in order. You cannot separate the psychological from the physical. You, as a total person, consist of both. When you suffer from stress (real or imagined), your physical body reacts with what is known as the "fight or flight" response. The adrenal glands secrete the catecholamines epinephrine and norepinephrine (adrenaline), which raise the blood glucose levels to prepare the body to fight or flee. Once that occurs, the pancreas begins to over-secrete insulin, and the blood glucose yo-yo begins. The drop in blood glucose is real! So, you need to be even more diligent with your diet during times of stress.

I also believe that once you understand how stress, like poor diet, can set off hypoglycemia, you will comprehend the need to control both. Also, the more overanxious you become about this condition, the more difficult it will be to get it under control. *Dr Lorna Walker.*

Q. What is your opinion about eating protein to manage low blood sugar?

A. Protein is not a "solution" to hypoglycemia. Protein can be used as a body fuel and is digested more slowly than carbohydrates and sugars. It is broken amino acids that can be turned into "fuel" later by the body if needed. Too much protein in the diet can lead to ketosis; too little can lead to protein starvation. The idea is to maintain a diet moderate in protein, low in carbohydrates (but not too low, as in the Atkins' diet) and devoid of simple sugars. This will help rest an overactive pancreas and help maintain steady blood glucose levels. *Dr. Lorna Walker.*

Q. I was recently diagnosed with hypoglycemia. My doctor prescribed a drug that has proved, in many cases, to reduce all signs of hypoglycemia. The drug is called Proglycem, which is not covered under my current insurance policy. I would like to know if you have any available information on this drug.

A. Proglycem (also known as Hyperstat) is a powerful drug used in the treatment of Hypertensive Emergency and "pathologic hypoglycemia due to insulinoma." An insulinoma is a tumor of the insulin-secreting cells of the pancreas. Functional hypoglycemia is not listed as one of the pharmaceutical indications for administration of this drug. In functional hypoglycemia, the insulin-secreting cells over secrete insulin in response to eating sugar and/or excessive refined carbohydrates. That is one reason why the fasting glucose levels of functional (reactive) hypoglycemia are usually within normal range. It is also why the condition is best treated with diet and lifestyle changes. I would surely consult a reputable endocrinologist before taking Proglycem for this condition. *Dr Lorna Walker.*

Q. I was diagnosed with hypoglycemia several years ago. I am currently suffering from a case of severe hives and am wondering if hypoglycemia has ever been known to cause this. Both my primary doctor and allergist don't seem to know what is causing this, so I am doing my own investigative work.

A. Hives indicate an allergic reaction to something. It is not hypoglycemia, although many hypoglycemics also suffer from allergies.

Although there is no scientific evidence to support it, I sometimes suspect that sub-clinical adrenal insufficiency may play a role in both disorders. The adrenal glands secrete glucocorticoids, which raise the blood glucose in times of stress or increased need. And hypoglycemics respond to rises in blood glucose with hyperinsulinism. Result: low blood glucose. The adrenals (along with the liver and other pancreatic hormones) must then secrete glucocorticoids to raise the blood sugar again. The cycle has begun.

Some adrenal hormones also serve to suppress the immune system and, in therapeutic doses, are used in the treatment of severe allergies and autoimmune disorders. If there are not enough of these types of hormones, the immune system may overreact to substances normally well tolerated, or "turn" on itself.

You will need to try to discover what your body is reacting to and remove it from your environment. *Dr Lorna Walker.*

Q. I've been having more trouble with my low blood sugar lately. I was wondering if there was a dietary way to get back to normal after a bout of very low blood sugar (near passing out). I know I need some juice at first, but what is the next best thing I should be eating after that and for the rest of the day?

A. Try not to respond to drops in blood sugar with sugar. It only continues the cycle of highs and lows. If you must drink some juice, dilute it with water, and then EAT something! A mixture of complex carbohydrates and protein usually works best. All the more reason to stick to your dietary regimen. The main purpose of the diet for hypoglycemia is to prevent drops in glucose, NOT to fix them after the fact. *Dr Lorna Walker.*

Q. My girlfriend has been diagnosed with Natal Hypoglycemia. From what I can make of the information available, low blood sugar can be caused by pregnancy and/or childbirth. Do you have any information on this condition?

A. Glucose Mismanagement Disorders are common to pregnancy. Both Gestational Diabetes and Gestational Hypoglycemia can occur. Many times the condition disappears after giving birth, but sometimes the stress of pregnancy is suspected of bringing out a condition that the woman is prone to anyway. In either case, the diet for hypoglycemia is compatible with pregnancy, as it is a healthy one. Be sure to have your girlfriend check with her doctor. *Dr Lorna Walker.*

Q. It is very rare that people talk about long-term, cumulative effects of hypoglycemic episodes. If one has a few dozen average-to-severe episodes per year of low blood sugar, what is the effect on various body functions? I have heard brain damage can result. Any suggestions?

A. The first organ affected by hypoglycemia is the brain, as its exclusive fuel is glucose. Unlike other organs, the brain cannot convert fats or protein to glucose. A few dozen short episodes a year have not proven to be detrimental. However, evidence is beginning to show that long-term, uncontrolled hypoglycemia could be a precursor to diabetes, the effects of which are well documented. All the more reason to stick to your dietary regimen. I say it repeatedly—the main purpose of the diet for hypoglycemia is to prevent drops in glucose, NOT to fix them after the fact. *Dr Lorna Walker.*

Q. Is there a way to do a glucose tolerance test at home?

A. Sorry, there is no way to do a glucose tolerance test at home. Many physicians familiar with this disorder often make the diagnosis by placing their patients on a hypoglycemic diet. If they improve, the diagnosis of hypoglycemia is made. Since the diet for hypoglycemia is a healthy one, I suggest you try eating as recommended and see if you feel better. *Dr Lorna Walker.*

Q. My son (18) has prostate cancer and was treated with chemotherapy. Now he has symptoms of hypoglycemia. Is there any connection?

A. Not necessarily. With the reference to the chemotherapy being the causative agent of the hypoglycemia, it would be extremely important to know which chemotherapy was used. Symptoms of hypoglycemia can occur that are not necessarily connected to the therapy given. Further, it would be important to determine if this is truly hypo-glycemia or general immune suppression related to the chemotherapy. *Dr. Herbert Pardell.*

Q. I have hypoglycemia and chronic fatigue syndrome. Even though I'm on a strict hypoglycemia diet, I still can't seem to feel better. Is there anything I can do to speed the healing process?

A. Although you have not elucidated what you are doing at this time, I would assume that, under the circum-stances, you are following protocols that include both diseases. The use of multiple antioxidants (which should of course include lipoic acid, selenium and chromium along with a strict diet) would help in this endeavor. Other parts of the protocol include a good exer-cise program along with proper rest. Each person is an individual, and the rate of healing depends on the general state of health and cannot be generalized for any one person. *Dr. Herbert Pardell.*

Q. I have hypoglycemia and hypothyroidism. Is this common?

A. The determination of commonality is very difficult because symptoms of both of these diseases seem to cross over and can be exhibited in either hypoglycemia or hypothyroidism. Decreased thyroid function will affect glucose metabolism and, in fact, will affect every part of the metabolic system, causing symptoms such as fatigue, sweating, weight gain, etc. Hypoglycemia can give you similar symptoms. At this time, I don't know of any studies that give an exact percentage of how many people have both entities. However, again the symptomatology of these diseases can be seen in either one. *Dr. Herbert Pardell.*

Q. I am hypoglycemic. I've heard and read that I should take chromium picolinate. How does it help, and how much should I take?

A. Chromium, whether it is given as chelate, picolinate or polynicotinate helps insulin work better to transport glucose to the cells. A big problem with insulin resistance is a deficiency of chromium and other trace elements. Without a mineral analysis, it is safe to take chromium as picolinate or chelate or polynicotinate at 200 to 400 mcg per day for adults. If you had a mineral analysis, we might recommend higher amounts. One word of caution: if you have high insulin levels and all your insulin is not sensitive, the chromium may initially activate it and you could experience worse blood sugar symptoms. If that happens, reduce or eliminate the chromium until you get further testing to see what you need. *Jay Foster, Nutritional Biochemist.*

Q. I am hypoglycemic and have been taking an herbal phen from the local health food store that has St. John's Wort and Ma Huang in it. Are there any health risks with this combination?

A. The Ma Huang may be dangerous. Many people using it report cardiac stress symptoms, including rapid heartbeat. The FDA is trying to get it banned. St. John's Wort is okay, but 50 mg. (a.m. & p.m.) of 5-HTP is better, although you cannot take either if you are on an SSRI drug like Paxil, Prozac or Zoloft. *Jay Foster, Nutritional Biochemist.*

Q. I've eliminated Aspartame and Nutrasweet. Can I have Splenda?

A. Research shows that the artificial sweetener Splenda, also known as sucralose, is a chlorinated sucrose derivative. I do not recommend it. For more information, use a search engine to look it up on the web. What you might try is Stevia. Stevia comes from a South American tree. It is natural, comes in pills, powder and liquid. I do not find the taste great, but other people find it very appealing. Also, research shows that it will do no harm. *Dr. Nancy Appleton.*

Q. How much sugar can a hypoglycemic ingest safely in one day?

A. I think a hypoglycemic should ingest very little sugar. This includes all forms of simple sugar such as sucrose, glucose, fructose, maltose, dextrose, honey, barley, malt, maple syrup, rice syrup, brown sugar, raw sugar, turbinado sugar, corn sweetener, corn syrup solids, liquid cane sugar, concentrated fruit juice, and fruit juice. The less, the better. There is plenty left to eat. If you eat fruit, eat it with protein and fat to control your blood sugar level. The fruits that have the least amount of sugar are melons and berries. *Dr. Nancy Appleton.*

Q. I am so confused. One book says I can eat whole wheat, and another book says I should avoid it. As a hypoglycemic trying to figure out what to eat, this is so confusing. What's correct?

A. Many people have made themselves allergic to wheat and dairy due to eating sugar with these products (cakes, cookies, pies, pastries, ice cream, cheesecake, yogurt, etc.). I do not think a hypoglycemic should eat any sugar, wheat, or dairy. The best foods to eat are whole foods, not processed foods like bread, boxed cereals, pasta, pizza, etc. *Dr. Nancy Appleton.*

Q. Is hypnosis recommended for hypoglycemia? I'm having a very difficult time with my diet. I can't seem to break my caffeine habits. I'm willing to try this but would this be the easy way out?

A. Although you could use hypnosis to try to gain control over longstanding habits, it is not necessarily the best treatment choice. The essential issue here is controlling cravings. The cravings you have are biologically driven. You may think they are a matter of will or psychological in some way, but when your blood sugar drops, you have little control over your food choices. Therefore, if you are following a proper hypoglycemic diet, the "cravings" should dissolve away. There are some food habits that are emotionally based. You will be able to see these once you have cut away the biologically driven ones. Examples include: eating comfort foods when upset or bored, or having a "relationship" with food in the place of the relationship you yearn for. If you feel you are eating from emotional need, a brief course of individual psychotherapy is a better treatment choice.

Regarding coffee, you must remember that caffeine is a drug from which you must withdraw slowly. Go slowly and replace it with a healthy alternative. Don't overlook how powerful this morning ritual is and brew herbal/green tea instead of coffee if that is your replacement. *Dr. Nancy Scheinman.*

Q. I've just been diagnosed as having hypoglycemia after years of being told that my symptoms "were all in my head." I'm not only having a hard time with my diet but with my emotions. I am so a angry at all the doctors, my family included, who never really believed that this is a tried and true condition. I'm working on my diet but how can I get past my anger?

A. The only reason why the people in your past labeled your hypoglycemia as "all in your head." was because they had no understanding of what was actually taking place. Can you really be angry at someone because they have never been exposed to something? Or because, generally, our knowledge of the disease is in a developmental state? They weren't making a value judgement about you: they were merely reaching for the only reason they could find. I notice that the solution to a problem does not appear until a person is truly ready to see it and confront it. That is, ask yourself these questions: "Was I really ready to deal with this back then? How have I grown from the difficulty of living with this? Who am I as a result of this?"

Anger is a complex emotion. While it may be destructive, it may also be motivating and empowering. The key is to change the energy of the anger into a positive force. Interestingly, if you do not, and you remain stuck in the anger, it may actually interfere with your sugar. By remaining angry, you may create blood sugar instability. Therefore, via another route, you will allow these individuals to continue to block your healing. *Dr. Nancy Scheinman.*

Q. My nine year old daughter was diagnosed as having hypoglycemia. I changed her diet, which consisted of a large amount of sugar and fruit juices. She was doing quite well until I started giving her a vitamin/mineral supplement. I thought this was a good idea. Why does she seem worse since I added this chewable?

A. I just addressed this problem in a recent article that I wrote in *the Journal of Longevity*. You child may be allergic to some of the additives in the supplement. Our research has shown that about seven percent of the population has chemical sensitivities to a variety of things like synthetic food colors, food dyes, binders, and fillers. (Incidentally, many food dyes, binders, and emulsifiers have been linked to Attention Deficit Hyperactivity Disorder (ADHD) and hyperactivity alone.) For example, although kids prefer chewable vitamin supplements, all chewables contain the exact same chemicals, which we know promote hyperactivity. Unfortunately, there's no known technology for creating a chewable without using these chemicals. For those kids who are chemically sensitive, hypoallergenic nutritional supplements are the answer. *Dr. Stephen J. Schoenthaler.*

⁓✿ Chapter 17
RECOMMENDED
FOODS/MENUS

Recommended Foods

N ote: The following list of recommended foods and menus is just a guideline. You must remember that everyone's body chemistry is different, therefore, adjustments must be made to meet individual needs. Size of portions depend on weight and symptoms. READ the chapter on INDIVIDUALIZING YOUR DIET before incorporating the menus into your diet program.

Meats: All kinds of fresh meats—veal, lamb, lean beef, pork (if no nitrates).

Poultry: Without skin—chicken, turkey, Cornish hens, duck, pheasant.

Fish: Flounder, turbot, sole, halibut, grouper, cod, haddock, salmon, red snapper, scallops, tuna, shrimp, lobster, crab.

Dairy: Whole milk, skim milk, cheeses (farmer, cottage, ricotta, mozzarella), eggs, butter and yogurt.

Grains: 100 percent whole wheat bread, brown rice, millet, oatmeal, buckwheat, oats, whole wheat pasta and noodles.

Nuts & Seeds: Almonds, cashews, walnuts, pecans, chestnuts, sunflower seeds, pumpkin seeds.

Vegetables: Artichokes, asparagus, avocado, beans, beets, broccoli, brussels sprouts, cabbage, carrots, cauliflower, celery, chives, collard greens, corn, cucumber, eggplant, endive, garlic, kale, lettuce, mushrooms, mustard greens, okra, onion, parsley, peas, peppers, potatoes, pumpkin, radish, rhubarb, spinach, sprouts, tomatoes, zucchini, and yams.

Beverages: Water, vegetable juice, herbal tea, seltzer, clear-broth. Occasionally, decaffeinated coffee or weak tea.

Fruits: Avocado, strawberries, apples, peaches, pears, oranges, watermelon, tangerines, berries, plums, grapefruit, honeydew.

Foods to Avoid

Desserts: Anything containing white sugar, such as, candy, cakes, pastries, custard, jello, icecream, sherbet, pudding, cookies, breakfast cereals, and commercially baked breads. Avoid honey and other forms of sugar, such as brown, raw, and turbinado.

Grains: Anything containing white flour, such as packaged breakfast cereals, gravies, white rice, refined corn meal, white spaghetti, macaroni, noodles and refined bakery goods.

Meats: Lunch meats, bacon, sausage, processed meats (most contain corn sugar), meat or meat products with artificial colors, flavorings or preservatives.

Beverages: Alcohol, caffeine, all sugared soft drinks, and fruit juices.

Fruits: Dried fruits (figs, dates, raisins). Fruit juices can be tolerated at times if diluted. Avoid EXCESSIVE amounts of fresh fruit.

Note: Tobacco should be avoided entirely.

Suggested List of Snacks

FRESH VEGETABLES: tomato wedges, sliced cucumbers, carrot, celery sticks, radish flowers, sliced summer squash, zucchini, cauliflower, broccoli flowerettes (steamed) mushrooms, and pepper rings.

FRESH FRUITS: apple wedges, orange slices, cantaloupe, watermelon, and strawberries (in moderation)

COTTAGE CHEESE
HARD BOILED EGG
YOGURT
GRANOLA SEEDS (sesame, sunflower, pumpkin)
NUTS (almonds, cashews, pecans, walnuts)
POPCORN
COLD CHICKEN, TURKEY, ROAST BEEF
CHEESE SLICES
WHOLE GRAIN BREAD (with nut butter)
RICE CRACKERS (with natural peanut butter, tuna fish or cheese)
RICE WAFERS (with natural peanut butter, tuna fish or cheese)
WHOLE WHEAT PRETZELS
APPLESAUCE (no sugar)
CELERY STICKS (stuffed with peanut butter, tuna fish or cheese)
BAKED POTATO (with steamed vegetables)

Suggested Breakfast

1/2 cup of oatmeal
1 poached egg
1/2 grapefruit
Beverage

1 egg omelet with green peppers, onions or mushrooms
1 slice whole wheat bread or rice cake
1 orange
Beverage

1/2 cup of cream of rice (millet, grits, dry rolled oats)
Cheese omelet
1 cup strawberries
Beverage

1 - 2 slices of whole grain bread
1 cup cottage cheese
Beverage

Suggested Lunches & Dinners

Chef salad (egg, turkey, chicken, lettuce, carrots, etc.), with oil and vinegar dressing
1 slice whole wheat bread or rice cake
Beverage

Soup (bean, lentil, chicken or beef)
Small tossed salad
1 slice whole wheat bread
Beverage

4 - 6 oz. broiled shrimp (or fish of any kind)
Green beans with almonds (or mushrooms)
Small tossed salad
Beverage

4 - 6 oz. chicken (one leg, thigh or breast)
1 small potato
Broccoli
Small tossed salad
Beverage

Broiled lamb chop
Brown rice
Brussels sprouts
Small tossed salad
Beverage

Health Emergency Card

This card was custom-designed with the hypoglycemic in mind. It should be kept close to your side at all times! Feel secure knowing that your diagnosis, allergies, medications, and physician are listed on this card in the event of an emergency. Enjoy peace of mind knowing that this card will contain vital information that could *save your life!*

To order your Health Emergency Card, please mail in a check for $12.00 plus postage:

First Class: $2.50
Priory Mail: $4.50
Out of the U.S.: $8.50.

Please include a picture of the card holder (no larger that 5"x7") and your check or Money Order to:

The Hypoglycemia Support Foundation, Inc.
P.O. Box 451778
Sunrise, Fl 33345
Please allow 2-4 weeks delivery

To use your credit card, please visit our website:
www.hypoglycemia.org

Health Emergency Card
Order Form

First Name:
Last Name:

Address:
City: State: Zip:
Country:

Email:
Date of Birth:
Sex: Male   Female
Home phone: Work Phone:
Emergency Contact: Emergency Phone:
Diagnosis:
Allergies:
Medication:
Physician Name:
Physician's Phone:

HEALTH EMERGENCY CARD

Roberta Ruggiero
P.O. Box 451778
Sunrise, FL 33322

Home Phone	Work Phone	D.O.B.	Sex
		06/16/42	F

Emergency Contact	Emergency Number
Anthony Ruggiero	

Diagnosis	Hypoglycemia
Allergies	Penicillin
Medication	Cytomel
Physician	

The Hypoglycemia Support Foundation, Inc.

172

Hypoglycemia Questionnaire

HYPOGLYCEMIA: DO YOU HAVE IT?

In the space provided below, please mark (1) if you have this condition mildly, (2) if moderate, and (3) if severe. If you do not have the condition, leave it blank. The accuracy of this questionnaire depends upon complete honesty and serious objective thought in answering the questions. (Many of these symptoms may relate to other health problems).

1____Abnormal craving for sweets

2____Afternoon headaches

3____Allergies: tendency to asthma, hay fever, skin rash, etc.

4____Awaken after a few hours sleep/difficulty getting back to sleep

5____Aware of breathing heavily

6____Bad dreams

7____Blurred vision

8____Brown spots or bronzing of skin

9____"Butterfly stomach," cramps

10____Difficulty making decisions

11____Need coffee/caffeine to start morning

12____unable to work under pressure

13____Chronic fatigue

14____Chronic nervous exhaustion

15____Convulsions

16____Crave candy or coffee in afternoons

17____Cry easily for no apparent reason

18____Depressed

19____Dizziness, giddiness or light-headedness

20____Drink more than three cups of coffee or cola a day

21____Get hungry or feel faint unless you eat frequently

22____Eat when nervous

23____Feel faint if meal is delayed

24____Fatigue relieved by eating

25____Fearful

26____Get "shaky" if hungry

27____Hallucinations

28____Hand tremor (or trembles)

29____Heart palpitations if meals are missed or delayed

30____Highly emotional

31____Nibble between meals because of hunger

32____Insomnia

33____Inward trembling

34____Irritable before meals

35____Lack of energy

36____Moods of depression, "blues" or melancholy

37___Poor memory or ability to concentrate

38___Reduced initiative

39___Sleepy after meals

40___Drowsy during the day

41___Weakness, dizziness

42___Worrier, feel insecure

43___Symptoms of hypoglycemia appear before eating

44___Total Score.

Add the total of all answers. A total score of less than (20) twenty is within normal limits. A higher score is evidence of probable adrenal insufficiency and/or deranged carbohydrate metabolism (Hypoglycemia), and would indicate further testing.

~⁀C Appendix A

RECOMMENDED BOOKS ON HYPOGLYCEMIA

Blood Sugar Blues, Miryam Ehrlich Williamson, Walker & Company, New York 2001.

Body, Mind and Sugar, by E.M. Abrahamson, M.D. and A.W. Pezet. New York, Avon Books, 1977.

Carlton Fredericks' New Low Blood Sugar and You, by Dr.Carlton Fredericks. NewYork, Perigee Books, 1985.

Dr. Atkins' New Diet Revolution by Robert C. Atkins, M.D., M. Evans, 1992.

Food, Mind and Mood, by David Sheinkin, M.D., Michael Schacter, M.D., and Richard Hutton. New York, Warner Books, Inc., 1979.

Fighting Depression, by Harvey Ross, M.D., New York, Larchmont Books, 1975.

Get the Sugar Out by Ann Louise Gittleman, M.S., New York: Crown trade Paperbacks, 1996.

The Hidden Menace of Low Blood Sugar, by Clement G. Martin. New York, Arco Publishing Co., 1976.

Hypoglycemia: A Better Approach, by Paavo Airola, Ph.D. Phoenix, Health Plus Publishers, 1977.

Is Low Blood Sugar Making You a Nutritional Cripple? by Ruth Adams and Frank Murray. New York, Larchmont Press, 1970.

Lick The Sugar Habit, by Nancy Appleton, Ph.D. New York, Warner Books, Inc., 1986.

Low Blood Sugar Handbook, by Ed and Patricia Krimmel. Bryn Mawr, PA, Franklin Publishers, 1984.

Low Blood Sugar; What it Is and How to Cure It, by Peter J. Steincrohn, M.D., Chicago, Ill., Contemporary Books, Inc.,1972.

Nutraerobics, by Dr. Jeffrey Bland, New York, Harper and Row, 1983.

Psychodietetics, by Emanuel Cheraskin, M.D., D.M.D., William Ringsdorf, Jr., D.M.D. with Arline Brecher. New York, Bantam Books, 1978.

Seven Weeks to Sobriety; The Proven Program to Fight Alcoholism Through Nutrition by Joan Mathews Larson, Ph. D., Ballantine publishing Group, 1997.

Sugar and Your Health, by Ray C. Wunderlich, Jr., M.D. St. Petersburg, FL, Good Health Publications, Johnny Reed, Inc., 1982.

Sugar Blues, by William Dufty. New York, Warner Books, Inc., 1975.

Sugar Isn't Always Sweet, by Maura (Jinny) Zack and Wilbur D. Currier, M.D. Brea, CA, Uplift Books, 1983.

Sweet and Dangerous, by John Yudkin, M.D. New York, Bantam Books, 1972.

The Sugar Addict's Total Recovery Program, by kathleen Des Maisons, Ph.D., Ballantine Publishing Group.

Cookbooks for the Hypoglycemic

The Allergy Cookbook, by Ruth R. Shattuck. NewYork, A
Plume Book, 1984.

Cooking Naturally For Pleasure and Health, by Gail C.
Watson. Davie, FL, Falkynor Books, 1983.

Foods For Healthy Kids, by Dr. Lendon Smith. New York,
Berkeley Books, 1981.

Hypoglycemia Control Cookery, by Dorothy Revell. New
York, Berkeley Books, 1973.

The Low Blood Sugar Cookbook, by Francyne Davis. New
York, Bantam Books, 1985.

Dr. Lendon Smith's Diet Plan For Teenagers, by Lendon
Smith, M.D. NewYork, McGraw-Hill, 1986.
Step-By-Step To Natural Food, by Diane Campbell.
Clearwater, FL, CC Publishers, 1979.

Sugar Free. . .That's Me, by Judith S. Majors. New York,
Ballantine Books, 1978.

The Low Blood Sugar Cookbook, by Ed and Patricia
Krimmel, Bryn Mawr, PA, Franklin Publishers, 1984.

Exercise Books for the Hypoglycemic

Aerobics, by Kenneth H. Cooper, M.D., NewYork, Bantam, 1972.

Aerobics For Women, by Kenneth H. Cooper, M.D., New York, Bantam Books, 1973.

The Aerobics Program For Total Well-Being, by Kenneth H. Cooper, M.D., New York, Bantam, 1983.

The Complete Book of Exercisewalking, by Gary D. Yanker. Contemporary Books, Inc., 1983.

Fit or Fat? by Covert Bailey. Boston, Houghton Mifflin Company, 1977.

Gary Yanker's Sportwalking, by Gary Yanker, New York Contemporary Books, 1987.

Books to Help Develop a Positive Attitude

Anatomy of An Illness, by Norman Cousins, New York, W.W. Norton & Co., 1979.

Bus 9 To Paradise, by Leo Buscaglia, New York, Fawcett, 1987.

Enthusiasm Makes the Difference, by Norman Vincent Peale, NewYork, Fawcett, 1987.

Gifts Form Eykis, by Dr. Wayne Dyer, New York, Pocket Books, 1983.

Goodbye to Guilt, by Gerald G. Jampolsky, M.D., New York, Bantam Books, Inc., 1985.

The Healing Heart, by Norman Cousins, New York, Avon Books, 1983.

Love, by Leo Buscaglia, New York, Fawcett Crest Books, 1972.

Loving Each Other, by Leo Buscaglia, NewYork, Fawcett Columbine, 1984.

Personhood, by Leo Buscaglia, New York, Fawcett Columbine, 1978.

The Power of Positive Thinking, by Norman Vincent Peale, NewYork, Prentice-Hall, Inc., 1952.

Pulling Your Own Strings, by Dr. Wayne Dyer, New York, Thomas Y. Crowell Co., 1978.

The Road Less Traveled, by M. Scott Peck, M.D., New York, Simon and Schuster, 1978.

Tough Times Never Last, But Tough People Do!, by Robert H. Schuller, NewYork, Bantam Books, 1983.

The Seat of the Soul by Gary Zukav, Simon & Shuster, 1990.

The Sky's The Limit, by Dr. Wayne Dyer, New York, Simon and Schuster, 1980.

Teach Only Love: The Seven Principles of Attitudinal Healing, by Gerald G. Jampolsky, M.D., New York, Bantam, 1983.

When Bad Things Happen to Good People, by Harold S. Kushner, New York, Avon Books, 1981.

Your Erroneous Zones, by Dr. Wayne Dyer, New York, Funk & Wagnalls, 1976.

§

Books on the Correlation Between Hypoglycemia & Learning Disabilities, Juvenile Delinquency, Mental Illness, Alcoholism and Candida Albicans

Allergies and the Hyperactive Child, by Doris J. Rapp, M.D. NewYork, Simon & Schuster, 1979.

Brain Allergies, by William H. Philpott, M.D. and Dwight K. Kalita, Ph.D. New Canaan, CT, 1980.

Chocolate to Morphine, by Andrew Weil, M.D., and Winifred Rosen. Boston, Houghton Mifflin, 1968.

Diet, Crime and Delinquency, by Alexander Schauss, Ph.D. Berkeley, CA, Parker House, 1981.

Eating Right To Live Sober, by L. Ann Mueller, M.D., and Katherine Ketchum, NewYork, NAL, 1986.

Fighting Depression, by Harvey Ross, M.D., New York, Larchmont Books, 1975.

Food, Teens and Behavior, by Barbara Reed Stitt,Ph.D. Manitowoc, WI, Natural Press, 1983.

Hypoglycemia: A Better Approach, by Paavo Airola, Ph.D. Phoenix, Health Plus Publishers, 1977.

Mind, Mood and Medicine: A Guide To The New Biopsychiatry, by Paul H. Wender, M.D. and Donald F. Klein, M.D., NewYork, NAL, 1982.

Psychodietetics, by E. Cheraskin, M.D., D.M.D., William Ringsdorf Jr., D.M.D. with Arline Brecher. NewYork, Bantam Books, 1978.

Sugar and Your Health, by Ray C. Wunderlich, Jr., M.D. St. Petersburg, FL Good Health Publications, 1982.

The Yeast Connection, by William G. Crook, M.D., Jackson, Tenn., Professional Books, 1983.

The Yeast Syndrome, by John Parks Trowbridge, M.D. and Morton Walker, D.P.M., 1986.

§

~C Appendix B

ORGANIZATIONS THAT SUPPLY NUTRITIONAL
INFORMATION & REFERRAL LISTS

Hypoglycemia Support Foundation, Inc.,
Frederick Fell Publishers, Inc.,
2131 Hollywood Blvd. Suite 305
Hollywood, FL 33020.

Hypoglycemia Association, Inc.
18008 New Hampshire Ave
Box 165
Ashton, Maryland 20861-0165
Recorded Message
Phone: (202) 544-4044

International Academy of Preventive Medicine,
34 Corporate Woods, Suite 469,
10950 Grandview,
Overland Park, KS 66210.

International Academy of Applied Nutrition,
P.O. Box 386
La Habra, CA 90631.

The Price-Pottenger Nutrition Foundation
P.O. Box 2614
La Mesa, California 91943-2614
Phone: (619) 574-7763
E-mail: www.Price-Pottinger.org

American Holistic Medical Association
12101 Menaul Boulevard NE
Mc Lean, Virginia 22101
Phone: (703) 556-9245
E-mail: www.holisticmedicine.org

American Academy of Osteopathy
3500 DePauw Boulevard Suite 1080
Indianapolis, Indiana 46268
Phone: (317) 879-1881
Fax: (317) 879-0563
E-mail: www.academyofosteopathy.org

American College for Advancement in Medicine
23121 Verdugo Drive
Suite 202
Laguna, California 92653
Phone: 1-800-532-3688
E-mail: ACAM.org

The Life Extension Foundation
1100 W. Commercial Boulevard
Fort Lauderdale, Florida 33309
Phone: (954) 766-8433 or 1-800-226-2370
E-mail: www.LifeExtension.com

Well Mind Association of Greater Washington
18606 New Hampshire Avenue
Ashton, Maryland 20861-9789
Phone: (301) 774-6617
Fax: (301) 774-0536

§

〰 Appendix C

BIBLIOGRAPHY

Abrahamson, E.M., M.D., and Pezet, A.W. Body, Mind and Sugar. NewYork, Avon Books, 1977.

Adams, Ruth, and Murray, Frank. Is Low Blood Sugar Making You a Nutritional Cripple? New York, Larchmont Press, 1970.

Airola, Paavo, Ph.D. Hypoglycemia: A Better Approach. Phoenix, Health Plus Publishers, 1977.

Anderson, Linnea, M.P.H., Dibble, Marjorie V., M.S., R.D., Turkki, Pirkko R., Ph.D., R.D., Mitchell, Helen S., Ph.D., Sc.D., Rynbergen, HenderikaJ., M.S. Nutrition in Health and Disease, 17th Edition. Philadelphia, J.B. Lippincott Company.

Appleton, Nancy, Ph.D. Lick the Sugar Habit. New York, Warner Books, Inc. 1986.

Atkinson, Holly, M.D. Women and Fatigue. NewYork, G.P. Putnam's Sons, 1985.

Bailey, Covert. Fit or Fat? Boston, Houghton Mifflin Company, 1977.

Bennion, Lynn J., M.D. Hypoglycemia: Fact or Fad? New York, Crown Publishers, Inc. 1983.

Bland, Jeffery, Ph.D. Your Health Under Siege. Vermont, The Stephen Greene Press, 1981.

Brennan, Dr. R.O. Nutrigenetics. NewYork, M. Evans and Company, 1975.

Budd, Martin L., N.D., D.O., Lic.Ac. Low Blood Sugar. New York, Sterling Publishing Co., Inc. 1981.

Cheraskin, E., M.D., D.M.D., William Ringsdorf, Jr., D.M.D. and .W. Clark, D.D.S., Diet and Disease. Connecticut, Keats Publishing, Inc. 1986.

Cheraskin E., M.D., D.M.D., William Ringsdorf, Jr., D.M.D., with Arline Brecher. Phychodietetics. New York, Bantam Books, 1978.

Cheraskin, E., M.D., D.M.D., William Ringsdorf, Jr., D.M.D., and Emily L. Sisley, Ph.D. The Vitamin C Connection. NewYork, Harper & Row Publishers, Inc., 1983.

Crook, William G., M.D. The Yeast Connection. Tennessee, Professional Books, 1983.

Dufty, William. Sugar Blues. New York, Warner Books, Inc., 1975.

Fredericks, Carlton, Ph.D. Carlton Fredericks' New Low Blood Sugar and You. New York, Perigee Books, 1985.

Fredericks, Carlton, Ph.D. Psycho-Nutrition. NewYork, Grosset & Dunlap, 1976.

Krimmel, Patricia and Edward. The Low Blood Sugar Handbook. Bryn Mawr, PA, Franklin Publishers, 1984.

Lorenzani, Shirley, Ph.D. Candida; A Twentieth Century Disease. New Canaan, CT, Keats Publishing, Inc., 1986.

Martin, Clement G. Low Blood Sugar; The Hidden Menace of Hypoglycemia. New York, Arco Publishing Co., 1976.

The Merck Manual of Diagnosis and Therapy, Twelfth Edition. Rahway, NJ, Merck Sharp & Dohme Research Laboratories, Division of Merck & Co., Inc.

Milam, James R. and Katherine Ketcham, Under the Influence, New York, Bantam Books, 1981.

Nutrition and Mental Health. Hearing before the Select
Committee on Nutrition and Human Needs of the
United States Senate. California, Parker House, 1977.

Page, Melvin E., D.D.S., and H. Leon Abrams, Jr. Your
Body is Your Best Doctor. New Canaan, CT, Keats
Publishing, 1972.

Passwater, Richard A. Supernutrition. New York, Pocket
Books, 1975.

Pritikin, Nathan, with Patrick M. McGrady, Jr. The Pritikin
Program for Diet and Exercise. New York, Grosset &
Dunlap, 1979.

Rapp, Doris, J., M.D. Allergies and the Hyperactive Child.
NewYork,Simon&Schuster,1979.

Reed, Barbara. Foods,Teens and Behavior. Manitowoc,Wi,
Natural Press, 1983.
Ross, Harvey, M.D. Fighting Depression. NewYork,
Larchmont Books, 1975.

Schauss, Alexander,Diet, Crime and Delinquency. Berkeley,
CA, Parker House, 1981.

Saunders, Jeraldine, and Ross, Harvey, M.D. Hypoglycemia:

The Disease Your Doctor Won't Treat, New York Pinnacle Press, 1980.

Smith, Lendon, M.D. Feed Yourself Right. New York, McGraw-Hill, 1983.

Smith, Lendon, M.D. Foods For Healthy Kids. New York, Berkeley Books, 1981.

Truss, C. Orion, M.D. The Missing Diagnosis. Birmingham, The Missing Diagnosis, Inc., 1983.

Yudkin, John M.D. Sweet and Dangerous. New York, Bantam Books, 1972.

Weil, Andrew, M.D., and Rosen, Winifred. Chocolate to Morphine. Boston, Houghton Mifflin Co., 1983.

Weller, Charles. How To Live With Hypoglycemia. New York, Doubleday, 1968.

Wunderlich, Jr., Ray C., M.D. Sugar and Your Health. St Petersburg, FL, Good Health Publications, Johnny Reed, Inc., 1982.

Zack, Maura and Currier, Wilbur D., M.D. Sugar Isn't Always Sweet. Brea, CA, Uplift Books, 1983.

Index

§

The Hypoglycemia Research Foundation, Inc.
was founded
on June 6, 1980
but was renamed
The Hypoglycemia Support Foundation, Inc.
on December 13, 1991.